Deliver
Me

Karen Cole grew up in the Cotswolds and got a degree in Psychology at Newcastle University. She spent several years teaching English around the world before settling in Cyprus with her husband and two sons, where she works at a British army base as a primary school teacher. She recently completed the Curtis Brown writing course where she found her love of writing psychological thrillers.

Deliver Me is her debut novel.

KAREN COLE

Deliver Me

Quercus

First published in Great Britain in 2019 by

Quercus Editions Ltd
Carmelite House
50 Victoria Embankment
London EC4Y 0DZ

An Hachette UK company

A CIP catalogue record for this book is available
from the British Library

PB ISBN 978 1 52940 072 4
EBOOK ISBN 978 1 78747 656 1

10 9 8 7 6 5 4 3

Typeset by CC Book Production

Printed and bound in Great Britain by Clays Ltd, Elcograf S.p.A.

For my parents who have always believed in me
and encouraged me to write.

Prologue

They've been there all night. Fingers of grey daylight are already creeping through the trees, banishing the shadows, exposing roots, leaves and the shape of Abby's captor hunched over his phone.

The pain has subsided for a moment and tears of terror roll down Abby's cheeks as she realizes the full extent of the danger she's in.

She looks around, frantically trying to work out an escape route. In the distance she can hear the faint hum of traffic on the main road. If she could get there maybe she could flag down a car. *Could she make a run for it?* He's distracted at the moment, absorbed in whatever's on his phone. But she knows in her heart that it's not possible. There's no way she could run. Right now, she could no more run than fly.

There's another wave of intense pain and Abby's no longer thinking about escape. Something primal surges over her and she cries out in agony, but the sound is merely a muffled grunt through the tape over her mouth.

'Shut up,' he snarls, striding over and yanking her hair. 'Can't you be quiet for even a minute?!'

She hates this man so much. How could she ever have trusted him? She would kill him with her bare hands if she could. But, as she makes a last desperate attempt to wrench her arms free, searing pain, even worse than before, washes over her and he crouches between her legs, giving a low whistle.

'About time too,' he says. 'Your baby's coming.'

MARCH

Your baby is about the size of a peanut. There are tiny depressions where the eyes will be. The jaws and teeth are beginning to form, and a sense of smell is starting to develop. You might notice your waistline thickening, but it won't be obvious to anyone else.

Chapter One

'Does this hurt?' The doctor presses down sharply on her belly, so sharply that Abby Brooke gasps in shock.

'Not really,' she says through gritted teeth. She looks out of the window at treetops clawing the cold, grey sky. A gust of wind shakes the branches, and the new leaves shiver. She wishes she hadn't come. There's something very wrong with her, that's for sure, but whatever it is, she doesn't really want to know.

Cancer, she thinks. But she had that biopsy done just before Christmas and it came back clear, so it can't be cancer. Abby pulls down her top and sits up, swinging her legs round so they are dangling off the edge of the couch.

'Maybe it's stress?' she suggests. 'This is only my first year teaching and it's been ... Well, some of the kids are quite challenging.'

That's an understatement. Just halfway through the school year, Abby feels exhausted and disillusioned. She's spent the past few months trying to develop the natural authority that the other teachers seem to have, and failing miserably. It doesn't help that she teaches Art, a subject many of the children don't take seriously, or that she's only twenty-four and looks even younger, so small and fresh-faced that she's often mistaken for a student herself.

Rob thinks she would command more respect if she changed the way she dressed. But he doesn't understand that the vintage clothes she wears, and the over-the-top jewellery are part of her armour against the world. With them, she's funky, artistic Abby Brooke. Without them, she's just a shy young girl with mousy brown hair and grey eyes.

'And don't get me started on the paperwork.' She rolls her eyes and smiles.

'Hmm.' Dr Rowe doesn't seem interested in her teaching woes.

'Are there any other symptoms?' he asks, glancing up at Abby. 'Apart from the nausea?'

'Only that I feel tired all the time.' Lately when she gets home from work it's all she can do to wolf down her food and drag herself up to bed for a marathon twelve-hour sleep.

'I'm afraid I haven't finished yet. Could you lie back down please and lift your top up?' He smiles apologetically at Abby.

Dr Rowe begins kneading and prodding again. He's about thirty-five, with blond hair and an eager, friendly manner like a golden retriever. Right now, he seems puzzled, like a retriever that's lost its bone. He frowns and takes out something like a stethoscope, placing it against her stomach.

'You can sit up now, Abigail.' He pulls off his gloves and

propels his chair over to the desk, where he taps something into the computer.

On his desk, next to the computer, is a framed photo of him on a mountainside with his arms round a sporty-looking blonde woman and two children, a pale wisp of a girl about six years old and a boy who looks about ten. Abby recognizes the boy. He's a few years older now than he is in the photograph but she's fairly sure it's Aaron, a quiet, studious boy from one of her classes. She wonders if Dr Rowe knows that she teaches his son. If he does he hasn't mentioned it, and she's glad. The last thing she wants to do now is to get into a conversation about school. She looks away quickly and her eyes rest on a bronze bust of a man with a curly beard and a bald head.

'Hippocrates.' Dr Rowe notices her looking at it. 'The father of Western medicine.'

Abby nods. Her sister is a doctor, so she knows all about Hippocrates. She thinks about Ellie's graduation, her mum, still very much alive, sitting next to her in the audience, how she squeezed Abby's hand as Ellie walked up to the podium, how she was so proud to have a doctor in their working-class family. By the time Abby graduated ten years later her mum was unable to attend, already in the grip of the cancer that killed her. To her dismay, Abby feels tears welling up in her eyes. She blinks them away and looks at Dr Rowe to see if he's noticed.

He's giving her an oddly intense stare. He clears his throat. 'Are you sexually active, Abigail?' he asks.

'No, not lately,' she says, taken aback by the sudden switch in topic.

'And your periods? Are they regular?'

'Not really.' Come to think of it, they have been erratic lately, if not non-existent, but she's put that down to stress.

'When was your last period?'

She strains to remember. She's been so busy lately she's barely noticed.

'Maybe at the start of December sometime.'

'Well, Abigail,' he says. 'It looks like you're pregnant. About two months I would say.'

Abby stares at him, astonished. 'That's impossible.' She laughs nervously. 'Unless it's the virgin birth.'

'Oh?' Dr Rowe raises an eyebrow.

She flushes. 'I mean . . . I haven't had sex for over a year, so I can't be, can I?' Since breaking up with Ben she hasn't really wanted to get involved with anyone else. She's been on a couple of dates, had a couple of awkward snogs and fumbles, but that's about it.

The doctor shrugs. 'You can take a test if you want to make certain.'

She opens her mouth to argue, but then closes it again. What's the point? Dr Rowe clearly thinks she's some flighty young girl who can't keep track of her own sex life.

'We'll need a urine sample,' he says, scribbling her name on a plastic beaker and handing it to her. 'Give it in at reception when you've finished.'

In the hallway Abby pauses, fighting off a wave of nausea. She stares down at the pattern of hexagonal tiles on the floor. The sickness comes on suddenly and she doesn't always have time to reach the toilet. Yesterday she threw up in a plant pot at work, which is why Danny insisted on driving her to the doctor's today.

Well, there's no way she's pregnant. Dr Rowe is clearly mistaken. She knows Ellie thinks he's great, and she should know, but Abby's beginning to doubt he's as good as she thinks. She hesitates outside Ellie's door, looking at the brass plaque with the words 'Dr Elizabeth Campbell MRCGP' etched in it. She's tempted to tell Ellie about Dr Rowe's mistake. She usually shares most things with her older sister. She raises a fist to knock on the door, then lets it drop by her side. She can't talk to Ellie about this. Anything to do with babies or pregnancy is taboo with Ellie. Anyway, she shouldn't disturb her now. The door's closed, so she's probably in there with a patient.

Abby tosses the empty beaker into a bin and pushes open the door to the waiting room.

Danny looks uncomfortable, a thin, dark presence, squashed between an old man with a hacking cough and a mother with a snotty baby. He puts down the magazine he's reading as Abby comes in.

'You look pensive, sweetie. How was it?' he asks, giving her a searching look.

'I'll tell you once we're out of here,' she says, tugging his arm.

It's a relief to get outside. A brisk wind whips through her thin coat clearing her head. Clouds scud by over the rooftops. She's glad Danny came with her. He has a way of making her see the funny side of a situation and already the incident is transforming into an amusing anecdote in her head.

'You'll never guess what the doctor said,' she says as they turn and walk towards town.

'Nothing bad I hope?'

'Not exactly bad . . . no.'

Danny groans in frustration. 'Just tell me.'

Abby pauses for extra drama. 'He thinks I'm pregnant.'

She waits for Danny to laugh, give that infectious chuckle of his, and put this ridiculous idea in its place.

He doesn't laugh. Instead he stops and claps his hand to his mouth. 'I had no idea you were even seeing anyone!'

Abby frowns. 'That's just the point. I'm not. I'm not pregnant. I can't be.'

'Are you sure?'

'Of course I'm sure,' Abby snaps. She walks on quickly, feeling annoyed. He's supposed to be making her laugh about this.

Danny runs to catch up. 'Okay, I get it, you live like a nun. It's just a strange mistake for a doctor to make, that's all. Did you take a test?'

'No.' She uses her slow, talking-to-idiots voice. 'There would be no point. I'm not pregnant. I haven't had sex for over a year.'

They stop at the corner by the Red Cross shop near where Danny's car is parked.

'Do you want a lift home?' he asks.

'No thanks, I'd like to walk.'

'You sure you're okay?' he asks, his hand resting lightly on her arm.

'I'm fine,' she says tetchily. 'I'm feeling much better now. It was probably nothing.'

'Well, I'll see you tomorrow,' he leans forward and kisses her on the cheek. 'You take care.'

'You too.' Abby softens. 'And thanks for coming with me. I appreciate it.'

'What are friends for?' he says. Then he turns and saunters away towards the car. She watches him for a minute, taking in his thin shoulders, his light springy step, and she feels a lurch of unease.

'Danny?' she calls out.

He turns, his hand on the car door. 'Yes?'

'Don't tell anyone about this, okay?'

'Course not,' he says, grinning impishly. 'Would I?'

She makes her way through the pedestrianized town centre past the smug little tea shops, the antique shops and the gallery with its four-figure price tags, feeling the usual claustrophobia. This sleepy Gloucestershire town is just too small and too twee. You can't so much as sneeze without everyone knowing. Can she trust Danny not to tell anyone? Danny's a good friend, but he isn't exactly the most discreet person in the world.

Anyway, it doesn't matter. She's not pregnant. *She can't be.*

Nevertheless, she finds herself, a few minutes later, in the chemist's, staring at a display of pregnancy tests. She puts a couple in her basket and shoves deodorant and a bottle of conditioner on top in case she meets someone she knows. Then she heads for the checkout.

The cashier is overly friendly and chatty. She's seen Abby around. Doesn't she work at the school? Her son is in Year Seven. What does Abby think of the new head teacher? Abby answers her questions as politely as possible, all the time willing her to hurry up. Every extra minute makes it more likely a student or parent or someone she knows will walk in.

'The conditioner is two for the price of one,' the cashier says. 'Do you want to get another one?'

'No thanks,' says Abby impatiently, and the woman frowns as if not getting two when it's for the price of one is a sure sign of insanity.

A black cloud rolls over and Abby makes it home just as the rain starts pelting down. Rob's new Vauxhall is parked in the driveway, gleaming silver in the lashing rain. Abby sighs as she makes her way up the pathway. She'd hoped to have the house to herself. Rob usually has a management meeting on Thursday after school, but it must have been cancelled today.

She slips her key in the lock, wishing, not for the first time, that she could afford a place of her own. But it's impossible on her salary. She reminds herself how lucky she is that Rob and Ellie have let her live with them rent free. She should be grateful, and she is. It's just she wishes she didn't feel so suffocated all the time. Living and working with her brother-in-law is not exactly ideal.

Rob is in the kitchen, chopping chicken and humming along with the radio. He's wearing the apron Ellie had bought him last Christmas with the picture of a gladiator's body on it, a bit of a cruel joke on Rob's paunchy body but he doesn't seem to care. Hector, Ellie's dog, is watching him intently, waiting for some meat to drop. He wags his tail politely at Abby.

'Where the hell did you get to?' Rob switches off the radio and waves the knife at Abby. 'I would've given you a lift, but I couldn't find you.'

'Oh, sorry, I didn't think to tell you. I walked with Danny.' Abby clutches the bag with the test kits inside behind her back.

'Danny, eh? . . . "Oh, Danny boy",' Rob starts singing, '"the pipes, the pipes are calling" . . .' He puts the knife down, brushes a greasy hand through his thick brown beard and stretches out his arm like an opera singer. He sings that every time Danny's name is mentioned. The joke's wearing a bit thin.

'You've been seeing a lot of that young man lately. I haven't given my seal of approval yet.' He grins, his brown eyes glinting with amusement.

Abby rolls her eyes. 'You do know he's gay, don't you?'

Rob stares at her. 'Really? Danny? No way! I thought you two were . . . Well, you know . . . friends with benefits.'

'Yeah, well, a lot of people think that but it's not true.' In fact, Abby has encouraged the idea. Her friendship with Danny is a useful buffer against the attention of other men. Since Ben she's been in no rush to get into another relationship.

'Gay? Really?' Rob shakes his head. 'It's always the good-looking ones, isn't it?'

The microwave pings and when Rob turns to open it Abby takes the opportunity to escape. 'See you later,' she calls, and she runs upstairs, locking herself in the bathroom.

The test is simple, though it feels undignified squatting over the toilet and peeing on a small, plastic stick. Abby doesn't have to wait long for the results. Just two minutes. While she's waiting, she slumps against the bath, staring at the tangle of spiders' webs and dead flies under the sink. Ellie refuses to let Rob or Abby kill spiders.

'They have as much right as we do to be here,' she said a couple of months ago, during an argument with Rob.

'Well, not really,' Rob said. 'They don't pay the mortgage, do they?'

Abby had been unable to shake the feeling that they were really arguing about her.

She sighs and picks up the stick. A small but definite blue line has appeared in the control window.

And a plus sign in the result window.

A positive result.

It must be a mistake. She reads the instructions through again, trying not to panic. But she's done everything right.

'Shit. Shit. Shit,' she says, fumbling with a second test packet, and she repeats the test, warm wee splashing on her hand. After another two minutes, the results are back.

She's pregnant.

Chapter Two

It makes no sense. Abby looks down at her belly. There's a red pattern etched on her pale skin from trousers that are too tight and a tiny puncture mark from the belly-button ring she no longer wears, but otherwise nothing. It's as flat as ever. There's no sign of anything stirring under the surface.

The test claims to be 99 per cent accurate. A one-in-a-hundred chance the first test was wrong. But for both tests to be wrong . . . What are the odds?

She reads the section about medical conditions and medicines that could affect the result, but there's nothing that could conceivably apply to her. There's no escaping it. She must be pregnant. She sits down on the toilet seat with her head in her hands, reeling with shock. *This can't be happening*, she thinks. *Please God, let this not be happening*. How will she even begin to cope? She can barely take care of herself. The thought of having a small baby completely dependent on her is terrifying. And what will she do about her job? She can all too easily imagine the head's reaction when she tells her she needs to take time off to have a baby so soon after starting at Elmgrove.

Downstairs, the front door slams. It's Ellie arriving home, talking to Hector, murmuring something indistinct to Rob in the kitchen. Seconds later she hears her come thudding up the stairs.

Shit. Abby stuffs the tests back in the bag, ties it tightly and shoves it in the bin, covering it with scrunched-up toilet paper.

She waits for the sound of Ellie's bedroom door closing, then creeps across the landing to her room.

Lying on her unmade bed, Abby stares up at the blue ceiling with its fluffy white clouds. She painted them up there herself two years ago, when Ellie and Rob were still planning to use the room as a nursery. She remembers standing on the ladder painting up high, while a heavily pregnant Ellie painted the skirting boards. Abby blinks back tears at a sudden vision of her sister, rosy and happy, a smudge of magnolia paint on her cheek, struggling to reach down over her swollen belly.

'Our little miracle,' Ellie had called it.

They'd been trying for years to have a baby. They'd almost given up on the idea of conceiving naturally and were considering IVF when *boom*, just like that, she fell pregnant.

'She's going to be a black belt in karate, this one,' Ellie said during a break in painting.

They were sitting together on the bare floorboards, drinking milky tea. Abby put her hand on Ellie's belly and felt the taut skin judder as her niece tested her new limbs.

But Ellie's baby didn't become a black belt in karate. She never became anything. She kicked and wriggled so much in Ellie's womb that the umbilical cord wrapped itself around her neck and strangled her.

Abby sits up and wraps her arms around her knees, remembering those terrible months after Ellie lost the baby. Abby was still living in London at the time, but she came as often as she could to visit. And on her visits, she was deeply shaken by the change in her sister. For days on end Ellie just sat in bed staring into space, refusing to speak or eat. Ellie had always been so full of life and energy – always helping people, always with some cause to fight for. But when her baby died it was as if all that furious energy had been sucked inward somehow, like a star imploding. And it was awful to witness.

It's a cruel irony, Abby thinks, that Ellie who wants a baby so badly, who would make such a great mother, can't have one, and that she, Abby, who can't even so much as keep a plant alive, is pregnant. It makes no sense.

Unless . . . She sits up and switches on her laptop, types in 'What is the longest pregnancy on record?'

According to the internet, someone called Beulah Hunter gave birth in 1945, after a 375-day pregnancy. But even if the story is true, it still wouldn't make sense. She last had sex over a year ago and, according to Dr Rowe, she is only two months pregnant. Abby trawls the internet some more, getting distracted by some grim stories about stone babies, a rare condition where the foetus dies and calcifies inside the mother. She reads, horrified and fascinated, about how, sometimes, the baby can stay in the womb for years. There's a picture of a wrinkled Moroccan woman with a distended stomach and the stone baby she carried inside her for forty-six years.

Abby's stomach curdles, and she rushes to the bathroom, throwing up in the toilet bowl.

'Are you okay, Abs?'

Ellie's there, standing just outside the open door. She looks tired and anxious, her work suit creased, dark rings around her eyes and blonde hair scraped up in a messy bun.

Abby wipes her lips and flushes the toilet. Ellie is nine years older and has always been like a second mother to her. She normally tells Ellie everything. But this is different. She can't tell her this. It will only stir up all that pain and grief that Abby knows still lurks dangerously near the surface.

'I'm fine,' she says, standing up and offering a weary smile. 'Just a stomach bug.'

'You should go see Simon. Or if you want, I could examine you.'

'I saw him today, actually.' Abby washes her hands in the sink, watching the water get sucked down the plughole.

'You did?' Ellie frowns. 'What did he say?'

'Like I said, it's a stomach bug.'

'Why don't you take some time off work? They'd understand. I'm sure Rob could explain.'

'Rob could explain what?' Rob appears at the top of the

stairs. Now they are both looking at her, blocking her exit. Ellie with her anxious, blue eyes, and Rob with the superior, comical expression he reserves for his students and, with irritating frequency, Abby too.

'Jesus. Can't a girl get a little privacy?' Abby explodes in frustration. She pushes past them towards the stairs. 'Does everyone want to come and watch me throw up? Maybe I should sell tickets?'

'Abby was sick again,' says Ellie. 'She's overdoing it. Don't you think she should take some time off, Rob?'

Abby sighs angrily. 'I'm fine. I don't need time off, I just need some fresh air. I'm going to take Hector for a walk.'

The rain has stopped but the air is still damp, and the trees and shrubs are dripping. Abby strides along, Hector trotting along beside her, towards the old Abbey grounds.

Hector strains at the lead as they reach the park gates. Abby lets him off and he bounds away up the path round the lake. She follows, walking rapidly, as if she can shake off Rob and Ellie, as if she can shake off the questions and doubts crowding in her head. How can she be pregnant? If not Ben, then who? And when? How the hell has she got herself into this mess?

Abby follows the path over the bridge to the other side of the lake and sits on a damp bench looking at the dark, wind-ruffled water. The park is empty, the sun sinking behind the church and the trees. The shadows are growing, swallowing up the park and creeping over the newly mown grass. A swan glides by silently, its eyes cold and black. Abby shivers, batting away a sudden sense of unease. Something is very wrong.

She's walking back past the bandstand when it hits her. And suddenly it seems so obvious. Why hasn't she thought of it before? According to Dr Rowe, she's about two months pregnant. Two months ago was the beginning of January. Abby reaches the park gates and calls Hector, putting him back on the lead. Of course, that's it. It must be.

New Year's Eve.

Chapter Three

'Danny, you know your New Year's party? You remember how drunk I was?'

It's Friday afternoon, almost the end of the school week, and everyone else has buggered off to afternoon classes. Abby and Danny are the only people left in the staff room at Elmgrove Comprehensive, sitting in sagging armchairs and sipping cold coffee. They are done with classes for the day but Danny likes to stay late and get all his marking done on a Friday so that he can enjoy his weekend without having to think about work, and Abby is in no rush to get home. Gina, the head teacher, has left a box of chocolates on the table, and Abby is munching her way through them distractedly.

Danny's dark eyes crinkle in amusement. 'You certainly were the life and soul of the party, flirting for England, if I remember rightly.'

Abby cringes inwardly. 'Was I flirting with anyone in particular?'

Danny raises his eyebrows. 'Don't you remember?'

'Not really.'

She remembers arriving, feeling shy and hopelessly out of place amongst Danny's rich university friends, and she remembers that, encouraged by Danny's flatmate Mark, she tried boosting her confidence by downing several tequilas in quick succession. But after that, large parts of the evening are blank. She can only recall short fragments, like in a dream: sitting on the stairs; talking to a guy in a green T-shirt; then, later, lying on stiff, frosty grass gazing at the fireworks exploding in the sky; and then there's an image of a bottle shattering against a wall, shards of glass flying. *Bizarre*. Someone must have given her a lift home because she remembers waiting in a car at a garage forecourt, the headlights gleaming on the wet tarmac. Then nothing. Nothing until she woke up alone in her own bed with a massive hangover.

She woke up alone. She's sure about that.

'Someone gave me a lift home. Do you know who? Did you see who I left with?'

Danny shrugs. 'I was a bit preoccupied myself. Why do you want to know?'

She lowers her voice, even though there's no one else in the room.

'It turns out the doctor was right.'

Danny stares. His mouth falls open in astonishment. 'You mean . . . ?'

'I'm pregnant.' Saying it aloud makes it feel real. Abby feels dizzy and the room sways as if she's about to faint.

'But I thought you said . . .'

'... that I hadn't slept with anyone – I know.' Abby cuts him off impatiently. 'But I must have, mustn't I?'

Danny shakes his head, smiling. 'That's generally the way it works.'

'I think it must have happened ... at your party. It's the only logical explanation. The problem is ... I just don't know ... *who* ...'

Danny chews his nails, lost in thought. A worried crease appears in his forehead. 'Are you sure you want to know?'

'What do you mean?' Abby asks, confused.

'Think about it, Abs. You were out of your head. What kind of guy has sex with someone when they're almost unconscious? I mean it's practically rape.'

'I hadn't thought of it like that.' Abby feels sick at the thought, but at the same time strangely relieved. All day she's been blaming herself. Perhaps none of this is her fault, after all.

'Do you think I should go to the police?'

'And say what? You got drunk at a party and someone slept with you? Even if you knew who it was, it would be impossible to prove that you weren't in a fit state to consent, unless someone actually saw it happen. But I don't think you should worry.' He smiles. 'I'm probably being a drama queen as usual. Just ignore me. It's way more likely that it's a simple case of two people getting drunk and sleeping together.'

Abby nods. He's right, of course. She puts her head in her hands.

'Oh God, what a mess,' she groans, as tears well up in her eyes. 'What an idiot I am.'

Danny puts an arm around her shoulder. 'Everyone makes mistakes,' he says soothingly. 'I can't tell you the number of times I've woken up regretting the things I've done the night before.'

Abby nods and wipes her nose. 'Yeah, but you didn't end up pregnant, did you?'

'That's true. I'm sorry, Abs.' Danny gives her a lopsided smile. 'What are you going to do?'

'I don't know,' she shakes her head as she meets his eyes. 'I really don't know.'

'There's a parcel for you in your pigeonhole,' Jenny, the school secretary, calls as Abby passes reception on her way out of the building a couple of hours later. Jenny doesn't look up from the document she's typing, her pink, varnished nails tapping furiously at the keyboard.

'Okay, thanks. Have you seen Rob?' Abby asks.

'He left already.'

Abby empties her pigeonhole. There's a payslip, a circular from the head about raising standards, which she chucks straight in the bin, and a small, brown parcel. It has her name on it in block capitals but nothing else. She stuffs it into her bag along with the payslip. She'll open it at home.

Danny stays to finish his marking, so she walks home alone. Trudging in the drizzle down the dual carriageway, Danny's earlier question reverberates in her head. It's a good question. What the hell *is* she going to do?

A car whizzes past, spraying rainwater and soaking her dress.

Shit.

Could Danny have been right in the first place? Was she out of it at the time it happened? Abby's disgust at the thought is physical; it coils deep in her belly, snaking its way up her chest into her oesophagus. She doubles over and retches onto the pavement. Tears sting her eyes as she walks on. The worst of it is, she's allowed it to happen. She put herself in that situation and now she's pregnant. The question is: what's she going to do about it?

There's only really one option.

At home, Abby holes herself up in her bedroom with her phone and googles 'abortion clinics'. She writes down the number of a couple. Then she looks at her Facebook feed. There's a picture of Chloe and Ben with their arms entwined on the beach in Thailand. Chloe looks tanned and beautiful without make-up. Ben is looking at her adoringly.

Ben and Chloe. Her boyfriend and her best friend. The ultimate betrayal. They'd all hung out together at art college. Ben had always seemed happy to have Chloe around.

Perhaps *too* happy, she had realized with hindsight.

When she left to do her PGCE, and Chloe and Ben stayed on in London, sharing the same flat, she didn't think anything of it. She isn't quite sure when she first realized there was something going on between them. It was more of a gradual realization, an accumulation of small signs she tried

25

to ignore. She cringes with embarrassment remembering the showdown when Ben finally admitted he was sleeping with Chloe – the way she stormed around his room, tipping over furniture and emptying his wardrobe, flinging his clothes out onto the street.

She stares at the post, wondering why she tortures herself with this. She could just unfriend them. But maybe it's like a dog licking its wounds. Return often enough to the injury, and eventually it heals. She sighs and closes the window. She has other things to worry about now anyway. She opens another window and types in 'pregnancy eight weeks'.

Your baby now weighs approximately one ounce, she reads. *Its head is more erect, and the neck is becoming stronger. Its heart begins to separate into four chambers and an ultra-fine, soft hair called lanugo will begin to appear on the skin.*

There's a picture of an embryo – a strange, hunched-up creature with a tail like a sea horse. Its hand is up by its eye as if it's crying.

Oh God, she thinks. *This is real.* She turns off her phone and curls up on the bed. She wants to pretend this isn't happening – to burrow under the duvet and hide. But how can you hide from something inside you?

It's only later, after tea, that she remembers the parcel. She fetches it from her bag and takes it into the kitchen. The dishwasher's humming, and the TV is blaring out the theme tune from *Game of Thrones* in the living room where Rob and Ellie are watching. Abby gets the kitchen scissors to cut the Sellotape. She can't imagine what it could be; possibly some stupid teaching aid from the head teacher, or maybe a present from a pupil. It must have been hand-delivered. There's no postmark, no address. She tears at the brown paper and something white and soft falls out. She picks it up and her breath catches in her throat.

What the hell?

It's a Babygro with a yellow duck on the front. The duck is wearing red wellingtons and splashing in a puddle, winking cheekily.

Abby's hands are shaking as she scrabbles inside the discarded brown paper and finds a simple white card. On the card, typed in capitals, it says:

> *TO ABIGAIL,*
> *FOR BABY,*
> *WITH LOVE.*

Chapter Four

'Is this your idea of a joke?'

Danny's standing in the doorway of his flat rubbing his eyes. It's eleven o'clock in the morning but he's still wearing boxers, and his dark hair is all messy like he's just got out of bed. He blinks in confusion at the Babygro she's brandishing.

'You'd better come in,' he says croakily as Abby strides past into his dark, dinghy living room. The curtains are drawn, and the air is fuggy with the smell of cigarettes and beer. Cans and ashtrays are scattered everywhere.

'Bit of a late one last night,' he explains, wincing when Abby draws the curtains, letting bright sunlight flood in. 'Do you have to do that? My head is killing me.'

She's too angry to care. She's been fuming all night, letting her anger grow and ferment. 'What were you thinking, Danny? Why did you send me this?'

He stares at the Babygro in what seems like genuine bewilderment.

'What's that?'

'You know very well what it is.'

'No, I don't,' he scowls. He's starting to get angry too. 'I mean, of course I know what it is. But I don't know what you're doing with it, or what it has to do with me.' He sinks into the sofa rubbing his temples with his thumbs. 'Look, can this wait? I'm really feeling like shit.'

'You didn't send this to me then?' Abby perches on the edge of the sofa, the wind taken out of her sails.

'What? No of course not. Why would I?'

Abby gives him a searching look. She feels like she has a good nose for lies and it seems like Danny's telling the truth. Without a target, her anger quickly evaporates and turns to confusion.

'I don't know,' she shrugs. 'As a kind of sick joke, I suppose.'

'I'm insulted you think I would do something like that.'

'I'm sorry,' she says. 'But apart from you, no one knows I'm pregnant. Who else could have sent it?' She stands up and paces the room, thinking hard. 'Are you sure you didn't tell anyone?'

'Of course not,' he says. This time, though, she can tell he's not telling the truth. He does this thing where he tugs at his ear lobe when he's lying. It's a dead giveaway. She glares at him until he smiles sheepishly.

'Well, alright then, I told my mum, that's all, and I made her *promise* not to tell anyone else. I had to get it off my chest somehow. I was worried about you!'

'Your mother!'

Abby pictures Danny's mum, a tiny, garrulous woman who

works at the local newsagent's. She knows everyone in the town and loves to gossip.

'Jesus. Thanks a lot, Danny. You might as well have announced it to the world.'

Danny grips his head. 'I'm sorry, Abs, but I don't really see what you're worried about. This is the twenty-first century. Nobody's going to judge you for being single and pregnant.'

'That's really not the point. Oh, never mind. What's done is done, I suppose.'

She sinks back in the sofa. 'It wasn't just the Babygro. There was this, too.' She takes out the card she has in her back pocket and shows him.

'*To Abigail. For baby* . . .' he reads aloud. 'It is weird,' he admits, chewing a nail thoughtfully. 'When did it arrive? Was there a sender's address?'

'No, it wasn't even posted. I found it in my pigeonhole at school, yesterday.'

'Hmm. Do you think it could have been put there by a kid, as a joke?'

Abby nods slowly. 'Yes, I suppose so.' It seems like the most likely explanation. The children must have somehow found out that she's pregnant. Maybe they overheard her and Danny talking and thought it would be funny to send her a gift. The kids are not usually allowed in the staff room, but it would be easy enough to sneak in when no one was watching.

'Mystery solved.' Danny slaps his knees. 'I don't know about you, but I'm gasping for a coffee. Do you want one?' He stands up and heads into the kitchen.

Abby follows him, still thinking furiously. 'This whole thing is driving me crazy,' she says. 'I mean, I need to know who did this to me.'

'Like we said, it was probably just a schoolkid.'

'No, I don't mean just the parcel, I mean this.' Abby clutches her belly. 'Who's the father? How did I get pregnant?'

'Well . . .' Danny fills the kettle and switches it on. 'You think it was someone at my New Year's Eve party, right?'

Abby has thought about this. 'Yes. Do you remember who was there? I mean, would you be able to make a list for me?'

Danny spoons out the coffee into mugs. 'I'll try, Abs, but there were a lot of people coming and going that night.'

'I know.' Abby paces the room. She gets the milk out of the fridge and pours it into the mugs. She thinks about the memory she had earlier, about the man on the stairs. 'There's something I do remember, though. I was talking to a guy in a green T-shirt, on the stairs I think. He was good-looking, dark-haired.'

Danny picks up his coffee and slurps. 'Did he have tattoos?'

An image of a wiry arm covered in a black, geometric design flashes into her mind.

'Yes, I think so!'

'Sounds like my friend Alex,' says Danny. 'Alex Taylor. But we'll check with Mark. Mark will remember. He barely ever drinks. He has this annoying habit of remembering everything and then telling you all the stupid things you did the night before.' He hands a cup of coffee to Abby and then takes his into the hallway.

'Hey, Mark!' he calls up the stairs before Abby can stop him.

'Don't wake him up!' she exclaims.

'Oh, he's been up ages already. You know what he's like.'

Abby suddenly panics. 'I don't want him to know about this. You haven't told him already, have you?'

Danny shakes his head. 'It's okay. Relax, Abs, we won't have to tell him anything.'

'Tell me what? What's up?' Mark pads down the stairs. He's dressed neatly, as always, in jeans and a T-shirt that says *Mr Universe* in symbols from the periodic table. Small, geeky and obsessively neat. He's a strange sort of flatmate for Danny. And Abby often wonders how he can stand all the drama and chaos that living with Danny must entail. Opposites attract, she supposes.

Mark pushes his glasses up his nose and nods at the bodysuit Abby's still clutching. 'Bit small for you that, Abigail,' he says.

She reddens and forces a laugh. 'Oh, yes, it's a present for a friend. She's having a baby.'

'Oh.' He nods, and starts fiddling with his phone.

'Did you see who Abby left with on New Year's Eve?' asks Danny as they head to the living room. Abby throws him a look that he ignores. But if Mark is curious about why she wants to know after all this time, he doesn't show it.

'Don't you remember?'

Abby sighs and sits down on the sofa. 'No, I had a bit too much to drink.'

Mark nods, a faint smile hovering at the edge of his mouth. 'Yeah, you had quite a few tequila slammers, if I remember rightly. We played Truth or Dare, remember?'

Abby stares at him and groans. She has absolutely no memory of that. 'Not at all. Did I say anything stupid?'

It wouldn't be the first time, she reflects. Just after Mum died she'd gone through a phase of drinking way too much and doing or saying reckless, embarrassing things. There was that time at uni when she got up on stage at a gig and tried to grab the mike from the lead singer, and another time when Ben and Chloe had to drag her out of a nightclub when she picked an argument with the biggest, meanest-looking bloke in there.

'Not too stupid, don't worry.' Mark grins. 'I didn't see who you left with, but you were talking a lot to Danny's friend, the one with all the tattoos.'

'There you go. Alex. I thought so.' Danny turns and gives Abby a meaningful glance. Abby ignores him.

'Why do you want to know, anyway?' says Mark.

'Er . . .' Abby thinks rapidly. 'I can't find the necklace I was wearing that night and I was thinking maybe I dropped it in his car.'

'Oh. Or maybe you dropped it somewhere here –' Mark bites his lip – 'though I think I would have found it by now.'

Danny nods. 'You definitely would have.' He winks at Abby and grins at Mark. 'Our Mark's a bit of an obsessive-compulsive cleaner on the quiet.'

'Well, someone has to be, or this place would be a tip,' Mark says mildly, and looks around the living room. 'In fact, it is a tip at the moment. What were you doing last night, Danny?'

Danny shrugs. 'I just had a few friends round.'

'What does your necklace look like, Abby?' Mark asks, picking up a few empty cans.

Abby thinks for a second. 'Er . . . it's a silver tree-of-life pendant. It's not valuable, but it has a lot of sentimental value. My mother gave it to me the Christmas before she died.' It's true that her mum gave her a pendant that fits that description, but the necklace is, in reality, safe at home in her jewellery box. Abby feels bad lying about it but it's the first thing that popped into her head.

'I'm sorry. I'll let you know if I find it.' Mark blinks owlishly at Abby, then wanders off.

Abby turns back to Danny. 'So, is he straight?' she asks when Mark's out of earshot.

'Mark? Yes, of course.'

'No, I mean your friend Alex!' Abby rolls her eyes.

Danny sighs. 'Unfortunately, yes.'

'Unfortunately?'

'Because he's absolutely gorgeous, obviously.'

Abby doesn't smile. 'Do you think he could be the one . . . ?'

Danny frowns and shakes his head. 'No, I don't think so. I mean, he's had his share of troubles, but nah, there's no way. I've known him for years, ever since we were kids. He wouldn't take advantage of someone like that.'

Abby sips her coffee and thinks about this. 'Unless he was out of it too? What do you mean by "troubles"?'

'Some minor stuff. Drug-related, I think. It was years ago. I was away at university when it all happened – but I'm telling you, Abby, he's a good guy at heart.'

'I think we should talk to him anyway,' says Abby. 'Even if it isn't him, maybe he'll remember something important. Have you got his number?'

'Yes, but I tell you what, I think we can do better than that. He's works at the Three Compasses. I'm not quite sure which days he works, but I know he's there every Saturday. We could go there for a drink and I can introduce you in a casual way – he needn't know why you want to talk to him.'

'Good idea,' says Abby. 'When? Tonight?'

Danny shakes his head ruefully. 'I'm really sorry, I can't tonight. My sister and her fiancé are coming to visit. How about next Saturday?'

Abby would rather go immediately and get some answers, but she doesn't really want to be alone when she meets Alex after what Danny said yesterday in the staff room, so she reluctantly agrees.

'Okay, it's a date.'

Danny leans back, lights a cigarette, and then quickly stubs it out.

'Sorry,' he says. 'I shouldn't smoke with you in your condition.'

Abby swallows a burst of irritation. 'It's okay. Go ahead. It won't make a difference. I'm not keeping it, anyway.'

This slips out, without premeditation. She hasn't meant to tell anyone until it's all over. A done deal.

Danny eyes narrow but he says nothing. He gets that dark,

brooding look he sometimes has. 'You mean, you're going to have an abortion?'

'What else can I do? I don't have any choice.'

'Well, I suppose it's your body, your decision.' Danny shrugs, not quite meeting her eyes.

Abby feels anger bubbling up inside her. 'Damn right it's my decision,' she says. She doesn't understand what his problem is. It has nothing to do with him, and as far as she's concerned, he has no right to judge her.

Danny drains his coffee and stands up. 'Well, I'm going to go back to bed now, Abs, if you don't mind,' he says coldly. 'I really feel like shit. You can see yourself out, can't you?'

Abby watches him go in anger and astonishment. Then she lets herself out, slamming the door. She feels betrayed and hurt. How dare he judge her? It's okay for him. He's a man. By definition, he'll never have to face this horrible dilemma.

She walks back towards her house, through St Michael's Park and past the empty tennis courts and the crazy golf. It's not actually raining but the sky is heavy, oppressive and grey. Everything is still. She feels a wave of hopelessness wash over her. She's got no one to talk to. Danny is acting weird, and Ellie is out of the question. There's no one else she can really trust. If only Mum were still alive, Mum would know what to do.

Grief grips her as she thinks of her mum, always upbeat, never complaining, even towards the end when she must have been in so much pain. But that was typical Mum, always thinking of other people, never of herself.

She pictures Mum a few days before the end, lying in the

hospital bed attached to all sorts of tubes and machines. Her face was so heartbreakingly thin and gaunt, and she was lying so still – she looked like one of those medieval stone effigies you see on top of tombs. Sitting next to the bed, Abby had reached out to touch her, terrified she was already dead, but Mum's eyes had flown open and she'd grasped Abby's hand.

'Remember what I told you,' she said. 'You're strong and beautiful and you can do anything you want with your life.'

Abby's pretty sure that an accidental pregnancy wasn't what her mum had in mind when she'd said that.

There's a small wooded area just after the crazy golf with a bench overlooking a sort of adventure playground made of logs and zip wires. She sits down on the bench and rings her dad. He'll be surprised to hear from her, she reflects. They don't talk often these days. Not since Sue came into the picture about a month after Mum died. Dad's new girl-friend, Sue, is twenty years younger than her dad and about as different from Mum as possible. Abby couldn't get over how quickly he managed to replace their mother. It was like a slap in the face and it created a big rift between them. But right now, she really can't think who else to turn to.

'Hello?' Her dad answers quickly, sounding a little breath-less and distracted.

'Hi, Dad.'

'Hello, Ellie,' he says.

'It's not Ellie, it's Abby.'

'Yes, of course, sorry, you sound so alike on the phone.' There's a pause. 'So, to what do I owe the pleasure?'

'I don't know . . . just thought I'd ring for a chat.' *Do I need a reason to phone my father?* Abby thinks, immediately angry.

'Oh.' There's another long pause.

'How are you, Dad?'

'Oh, I'm okay,' he says vaguely. 'They're repaving the centre of the village. Everyone is up in arms about it.'

'Oh. Why?'

'People keep tripping, and someone broke their hip the other day. Anyway, how are you, Abigail? How's work?'

'Um, I'm okay. It's okay. Listen, Dad, the reason . . .'

'Sorry, love. Someone's at the door and I'm late for my cookery class. Can I ring you back later?'

'Sure.'

Ever since her mum's death, her dad, inspired by Sue, has been involved in a whirlwind of activities. Badminton, golf, the local history society, and now cookery. It seems like a strange choice. She doesn't think she ever saw him so much as boil an egg when Mum was alive.

He hangs up and Abby sighs. She's almost sure he won't ring back. She was stupid to think he would help. Her mum was always the one she went to with problems. The pain of missing her is physical. She brushes away angry tears. Well, now she's going to have to grow up, finally. She's going to have to deal with this one on her own. And the decision really can't be delayed.

She pulls out the numbers she wrote down last night and punches in the numbers to the clinic.

Chapter Five

They have done their best to make the waiting room cheery and calming. Innocuous landscapes in soft, muted colours hang on the walls, and a few wilting pot plants are scattered around the room. Despite that, Abby feels far from calm. This is the last place she wants to be. But every day she leaves it, this pregnancy becomes more real. She's already had to wait a few days because the clinic was fully booked. She can't back out now.

There are only two other people in the waiting room with her: a pale-faced girl fiddling with her phone, who looks like she can't be more than fifteen, and her mother, who is reading a magazine. Abby picks up a magazine herself and tries to read, but she can't focus; the words blur, there's a faint throbbing at the back of her head, and she feels like she's going to throw up.

It feels like an age but it's probably no more than ten minutes before the intercom crackles and screeches: 'Abigail Brooke. Please come to room three on the right.'

Abby tries not to feel as if she's walking the green mile.

There's no need to be nervous, she tells herself. She's taking decisive action. *It's a good thing. A short, simple operation. Very soon this is all going to be over and done with.*

Dr Georgiou has bleached white hair, striking against her youthful, olive skin and dark eyes. Her desk is clear, apart from a photograph of a dark, handsome man in a silver frame. 'Take a seat, Abigail.' She smiles briskly. 'I need to ask you few questions, just to make sure you're clear about the procedure and are aware of all the options, is that okay?'

'Sure.'

Dr Georgiou looks down at her notes. 'Why have you opted for a termination, Abigail?' she asks.

The truth is uncomfortable to talk about and Abby is tired of being judged. 'I'm still young,' she finds herself saying. 'I'm not really in a financial position to bring up a baby, and the father is out of the picture.' It's not a lie. Just a partial truth.

Dr Georgiou nods and smiles. Her eyes are distant and there's something detached about her that Abby is grateful for.

'And has your doctor explained what surgical abortion involves?'

'Yes,' she lies. In fact, she hasn't mentioned this to Dr Rowe. There's doctor–patient confidentiality of course, but she knows that it sometimes gets broken, and there is no way she can let this get back to Ellie. Just the thought of what Ellie's reaction would be if she found out makes Abby's headache worse. She just wants to get it over with.

Dr Georgiou goes on to talk about the process. Abby tries to focus but her head is starting to throb, and something's clawing at her stomach.

'The whole procedure takes between ten to fifteen minutes. There may be some pain afterwards . . .'

'Excuse me,' Abby blurts. She rushes to the toilet and gets there just in time, as she coughs up a yellowish bile.

'Sorry about that,' she says when she returns.

Dr Georgiou flicks her hand dismissively. 'No need to apologize. These things happen. Are you okay?'

Abby nods.

'So, do you have any questions?'

Abby shakes her head.

'And you want to go ahead with the termination?'

'Yes.'

'I can book you in for about an hour's time.'

'Great.'

Outside in the waiting room, Abby's headache gets worse. It feels like a hammer is pounding inside her skull, about to crack it open. She pours herself a drink from the water cooler and swallows a couple of painkillers from her bag. The mother of the young girl gives her a sympathetic smile and she smiles back. But the headache just seems to get worse. The lights in the waiting room are too bright. It's stifling. Abby feels an overwhelming urge to be outside in the fresh air, so she heads out through the sliding doors. She'll just be a few minutes.

It's recently been raining, and she gulps in the still damp

air, trying to remember the breathing exercises Ellie taught her when she started having panic attacks after Mum's death.

A few minutes. Some manageable pain and it will all be over. So why can't she bring herself to go back? Instead, Abby finds herself walking, her feet carrying her away from the clinic up over the bridge, until she reaches the old Roman amphitheatre. It was originally made of wood and so there's nothing left of it now, just a grass-covered hollow. Kids sledge down it in winter and people walk here in summer. She sits on the edge of the green bowl, moisture from the damp grass seeping into her dress. Maybe it's the painkillers finally kicking in, but her headache is beginning to subside.

She looks at her phone. Forty minutes left. She watches a man as he walks his chocolate Labrador on the far side of the amphitheatre. *Hector would like it here,* she thinks. Why does she never bring him here? She feels strangely detached.

Twenty minutes left. Plenty of time to get back. She'll just wait a few more minutes . . . It's so peaceful.

Ten minutes left. There's still time to get back to the clinic if she walks fast. But somehow, she doesn't move.

About half an hour later, she stands up, stretches, and walks slowly towards home.

'You win,' she whispers to the thing inside her. And maybe it's her imagination, but she feels an answering flutter, like there's a trapped bird inside of her.

At home, Abby runs upstairs, shuts herself in her room and flings herself on the bed. She lies there trying to get her head around what has just happened. What has she done? She's an idiot. *There was a way out of this. Simple. Clean. Final.* Of course, she could always make another appointment for tomorrow, but somehow, she knows she won't. For better or worse, she's allowing this thing inside her to live.

Abby pictures it stretching like a maggot inside her, and she remembers a documentary she saw recently about the jewel wasp – a deadly but beautiful creature. She thinks about the way it injects a cockroach with venom, not enough to kill, but enough to immobilize. Then it drags the paralysed cockroach to its burrow and lays its egg inside its body. The larva hatches and feeds on the internal organs, while the roach is still alive. Abby shudders, and rolls over, clutching her pillow. The parallel is inescapable. She's the cockroach in this scenario. She's been immobilized, and now this thing is taking over her life.

She must have dropped off to sleep because the next thing she knows, she can hear loud laughter from downstairs – it's the distinctive sound of Carla's braying laugh.

They're in the living room. Rob, Ellie and Carla. Carla is sitting on the sofa, her long legs coiled gracefully under her, while her twin toddlers charge around the room causing havoc and her baby sleeps in its car seat in the corner. Rob and Carla are laughing raucously at some joke Rob has made, and Ellie is drinking steadily from a glass of wine.

'Hi, Carla,' Abby says. 'I didn't know you were here.' She doesn't particularly like Carla. She flirts too much with Rob, and Abby knows that seeing Carla with all her kids makes

Ellie feel worse about her own childless state, but for once Abby is glad of the distraction.

Carla flaps an elegant hand at Abby. 'Hi,' she says. 'Yes, well I just dropped by. I thought I'd find out what was going on with you all and what's happening in the world of work. I really miss the surgery. We used to have a laugh, didn't we?' she says to Ellie. 'I feel so out of it now I'm stuck at home all the time with . . . this pair.' She gestures to the twins, who are systematically taking books off the bookshelf and flinging them onto the floor.

'I don't know – they look like a nice pair to me,' says Rob, looking pointedly at Carla's low-cut top. 'Oh, you mean the twins!' He laughs loudly at his own joke and sits back, clutching his chubby stomach. Carla laughs too, and flicks her long, blonde hair.

Abby winces. Rob is an insensitive twat at times. Why does he feel the need to flirt with every female he meets? She glances anxiously at Ellie, who, poker-faced, is pouring herself another glass of wine. She pours a glass for Abby, too, and hands it to her. 'You're not missing much,' she says evenly to Carla. 'I've had a really shitty week.'

'How come?' asks Abby, taking a sip of wine. She really could use a drink. She guesses she's not meant to be drinking anymore, but surely one glass of wine won't do any harm.

'Where do I start?' asks Ellie. 'We've had to fire Helen, for a start.'

'Who?' asks Abby.

'You know. Helen Harris, the nurse I told you about.'

Abby nods. She remembers Helen; a thin, bird-like woman who did a pap test on her last year. She took over as the main practice nurse when Carla left to churn out a seemingly endless series of babies.

'She didn't take it well. Said she knew things that could bring the whole practice down. Get us all fired if she wanted.'

'She should have been fired a long time ago,' says Carla. 'She was always incompetent and unreliable. The number of times I covered for her, or Simon covered for her. You're well shot of her.'

Ellie tucks a stray hair behind her ear and frowns. 'I know, but I still feel bad. I mean, she's a friend, kind of, and she's got those two kids. I don't think her ex pays any maintenance.'

'What she really needs is help. You're doing her a favour. Now she can get the help she needs.'

'I'm not sure she sees it that way.' Ellie takes a deep breath. 'On top of that, I found out this morning that Mary died last night.'

Mary was one of Ellie's favourite patients. She came to her in the advanced stages of breast cancer and Ellie has made it her mission to try to get her the best treatment available. Abby knows Mary wasn't just another patient to Ellie, but a personal crusade.

'Oh, that's a shame,' says Carla. 'She was such a lovely woman, too. Why is it always the nicest people?'

There's a long silence. Abby is thinking about their mother. She knows Ellie is, too. The silence is broken when one of the twins picks up Ellie's wine glass from the coffee table and flings it across the room. It shatters into tiny pieces and red wine soaks into the carpet. Abby holds her breath, gripped again by the sudden memory of shattering glass.

'Oh goodness, I'm so sorry!' says Carla, not sounding very sorry as Ellie picks up the pieces. 'Well,' she laughs, 'I'd better get going before they destroy your house.'

'What happened to you, Abby?' asks Rob when Carla has gone. 'Jenny said you'd left early, a doctor's appointment or something?'

Abby flushes slightly. 'Oh, I had a headache, that's all . . . I'm fine now. I just needed a sleep.'

'There's some macaroni on the hob if you want some,' says Ellie. 'It might be a bit cold, though.'

Abby dishes herself some pasta, sits down at the kitchen table and picks half-heartedly at her food. Ellie follows her in.

'Why do you put up with Rob and Carla flirting like that?' Abby asks.

Ellie shrugs. 'Oh, you know Rob, he flirts with everyone. And anyway, I feel a bit sorry for Carla. It's been tough for her since the divorce. But forget them, are you alright? You're not eating your food.'

'I'm fine, just not that hungry.'

Hector pads into the kitchen and sits down next to Ellie, eyeing Abby's plate hopefully.

'That's not for you, boy. It's for Abby,' says Ellie, scratching him behind the ears and kissing the top of his head. Abby looks at them both and thinks, not for the first time, how much Ellie loves Hector. When Rob first brought Hector home from

46

the rescue centre, Abby thought he was an idiot. It was just a few weeks after Ellie lost the baby, and Ellie was refusing to get out of bed. The last thing she needed was a puppy, Abby thought – as if a puppy could possibly make up for all she'd lost.

'Take it away,' Ellie had muttered when Rob dumped the whimpering, wriggling creature at the end of her bed. 'I don't want it.'

But Rob, to give him his due, hadn't backed down, and somehow, slowly but surely, Hector had wormed his way into Ellie's affections. It had turned out that it was exactly what she needed – something to care for and love. And gradually the old Ellie had come back. She wasn't exactly the same, of course – something was still gone, some inner spark had disappeared, maybe forever – but on the surface, everything went back to normal.

'He can have it if he wants,' says Abby, and she stands up and scrapes her dinner into Hector's bowl.

'You've seemed a bit down lately. Are you sure you're okay?' Ellie watches her anxiously. 'You know I'm always here for you if you need me, don't you?'

Abby nods and tries to smile. 'I know, thank you.'

It's true. Ellie has always been there for her. When they were kids, and Abby was being picked on at school, Ellie was the one who marched into her school and demanded to see the head. When Mum died, she was the one who kept Abby on the straight and narrow. And when Ben dumped her, even though it was only a year and a half after she'd lost her baby, Ellie had been there with tissues, wine and funny stories. Abby toys with the idea of telling Ellie everything. She's going to guess sooner or later anyway. It'll be obvious once she starts to show. She opens her mouth.

'Ellie . . .' she starts.

'Yes?'

But at that moment Rob comes in and begins to stack the dishwasher.

'You got some post, Abigail,' he says. 'It's on the sideboard in the hall.'

Next to the pot where they keep keys and other random paraphernalia, there's a large brown envelope with a typed label. Abby's skin prickles as she reads her name. No address. Hand-delivered.

Again. Is it from the person who sent the Babygro?

She rips it open. A piece of paper falls out and flutters to the floor. Abby picks it up and sucks in her breath sharply. It takes her a moment to make sense of what she's looking at. When she does, she retches in disgust. It's a collage of pictures glued onto the page at strange jarring angles. There's a picture of a twenty-week-old aborted foetus. Next to it a black bin liner full of aborted foetuses that look like broken dolls. One of the foetuses looks like it's been covered in tar. *'Burned by saline abortion,'* reads the caption.

'What've you got there?'

Rob looks over Abby's shoulder.

'Nothing,' she says, and she shoves the page hastily back into the envelope.

Chapter Six

'I don't understand it. He's always here on a Saturday night,' Danny says, bringing their drinks. A pint of lager for him and a Diet Coke for Abby. He plonks them down on the table and pulls up a wooden stool, sipping the froth from the top of his beer.

They're in the Three Compasses, sitting by the large open fireplace. Danny has brought her here to meet Alex Taylor. But so far, there's no sign of him. Behind the bar a young blonde woman is serving drinks, and a middle-aged, bald man is polishing glasses, but there's no Alex, and Abby's beginning to wonder if they're wasting their time. She's still angry with Danny about the other day. They've barely exchanged a word all week and she doesn't want to sit and talk to him if she doesn't have to.

'I guess he's not working tonight. We might as well go home,' she says coldly.

'He'll be here. Let's wait a bit,' Danny answers. And maybe he has heard and understood the tone of her voice because he leans forwards and says, 'Listen, I'm really sorry about the other day. I had no business . . . If it's any excuse, I was extremely tired and hungover. Can you forgive me?' He smiles his most disarming smile, and Abby thaws slightly. It's always difficult to stay angry with Danny for long.

'I'll think about it,' she says, her lips twitching into a smile.

'How did it go, anyway? Are you feeling okay? Was it awful?'

Abby sips her Coke. She's nearly finished it already. She looks longingly at Danny's beer. She would give anything for a drink right now, but she's determined to be responsible. She may feel ambivalent, at best, about this creature inside her, but she doesn't want to harm it.

'Actually, I decided not to go through with it.'

'Really? Why not?' Danny asks carefully. Abby guesses he's trying not to put his foot in it again.

She thinks about the feeling she had in the waiting room and the way she walked to the amphitheatre in the rain. The strange reluctance she felt about returning to the clinic. She isn't sure she can explain. She isn't sure she understands it herself.

'I don't know.' She chews the edge of her thumbnail. 'Pretty stupid, right? Now I'm going to have a baby. I've got no money, no support, and no idea who the father is.'

'No – not stupid, not stupid at all.' He reaches out and pats her arm. 'I know this must be scary for you Abby, but you're not on your own, you know. I'm here for you. Whatever you need.'

'Right, so if I phone you up at two o'clock in the morning

and ask you to come and feed and change the baby, you'll be right over, I suppose?'

He grins. 'Well, maybe not. I was thinking of supporting you more in the moral sense, not in any practical or useful way.'

Abby laughs. It's good to be back on good terms with Danny. He can always make her smile, and she badly needs someone to talk to right now. She remembers the collage of photos in her handbag. She put it in there as she was going out. She's been itching to show him since she got it, but they haven't been speaking.

'Someone sent me this a couple of days ago.' She fishes in her bag, brings out the envelope, and hands it across the table to him.

Danny looks at the pictures and flinches in disgust. Then he slots the collage back in the envelope. 'God, they're horrible, Abby, how distressing for you.'

'It's disturbing, don't you think?' says Abby. 'First the Babygro, now this?'

'You think there's a connection?'

'Don't you?'

He looks thoughtful for a moment, then shakes his head. 'No . . . Doesn't it seem more likely these pictures were sent by an anti-abortion group? And I still think the Babygro must have been sent by the kids at school having a laugh.'

'But how would they even know? No one knows I was considering an abortion.'

Except you. Abby doesn't say it, but the accusation hangs in the air. But she doesn't seriously believe Danny could have sent those pictures. Whatever his views on abortion, Danny would never do something like this. He's her friend. She has to believe that.

'Don't look now, but that's him.' Danny suddenly nudges her and nods towards the bar to where a good-looking, dark-haired man has appeared, pouring drinks and chatting to an old bloke sitting on a bar stool.

Abby doesn't recognize him at all. How can she have forgotten him so completely? She scrutinizes his face, searching for something about him – anything – that seems familiar. He's good-looking in a disreputable kind of way with a narrow face, dark eyes, and tattoos on both forearms, but she could swear she's never seen him before in her life.

'That's him? Are you sure?'

'Positive. I've known him since I was eleven.' Danny drains his beer. 'You should go and buy us another round . . . see if he remembers you.'

'What am I supposed to say?' Abby asks, feeling suddenly nervous. '"Hello, sorry to bother you but I think we might have had sex and now I'm carrying your child"?'

Danny chuckles. 'Of course not. Just order some drinks and strike up a conversation.'

'About what?'

'I don't know. Use your imagination.'

As it turns out, Abby doesn't have to think of anything to say because Alex recognizes her immediately.

'Well, well, well. Abigail Brooke, isn't it?' He smiles as she approaches. It's a lazy, teasing smile which makes her stomach flip in a way that has nothing to do with the baby inside her. He's a man who's used to getting women's attention, Abby thinks. She can't imagine he finds it difficult getting a sober woman into bed. Why would he resort to taking advantage of someone who was paralytic? But maybe he was as drunk as she was. That would explain a lot.

'You remember me?' she asks carefully.

He grins wolfishly. His eyes are dark green and seem to bore into her. 'How could I forget?' he says. 'Danny's party, New Year's Eve, right?'

Jesus. How could he forget what? She clasps her hands behind her back. There's something threatening about him, like the air before a thunderstorm. She's attracted and repelled at the same time.

'You were a very entertaining drunk.' He leans on the bar, smiling.

Abby knows this is her opportunity to find out exactly what happened that night. But she finds herself tongue-tied. She wishes she were drunk now. That would make this a whole lot easier.

'Well, what can I get for you, Abby?'

'A pint and a Diet Coke please.' Abby props herself up awkwardly on a bar stool.

'How the hell is Danny, anyway?' he asks, pulling the tap handle. 'I haven't seen him for ages.'

'You can ask him yourself. He's over there.' She points to the table where Danny is just visible through the crowd, sitting fiddling with his phone.

'Oh, yeah.' Alex plonks the glasses on the bar. 'I might just do that. How long do you think you'll be here?'

'We weren't planning to go anywhere else.'

He grins. 'Good. Stick around. I'll see if I can get some time off later.'

'Well?' says Danny when she comes back with the drinks. 'Did you remember anything? Did seeing him jog your memory at all?'

'No. That's the scary thing. It's like meeting a complete stranger. If I don't remember talking to him, I suppose I could easily have had sex with him and forgotten about it.'

Danny sucks in one cheek. 'I'm telling you, if you were so drunk that you don't even remember meeting him, I just don't think Alex would have slept with you.'

'Maybe he didn't realize how out of it I was?'

'Hmm, maybe.' Danny looks unconvinced. 'Anyway –' he takes a small notepad out of his jeans pocket – 'I made that list you asked me to make.' He tears a page out and hands it to her.

Abby looks at the paper. It's a list of about twelve men's names, written in Danny's large flamboyant handwriting. Some of the names have been highlighted in yellow.

'It was a busy party – is this everyone?'

'I left out the women – for obvious reasons – and as you can see, I've highlighted some names for you. The rest of them are gay, so you can probably rule them out.'

'Probably?'

He sighs as if he's explaining the obvious. 'Well, some of

54

them might swing both ways. It's not impossible, you know. Even *I* slept with a couple of women in my early twenties when I was still in denial about my sexuality.'

'Really?' Abby leans forward, intrigued. 'What was it like?'

He shrugs. 'It was a bit dispiriting, actually. It's difficult to explain. I had to imagine I was doing it with a man to get any satisfaction, and there was no emotional connection.'

Abby absorbs this. It's not hard to imagine women being attracted to Danny. He's handsome and charming. She's embarrassed to admit it now, but she was attracted to him herself, when she first met him, before she knew he was gay.

She stares into the fire, the flames licking at the logs. Then back at the list Danny's given her.

There are four highlighted names:

Alex Taylor
Chris Baker
Andrew Wilson
Hugo Langley

Chris is a big teddy bear of a man married to her friend Thea, an English teacher at the school. She can't believe that he could be the man they're looking for. She can't imagine him cheating on Thea for a start.

'Who are Andrew Wilson and Hugo Langley?' she asks.

'Hugo's a friend of mine from uni.' Danny's mouth curls a little. 'I use the term "friend" loosely. He's a bit of an arse-hole, to tell the truth.'

Abby nods. 'And Andrew Wilson?'

'He's Mark's friend. About his only friend, as far as I can tell. They met at the medieval re-enactment society he belongs to.'

'Mark's a re-enactor?' Abby can't help smiling. She's still trying and failing to imagine Mark in a suit of armour holding a sword when Alex comes over carrying a couple of tequilas and a pint.

'On the house,' he says. 'I remember you like these.' He winks at Abby, pulling out a chair between her and Danny.

'How are you, Danny?' Alex asks. 'I haven't seen you for ages. I think the last time must have been New Year's Eve. It was a great night, wasn't it?' he adds, looking at Abby.

'I don't remember much about it,' Abby says, as casually as possible. 'I was so drunk, I don't even remember getting home. I think someone gave me a lift. It wasn't you, was it?'

Alex shrugs. 'No, it wasn't, unfortunately.' He smiles at her. 'You blew me off. You told me I was the best-looking man in the room, told me you wanted to have my babies, then you went to the toilet and didn't come back. The next time I saw you, you were leaving with some arsehole.'

Danny's eyes glitter with attention. 'Who was it?' he asks, leaning forward.

'I don't know his name. He works at one of the estate agents in town. He spent the whole evening handing out his card to everyone. Come to think of it, I've probably still got one.' Alex fishes in his back pocket and brings out a wallet, pulls out a selection of business cards, and flicks through them. 'Ah, yes here we go. *Andrew Wilson, Estate Agent, Brown and Lowe.*'

'Andrew Wilson?' Abby repeats, exchanging a look with Danny.

'Yeah, that's the guy. He looked like he was pushing forty, going thin on top. God knows what you saw in him. Wouldn't have thought he was much of a catch. But there's no accounting for taste.' Alex grins. His green eyes meet Abby's, and then he looks down at his beer glass, the liquid swirling. The old man at the bar is getting worked up about something. His voice raises as he bangs his fist on the bar.

'Anyway, how are you, mate?' Alex slaps Danny on the back. He turns to Abby. 'Has Danny told you we went to school together?'

'He did.' Abby looks at Danny, who is smiling uncomfortably.

'We've been mates since . . . God, since we were eleven, right? How many years is that? I'm telling you, Abigail, I could tell you a few stories.'

'Please don't,' says Danny. His tone is light, but Abby thinks she detects an edge to his voice. Danny has told her before that he was bullied at school, and she knows it must bring back painful memories. She has sometimes wondered why he chose to come back and work in the very same place where he had such a bad time, but maybe it's his way of squaring the circle.

'Don't worry. I won't tell her anything too embarrassing.' Alex grins. 'We used to call him Spielberg. He was really into making movies. Do you remember when we made a horror movie? What was it called?'

'The Ashridge Witch Project.'

Alex snorts with laughter. 'Yeah, that was it. He made us all go to Ashridge Park at night. We didn't have to act much. We were scared shitless.'

Danny chuckles. 'Remember Jess, when we found the severed hand you made? The look on her face!'

They both laugh.

'You were going to be a great movie director, do you remember?'

'Yeah, and look at me now.' Danny grimaces. 'Reduced to directing the school play.'

'Well, we all had dreams. I was going to be the next Jimi Hendrix.' Alex laughs ruefully. 'And instead I'm stuck in a dead-end job pulling pints.'

'You started that band in the sixth form and were too cool to hang out with me,' says Danny. 'The Impossible Moon. Whatever happened to that?'

'Yeah, well, life takes over.' Alex starts ripping up a beer mat. 'How about you, Abby? Did you always want to teach Art?'

Abby starts, surprised. 'How do you know I'm an Art teacher?'

'You told me at Danny's party. We were talking for ages. Do you really remember nothing?'

Abby shakes her head. 'I'm afraid not.' She wonders what else she might have told him. She has a horrible out-of-control feeling, not knowing what she said or did that night.

The conversation drifts onto other topics until Alex drains

his drink and stands up. 'Well, I'd better get back to work. Graham is giving me evils.' He takes his phone out of his back pocket.

'Do you have a phone number, Abby? We should get together sometime. Go see a movie or something.'

'Er . . . yes.' Abby is taken aback. 'That would be nice,' she says automatically. She tells him her number and he adds it to his contact list.

'Great.' He grins, and saunters away.

'That was quick work,' Danny comments once he's out of earshot. 'Are you really going to go out with him?'

Abby fiddles with her beer mat, tearing at the corners. 'I don't know. Maybe.'

'Are you sure that's a good idea?'

'Why not?'

'Well, he's a great guy, but he's not exactly boyfriend material. You know I told you he was in trouble with the police before.'

'I'm not looking for a boyfriend right now.' Abby shrugs. 'I just think it might be useful to meet him again and talk. I need to find out if anything happened between us.' As she says this, she wonders if it's entirely true. She does want to find out what happened, but she wouldn't be being honest with herself if she didn't admit that she's also more than a little attracted to Alex Taylor.

Danny sighs. 'It wasn't Alex, Abby. You heard him. He said you left with Mark's friend, Andrew Wilson. Isn't it much more likely to be him?'

Abby turns this idea over in her head. 'But I was flirting with Alex all night. Why would I sleep with someone else? Unless . . . you were right. About me being raped, I mean.' She breaks off.

'Abby, I shouldn't have said that before. I really think you would remember someone attacking you, no matter how drunk you were.' Danny's voice is sympathetic, but Abby can detect a hint of impatience.

'Not if I was already unconscious,' she says.

'You really think you drank that much?'

Tears prick at the back of Abby's eyes as another idea, even more horrible, occurs to her. 'Someone could have slipped something into my drink.'

'You mean like a date-rape drug?' Danny looks incredulous.

'It would explain why I don't remember anything.' It would explain, too, why she didn't come back from the toilet after talking to Alex, when she was obviously so into him.

'I don't know.' Danny shakes his head, his leg jiggling nervously. 'It's possible, I suppose, but surely you would have noticed something at the time?'

Abby nods. 'You're probably right.' She wants to believe Danny. But the idea won't go away. She's been drunk before, she has even blacked out before, but she's never had such a giant hole in her memory. If she'd been drugged, it would explain a lot. She looks down at her drink, feeling dizzy. The atmosphere in the pub is suddenly suffocating, like there's not enough air to breathe. It's too hot, and the room feels too small, as if the walls are closing in on her. Someone laughs loudly, and the sound makes her shudder.

'Let's get out of here.' She gulps down her Coke. 'I've had enough of this place.'

'Alright,' Danny agrees, draining his beer.

Danny's right, of course, Abby convinces herself as they walk to the car through the rain. What are the chances she was raped? Isn't it much more likely she was simply drunk?

APRIL

By the end of the third month, your baby already has arms, hands, fingers and toes. Tiny hands open and close. Fingernails and toenails are growing, and external ears develop. Reproductive organs are developing as well, but it will not yet be possible to determine the sex of the baby from an ultrasound.

Chapter Seven

Abby is fighting back nausea. The children are using oil paints and there is a strong smell of turpentine in the classroom. With an effort of will she controls the urge to throw up. She stands up and walks around, looking at the children's work, giving encouragement and advice where needed.

At least so far, the lesson is going well. The rain of the past few days has finally stopped, and a weak, cold sun is seeping through the grimy windows painting haloes around the children's heads. Nine Yellow are far from angelic, but they are unusually subdued and compliant today. Even the biggest troublemakers, Carl Hunter and Kiera Brown, are quiet. Okay, Carl has chosen to paint a phallus rather than the still life in the style of Manet that he's supposed to be doing, but Abby is choosing to ignore this. At least he's not being disruptive.

But it turns out to be the calm before the storm. Ten minutes before the end of the lesson an argument breaks out between Kiera Brown and Hannah Logan. Abby tries her best to ignore them, but soon their voices are raised so loud she's forced to go and intervene.

'What's the problem, girls?' she asks, wrapping her cardigan around her belly. She hasn't bought any maternity clothes yet, and under her baggy top, her trousers are held together with a safety pin because she can no longer do them up.

'Kiera says you're pregnant – you're not pregnant, are you, miss?' says Hannah, her grey eyes gleaming with malicious pleasure.

The question catches her off guard.

'What?' she says.

'There's a rumour going around that you're pregnant. But I told her it weren't true. It ain't, is it?'

Now the whole class is silent, listening. They're all staring at her. Abby feels the heat rise in her cheeks. 'That has nothing at all to do with the lesson,' she says. 'Now, will you please get on with your work.'

'I told you, it *is* true. She's pregnant,' says Kiera gleefully, sensing an opportunity to create trouble. 'How many months are you, miss?'

'That's really none of your business . . . Now, can you all just get on with your work.' Abby realizes she's getting flustered, and predictably Carl pounces, enjoying her discomfort.

'Who's the father, miss? Is it Mr Campbell? Is he your boyfriend, miss?'

'No, of course not. He's my brother-in-law.'

'Mr Thomas then, it's Mr Thomas, isn't it?'

'Don't be dumb, Mr Thomas is gay,' Aaron Rowe interjects, pushing his glasses up his nose. He's usually a quiet, studious boy and it's so unexpected, him challenging Carl Hunter, that for a moment everyone is silent. Even Carl looks taken aback.

'Like you, you mean,' he hurls back after a couple of seconds. Then he stands up. He's about six feet tall and broad, too, with serious anger-management issues. Abby has no idea why Aaron, who usually wouldn't say boo to a goose, has chosen to provoke the biggest, meanest kid in Year Nine, but she wishes he hadn't.

'Sit down please, Carl,' she says, as calmly as possible.

'But, miss, you heard him, he called me dumb. That's well out of order, that is.' But even as Carl is about to do as he's told, Aaron opens his mouth again.

'Idiot,' he mutters under his breath.

'What did you say?' Carl's face is red now with anger. He stands up again and stomps over to Aaron. 'Say that again to my face.'

'I didn't say anything,' Aaron says.

'Sit down please, Carl, or I'll have to give you a behaviour point,' Abby says, desperately trying to avert a disaster.

But it's too late. Carl has gone beyond listening to reason. He wrenches Aaron out of his chair. Then he tears the glasses off his face and holds them up above his head, laughing.

'Give them back!' Aaron tries to grab the glasses, but Carl pushes him away. Then Aaron pushes him back and they start punching and kicking each other.

'Stop that right now!' shouts Abby, but her voice is shrill, and it's drowned out by the shouting that erupts from the kids.

This is getting out of control. Abby tries to fight back

panic, unsure what to do. On the one hand, she'd like to be able to handle the situation herself. On the other, somebody might get hurt if she doesn't do something quickly. She needs to get help.

'Skye, can you go and get Mr Campbell,' she says urgently to one of the more responsible girls.

'Yes, miss,' says Skye, wide-eyed, and she scampers off.

By the time the girl returns out of breath, with Rob in tow, the boys are on the floor and Carl is pummelling Aaron's face, while Abby and a couple of the children are trying to pull him off. With Rob's help they manage to separate them. Rob does some bellowing, which silences the class, and then frogmarches Aaron and Carl down to the inclusion unit. The class settles back down and a few minutes later, thankfully, the bell goes for lunchbreak.

'Are you okay?' Rob asks in the staff room.

Abby nods, nursing a cup of tea. She feels embarrassed that she had to turn to Rob to control the situation.

'Yes, I'm fine. I just don't know what happened. One minute they were getting on with their work and the next, well, it was pandemonium, as you saw. God, please don't tell Gina about this. She already thinks I'm incompetent as it is.'

'Don't worry. It was bound to happen sooner or later. If it hadn't happened in your class it would have happened in someone else's,' says Rob filling his cup from the urn. 'Carl Hunter has been asking for trouble since the beginning of term.'

'You're telling me. That boy's always spoiling for a fight,' agrees Abby. 'What I don't understand is what got into Aaron Rowe. He's usually so quiet.'

Rob sits down opposite her and slurps his coffee.

'His mum has just remarried and there are some problems at home, apparently. He doesn't get on with his stepdad. Maybe that has something to do with it. What were they fighting about anyway?'

'Oh, nothing much. Aaron called Carl dumb.' She really doesn't want to get into the conversation that started the fight. She's been so shaken she'd almost forgotten about it, but now she's calming down she starts brooding. How has Kiera found out about her pregnancy? Has Danny told more people than he let on? Or is it just inspired guesswork?

Then another thought occurs to her. Perhaps Aaron is the source of the rumour. He's Dr Rowe's son, after all. It would be a breach of doctor–patient confidentiality for him to have told his son, but Abby knows, from the things that Ellie sometimes tells her, that doctor–patient confidentiality is not always as sacred as it should be.

Abby broaches the subject with Dr Rowe when she's having a check-up, a couple of days later.

'You didn't tell anyone about me being pregnant, did you?' she says as he takes her blood pressure. She sucks in her breath as the band tightens, squeezing her arm until it's almost painful.

'Of course not,' he says, loosening the band and noting something down.

'Not to Ellie, maybe . . . or to Aaron?'

'No. Your blood pressure is a little high but nothing to worry about. We'll just keep an eye on it.'

'It's just that all the kids in Aaron's class seem to know, or at least suspect, and I don't know how. I haven't even told Ellie yet.'

Dr Rowe sits down and types into the computer. 'Well, I promise you I said nothing to my son.' He grimaces. 'Anyway, chance would be a fine thing. I hardly see him. His mother and I divorced a couple of years ago.'

Abby remembers what Rob told her about Aaron's stepfather.

'Is Aaron okay? Did you know he got into a fight the other day?'

Dr Rowe stares at her. 'I didn't. But it doesn't surprise me. His mother remarried recently, and he doesn't get on with his stepfather. Can't say I blame him. He's a nasty piece of work.' For a second the normally sunny Dr Rowe looks downright miserable. Then he gives himself a little shake.

'Anyway, take a look at this.' He smiles. He turns his monitor to show her the website he's looking at. 'This is a foetus at sixteen weeks. This is what your baby looks like now.'

Abby stares at the screen, fascinated. In some images it looks almost like a fully formed baby, its hands clasped as if praying. In others, it looks like an astronaut floating in space, its overlarge head like a helmet, its black eyes covered with a thin film of skin.

'It doesn't seem long ago that Aaron and Katie were that

size.' Dr Rowe smiles wistfully, and a dimple appears in one cheek. 'They grow up before you know it.'

Abby nods politely. As far as she's concerned, the quicker this thing grows and is out of her, the better.

The doctor rubs his hands together. 'Now then, would you like to hear your baby's heartbeat?'

Abby's really not sure she wants to hear the baby's heartbeat, but he seems so enthusiastic that she lies down on the couch and lets him rub gel on her stomach. Then he twiddles a dial on an old-fashioned-looking machine and Abby hears a faint beat like tiny horses galloping.

'There, that's it!' He beams. 'That's your baby's heartbeat.'

'It's very fast.'

'Oh, that's completely normal. It's about twice the speed of an adult heartbeat. Anyway, everything seems fine.' Dr Rowe takes off his gloves and Abby sits up.

'So, do you have any other questions?' he asks.

Abby takes a deep breath. She knows he means questions about the baby, but there are other things on her mind, questions Dr Rowe might be able to answer. Questions she badly needs answered.

'This is kind of unrelated,' she says, 'but I was wondering how much alcohol a person would have to drink to lose their memory?'

Dr Rowe eyes her curiously. 'Well, that depends on the size of the person and how their body reacts to alcohol. It also depends on how quickly you drink and whether you're drinking on an empty stomach. Someone your size, not all that much, I should think. Maybe, eight or nine glasses of wine.'

Abby doesn't remember exactly how much she drank on New Year's Eve. She definitely drank quickly. But she can't shake the feeling that what happened wasn't a normal case of getting drunk. She's probably being paranoid, but she needs to know if her suspicions are plausible.

'And . . .' She flushes. 'A friend of mine thinks she might have been given a date-rape drug. How would she know?'

'Well . . .' Dr Rowe gives her a sharp look. 'It depends on the type of drug used. Rohypnol, for example, can be detected in the body for up to seventy-two hours, so I would advise your friend to go and get herself tested as soon as possible.'

'What if it happened months ago? How would she know?'

He shrugs. 'There would be no way for her to know for sure if she'd been drinking or taking drugs as well. Often people feel sick and very tired for days after, with flu-like symptoms. Does that answer your question?'

There's an awkward silence.

'If you need to talk about anything, Abby, you know I'm always here, and anything you tell me is completely confidential,' Dr Rowe says gently. Clearly, he doesn't believe in the existence of her friend and has guessed that she's talking about herself. For a moment, she contemplates confiding in him. Then decides against it. The fewer people who know about this the better.

'Thank you,' she says. 'I know.'

Dr Rowe waits, and then, when she says nothing else, he

sighs and says, 'I didn't tell Aaron or Ellie about your pregnancy. I never discuss my patients with anyone. But I think you should consider speaking to your sister yourself. She's going to know soon enough anyway.'

Abby nods. 'I know, but I want to tell her in my own time. I'm not sure how she's going to take it after losing the baby.'

Dr Rowe nods. He knows all about Ellie's loss, and was very understanding when it happened, giving her time off when she needed it. If it wasn't for Dr Rowe, Ellie could easily have lost her job as well as her baby.

After a pause, he says, 'Isn't it better that you tell her than if she guesses or hears it from someone else?'

Abby knows that Dr Rowe is right. She needs to talk to Ellie soon. The longer she leaves it, the worse it will be. On her way home Abby resolves to tell her as soon as she sees her. It will be okay, she thinks, trying to convince herself. *Just spit it out and get it over with.*

But when she gets home Ellie is lying on the sofa in the living room, clutching her head. The curtains are drawn, and the room is dark. 'One of my migraines,' Ellie groans as Abby comes in.

'You poor thing. Can I get you anything?'

'Just some water. And a bucket.'

Abby goes to fetch some water from the tap in the kitchen. Her revelation will have to wait until Ellie feels better.

On the kitchen table, there are flowers. Bright red tulips in a vase. Abby runs the tap wondering vaguely where they've come from. Perhaps Rob brought them for Ellie, or more likely Ellie bought them herself to brighten the place up. Rob is not generally one for romantic gestures. He buys Ellie flowers on Valentine's Day and that's about it.

Abby takes the glass through to the living room and places it on the coffee table next to Ellie.

Ellie groans and rolls over. 'Thank you,' she says. She sits up and sips at the water. 'I'm feeling a bit better. Think it's the ibuprofen kicking in.'

'Who bought the flowers?' Abby asks, sitting in the armchair.

'Oh,' Ellie feels in her pocket. 'I forgot, They're for you. I put them in a vase. I hope you don't mind. I didn't want them to die.' She fishes in her pocket and pulls out a small, white sealed envelope with 'Abigail' typed neatly on the front. 'This came with them.'

Abby tears open the envelope, and pulls out a small white florist's card and reads the message:

Abigail,
with love.

She turns the card over in her hand. There's nothing else, just those words, '*Abigail, with love.*' There's no clue as to who sent it. And there's nothing obviously threatening about it, but all the same Abby feels unsettled, even disturbed. *Why haven't they signed their name?*

'Where did they come from?' she asks Ellie.

'They were on the doorstep when I got back from work. Who are they from?'

'It doesn't say.'

'Well, it looks like you've got a secret admirer. How exciting.' Ellie smiles. 'Who do you think it could be?'

Abby smiles back faintly. 'I've got no idea,' she says. She throws the card in the bin and then puts it to the back of her mind.

Chapter Eight

Mark opens the door before Abby gets the chance to ring the bell.

'I saw you coming up the road,' he explains. He's dressed in jogging bottoms and a T-shirt, holding a roll of kitchen towel in his hands. He reeks of bleach and Abby, who is newly sensitive to smells, tries not to retch. 'I was cleaning the windows.'

With bleach? Abby thinks. *Who cleans their windows with bleach?* Out loud she says, 'Is Danny about?'

'I haven't seen him this morning. I think he's still in bed,' Mark mumbles vaguely.

'Oh,' she says. She looks at her watch. She's sure they agreed 10.30. Yesterday evening at school, they arranged to go to Brown and Lowe's, the estate agents, today. They planned it all out. They were going to talk to Andrew Wilson, pretend that Abby was looking for a new flat and somehow bring the conversation around to New Year's Eve, but Danny has obviously forgotten.

'Shall I wake him up?' asks Mark.

'Not yet. Give him a few more minutes. I'll come in and wait if that's okay.'

'Sure,' he says, standing back to let her in and flushing slightly. 'Do you want a cup of tea?'

She follows him into the kitchen and sits at the table watching as he fills the kettle.

He pours hot water into two cups, then sits opposite her, his elbows resting on the scratched pine table.

'How are you?'

'Um, okay, you?'

'Alright.'

There's an awkward silence. She never sees Mark without Danny, she realizes, and, like most people, Mark fades into the background when Danny's around. She wonders vaguely if he's a bit shy. She chews her nail, searching for something to say, and comes up blank.

'Have you found your necklace yet?' he asks at last.

'What?' she says momentarily confused. Then she remembers the lie she told last time she was here. 'Oh . . . no. Not yet.'

'I've been looking for you but so far no luck.'

'Thank you.' Abby hopes he hasn't spent too much time looking for something that he'll never find. But it gives her an idea.

'I wish I could remember what I did that night,' she says. 'If I could retrace my steps, maybe I'd know where else to look. I know I started off in the kitchen with you but after that, it's a bit of a blank.'

Mark scratches his head.

'Well, like you say, we were in the kitchen at the start of the evening. I don't remember whether you were wearing the necklace or not at that point. Then Chris and Thea turned up and we drank some more.'

'How much did I drink?'

He shrugs. 'I don't know. Quite a few. Then you wandered off and the next time I saw you, you were sitting on the stairs with Danny's friend, Alex.'

'How long was I talking to him?'

If Mark thinks this is an odd question, he doesn't let on. 'I'm not sure. I spent the next couple of hours in my room talking to Andy and Chris and a bunch of Danny's friends, that tall, red-haired guy . . .'

'Hugo?'

'Yes, that's it. Then you came in, looking for him.'

'For Alex?'

'Yes. I suppose you could have dropped the necklace then, somewhere in my room. Do you want to have a look?'

Abby hesitates. It feels strangely intimate, going to Mark's bedroom. Until recently she wouldn't have thought twice, but lately she's become warier. She doesn't really trust anyone anymore, even Mark. But he's already bounding up the stairs, taking them two at a time. It seems rude not to follow him. It's only Mark, after all.

As soon as she enters the room she's hit by a strong feeling of déjà vu. There's a musket hanging on the wall. She's sure she's seen it before, as well as the neatly made white bed. The blue curtains flutter in a breeze from the open window. And she remembers something. There was a woman sprawled on the bed, her long, dark corkscrew curls splayed over the pillow. She was laughing loudly. And there was a man with red hair sitting on the rug over there, under the musket. She can see him quite clearly, his long, lanky legs drawn up, smoking a roll-up, exhaling smoke languidly, looking at her through narrow eyes. For a second the image is so intense she feels dizzy, and she feels like she's about to faint. She steadies herself by putting her hands on the bed.

Then she looks up and notices Mark watching her curiously. 'Are you okay?' he asks.

She flushes with embarrassment. He must think she's so weird.

'Yes, I'm alright. It's nothing, I just felt a little faint for a moment.'

She scans the room in search of a distraction and makes a pretence of admiring the gun on the wall. 'This looks old, is it real?'

'It's a matchlock musket, seventeenth-century,' he says proudly. 'From the English Civil War. That one's real. The rest are replicas.'

'The rest?'

He unlocks a cupboard, revealing an alarming display of weapons – swords, guns and bayonets.

'Wow,' Abby exclaims, not knowing what else to say. 'Danny told me you were a re-enactor, but I had no idea you took it so seriously.'

He grins. 'Keeps me out of mischief.'

'You go with that friend of yours, don't you? The estate agent . . . I met him at your New Year's party . . . What's his name?' Abby tries to sound nonchalant, like she's not really interested but isn't entirely sure she pulls it off.

'Andy?' Mark suggests.

'Yes. Andy. What's he like?'

Mark shrugs. 'He's alright.'

She waits for him to expand on this statement, but he doesn't seem to think it requires elaboration.

'I mean . . . How well do you know him? Is he a trustworthy kind of person?'

Mark frowns. 'You do know he's married, don't you?'

'Oh, I'm not interested in him in that way.' Abby flushes. 'It's just . . . I was wondering if he would be a good person to help me find a flat, that's all.'

'Why?' Mark closes the cupboard door and locks it. 'Are you thinking of moving?'

'Yes.'

'How come?'

Abby thinks quickly. 'I've not been getting on so well with Rob and Ellie lately. I think I've outstayed my welcome. Sometimes I feel like I need a bit of space.' It's true, of course, she does need space, but Abby is not really thinking of moving out. Rent-free accommodation is just too attractive an option. And with her student loan still to pay off, she's willing to take any amount of inconvenience to save money.

'Three's a crowd, huh?' Mark says.

'Something like that.'

Mark looks at the floor, not meeting her eyes. 'You know we've got a spare room here. We could always use the extra rent money.'

'Thanks, I'll bear that in mind.'

They spend the next few minutes in a totally pointless search under the bed and behind furniture for a non-existent necklace and Abby is relieved when Danny appears in the doorway, looking pale and haggard.

'Danny,' Abby says. 'Are you still up for helping me with the house hunting?'

Danny groans and slaps his head, 'Shit, I forgot about that. Listen, Abby, I'm sorry, I don't think I'm going to be able to. I'm feeling like death. I've been up half the night vomiting. I think I've got a bug of some kind. Can we postpone till next weekend?'

But Abby doesn't want to put this off. It's been over a month already since she discovered she was pregnant and she's still no closer to discovering what happened.

'I might just go myself,' she says, standing up and brushing dust off her knees. It seems even Mark has dust under his bed.

Danny winces and clutches his belly. 'Are you sure that's a good idea, Abs? I mean . . .' He breaks off, realizing that Mark is listening. 'I mean, you'll need a second opinion, won't you?'

'Why not?' says Abby with more confidence than she really feels. She can think of quite a few reasons why not. For one, if Andrew Wilson really did rape her, then he could be dangerous. If he's capable of doing that, then what else could he be capable of? But she needs to know. It's eating away at her – the not knowing – and she's worried that if she doesn't act now she'll chicken out.

'Hope you feel better soon, Danny,' she says, heading downstairs.

'Just be careful, Abs,' Danny calls, shuffling back to his bedroom.

'Say hi from me,' says Mark, showing her out. 'If he knows you're my friend I'm sure he'll give you a good deal.'

Chapter Nine

Brown and Lowe's is in an old part of town squeezed between an antique shop and a solicitor's. From the look of the houses advertised in the window it deals mainly in expensive properties, the kind with aerial shots of acres of land and no price attached. Not for the likes of Abby. But she's not here to buy property.

She hesitates for a moment outside, trying to build up her courage. Then she takes a deep breath and pushes open the door.

Inside is a large office with two big empty desks. A couple of framed photos of local beauty spots hang on the walls but otherwise the space is bland and colourless. A man in his late thirties or early forties is sitting at one of the desks, on the phone. He's wearing a suit and a pink tie. He looks up as she walks in and she thinks she detects a flash of recognition in his eyes.

'Hold on one moment.' He covers the phone with his hand. 'Please take a seat,' he says smoothly. 'I'll be with you in a moment.'

While his attention is diverted she looks at him carefully and notices he's wearing a name badge that says *Andrew Wilson*. It's him. She draws in her breath, suddenly wishing she'd waited for Danny. She was stupid to come here alone. But it's too late now. Anyway, he looks harmless enough, wide set, with reddish cheeks. He looks wholesome, even. More like a farmer than an estate agent.

When he's finished on the phone he stands up and holds out his hand for her to shake. She's frustrated to note her hand is trembling a little as she takes his. Since when did she become such a scaredy-cat?

'How can I help you?' he asks pleasantly.

She clears her throat. 'I'm a friend of Mark's.'

'Yes, I remember you. We met on New Year's Eve, didn't we? Abigail, isn't it?'

Abby nods. 'That's right. Mark said you might be able to help me. I'm looking for a flat, a one-bed.' She quotes the price of a flat she's seen online.

Andrew Wilson raises his eyebrows. 'Hmm. It might be tricky to find something in town in your price range, but I'll see what I can do.'

As he taps at the keyboard on his computer she notices the wedding band on his ring finger and the photo of his family on his desk: a wife and two teenaged children. And she feels disgusted. Even if he didn't take advantage of her – even if the sex was consensual, or at least he thought it was consensual – at the very least he's betrayed his wife and his family.

'A studio might be your best bet,' he says, showing her a selection of pictures on the computer.

'I like this one.' She stabs randomly at an image of what looks like a stately home. Ivy covers half the façade. 'But that can't be in my price range, surely.'

'Well . . .' He laughs. 'You don't get the whole thing, of course. It's divided into flats, but it is a bit of a bargain, that. It's a bit out of town in the village of Bibury. Do you know it? The property's empty at the moment so we can go and view it now if you like.'

Abby finds herself nodding.

'Where did you park your car?' he asks.

'Um, I walked.' She doesn't tell him she doesn't have a car, because if he knows that, he might wonder why she wants to look at a property so far out of town.

'I'll give you a lift then,' he says, picking up a briefcase. Now she's standing next to him, she realizes how tall he is. Tall and broad. She barely comes up to his chest. She wouldn't stand much of a chance in a fight. She swallows a sudden panic. What's to stop him driving her off to a secluded spot and raping her again, or worse? She tells herself she's being paranoid. Still, there's no harm in taking precautions.

'I'll just ring my boyfriend,' she says pointedly, as they step out onto the street. 'Let him know where I'm going. He might want to meet us there.' She takes out her phone and rings Danny. But his phone is switched off. *Shit, why's he switched his phone off?* Danny never switches his phone off. Maybe it's out of battery. She speaks anyway, pretending he's answered.

'I'm at the estate agents, Brown and Lowe's, with Andrew Wilson,' she says loudly. 'I'm going to see a flat.' She gives him the address. 'You can come and meet us there, if you've got time.'

Then she nods and smiles, pretending to listen.

'Yes, okay. I'll see you later,' she says, and hangs up.

It's enough, she hopes. Andrew Wilson is warned. He knows that she's told someone where she's going and who with. He would be stupid to try anything.

A sleek, black BMW is parked halfway down the street, squeezed into a tight parking space between two other cars. As soon as she climbs in and inhales the familiar smell of new leather seats and gardenia air freshener she knows: she's been in this car before.

Abby is silent as they head through the town centre. She's fighting a growing sense of unease, thinking about what could have happened in this car.

'You gave me a lift home on New Year's Eve, didn't you?' she blurts.

'Yes, that's right,' says Andrew evenly. 'I'm surprised you remember, though. You were a bit worse for wear that night.'

Abby grips the seat. She must be crazy accepting a lift from this man. But it's too late now. They're already on their way, heading out of town towards the ring road.

'I know,' she says, keeping her voice steady. She must keep it casual. Avoid letting on that she suspects anything – that if they did sleep together, she just regards it as a normal one-night stand. 'I had a bit too much to drink. I really don't remember much at all. Did you come into the house?'

Andrew Wilson stares straight ahead at the road, smiling slightly.

'No, nothing like that. I'm nearly old enough to be your father.'

'So, nothing happened between us? We didn't sleep together?' Abby clasps her hands in her lap and looks across at him, studying his face.

His neck flushes red and he gives a short, embarrassed laugh. 'No. I'm a married man. I only gave you a lift because I was worried about you. You said you were going to walk home alone. You were upset about something ... and, well ... my niece is about your age. I wouldn't want her walking home on her own at that time of night.'

'So, you just dropped me at my door and that was it. You didn't come in?'

'Well, I waited until you were inside and then I drove off.'

He sounds convincing. He even sounds genuinely shocked that she would suggest that they'd slept together. And Abby finds herself wondering if he's exactly what he seems – a nice, normal, middle-aged man. But she's lost faith in her ability to judge truth from lies. She's entered a crazy new world where the impossible can happen and no one is to be trusted.

They are driving along a country lane now, hedges whizzing past. Andrew drives fast, not slowing down for sharp bends. Abby grips the seat and tries to remain clear-headed, logical. She needs to make the most of this situation, find out as much as possible.

'What time was it when you dropped me off?'

If he thinks it's strange that she wants to know the time she arrived home more than three months ago, he hides it well.

'Let me see. It must have been about two o'clock, I think. I got to my house around half past two and it probably took me a half-hour to drive home.'

He slows down a little to pass through a quaint Cotswold village and over a river.

'Look, I promise you, nothing happened.'

He sounds so plausible, but as they turn into a gravel driveway and through an imposing stone gateway, Abby wonders what a married middle-aged man is doing at a party with twenty-somethings. *And why didn't his wife come with him that night? Surely it's normal to spend New Year's Eve together with your nearest and dearest?*

He pulls up outside the large Cotswold stone mansion and kills the engine. They step out and Abby looks at the wide sweeping lawns that lead down to a lake. The wind is gusting across the open space and she shivers in her thin jacket.

'You would have shared access to the gardens,' says Andrew Wilson. 'And there's plenty of parking space, as you can see.'

They climb a dark carpeted staircase and he slips a key into the lock. The flat is cold, empty of furniture and slightly musty. There's a dead fly on the windowsill. The door swings shut with a thud and Abby tries not to think about the fact that she is all alone with him or that she is only five-foot-two and he is over six foot. She wishes she'd carried on with those self-defence classes. She had attended the classes with Ellie years ago, after Ellie was almost attacked just outside their home, but she doesn't remember much.

'It's a great view, isn't it?' says Andrew Wilson half-heartedly. She follows him to the window and stares out at the grey sky and the wide, sweeping lawns. 'Well, feel free to have a look around.'

Abby pretends to take an interest in the kitchen – the grimy-looking electric hob and the cheap-looking counters. She's trying to ignore the rising feeling of unease inside her. She wraps her fingers round the keys in her pocket, making them into a knuckle duster. You're supposed to go for the eyes, she remembers that much.

'Is there a dishwasher?' she asks.

'Um, I believe so.' He opens a few doors. 'Yes, there you go.'

Abby looks in the bathroom and the bedroom as quickly as possible.

'Okay,' she says. 'Let's go.'

Andrew Wilson looks at his watch. 'What about your boy-friend? Aren't we meeting him here?'

'What? Oh, no, he messaged me to say he can't make it.'

'Okay,' he shrugs. 'If you've seen enough.'

'So, what did you think of the flat?' Andrew asks as they drive back to town.

'I'll need to discuss it with my boyfriend.'

'Yes, of course.'

It starts raining a light splatter against the windscreen and Andrew Wilson turns on the windscreen wipers. Abby stares at them, mesmerized. They remind her of something. Then she realizes what it is. An image flashes into her mind: snow-flakes, lit up in the car headlights like a swarm of insects, the wipers squeaking as they pushed away the snow.

'It was snowing on New Year's Eve, when we drove home,' she says.

Andrew Wilson glances sidelong at her. 'Yes, that's right. It had just started to snow. So, you do remember some things?'

'Not much,' she says. 'I wish I could. Can you remember anything else about that night – the New Year's Eve party? I'm trying to piece together what happened.'

He shrugs. 'What do you want to know?'

'Did you see me at all at the party? What was I doing, who was I talking to?'

'Let me see . . . When I arrived you were talking to some bloke on the stairs. I went into the living room and chatted with Mark and another bloke, a Chemistry teacher . . .'

'Chris?'

'Yes, I think that was his name.'

'And after that?' Abby glances over at him.

'I don't know. You were outside watching the fireworks at midnight, like everyone else. You looked a bit out of it. You were with a dark-haired woman. After the fireworks, I went to Danny's room with Mark and we watched a boxset, so I don't know what you were doing then.'

'Was it just you and Mark watching the boxset?'

'No, that bloke Chris was there too.'

'And then?'

'I didn't see you again, until I was leaving. You were at the door. It was starting to snow, and you didn't have a coat on. I offered you a lift. It seemed like the right thing to do.' He stops for traffic lights as they drive into town and looks at her directly. 'I promise you it was nothing more than that.'

Abby nods. 'And did we stop at a petrol station?'

'Yes, that's right. So, you *are* starting to remember?'

Is it her imagination, or does he look worried for a second? Why would he be worried that she's begun remembering things?

Abby grips her phone tightly. Suspicion coils in her mind and there's a tight knot of anxiety in her chest. She's so deep in thought as they drive the rest of the way back that she blinks with surprise when they finally reach the town centre and stop opposite the church. 'Let me know if you want to take the flat,' Andrew says as she gets out of the car. 'But you'll have to be quick. A property like that won't stay on the market very long.'

'Thanks,' says Abby, 'I will.'

It's only as she walks back home through the rain and can finally breathe that she realizes just how tense she's been the whole time.

She finds Ellie outside, battling to bring in the washing, her mouth full of pegs. The wind is so strong the wet clothes keep wrapping themselves around her face.

'Here, let me help,' says Abby. It bothers her that Ellie does most of the housework even though her job is arguably more demanding than Rob's, but it's not her business to interfere and Ellie is that kind of person. She likes to look after everyone. She can see how it would be easy for Rob to slip into letting Ellie do a lot for him.

'Thanks,' Ellie mumbles. They work in silence for a while, racing against the wind and the rain, which is getting heavier.

'Remember New Year's Eve?' asks Abby, as she lugs the washing basket back inside and they start hanging the clothes on the rack. 'You and Rob went to Carla's for dinner, right?'

Ellie groans. 'Yes, I remember. I wish I could forget. It was the worst. Carla invited Simon and his ex, and they had a huge row. Then Rob got into an argument with the guy Carla was seeing at the time. You know what Rob's like. It almost ended in a physical fight.'

Abby grins. She does know what Rob's like. He enjoys provoking people. Sometimes it's amusing, but other times it's just downright annoying. 'What time did you get home?'

'Just after twelve. We left as soon as we could. Why?'

'And did you go straight to bed? Or do you remember me coming home?'

'I don't, but Rob might. He stayed up after I went to bed. Started watching a movie. God knows how long he was up.' Ellie drapes one of Rob's shirts over a hanger and glances curiously at Abby. 'Why do you ask?'

'No reason.' Abby slips away into the living room before Ellie can probe any further.

Rob is sitting with his feet up on the coffee table, watching the news.

'You were completely off your trolley,' he says when she asks him about New Year's. 'You could barely stand up. I gave you a glass of water to sober you up, but I still had to help you upstairs.'

Abby cringes with embarrassment and picks at some imaginary fluff on the sofa. 'So, there was no one else with me? I didn't invite anyone in?'

'No.' He gives her an odd look. 'That's a weird question, Abs.'

Abby opens her mouth to reply, but to her relief Rob turns back to the news, distracted by the report of a terrorist attack in France.

It seems as if Andrew Wilson was telling the truth. He dropped her off and didn't come in. If he is the man she's looking for, then either he parked in a lay-by somewhere or it happened sometime earlier at the party.

'By the way, there are some more flowers for you in the kitchen,' Rob says as she's leaving the room.

Abby stares at him. 'Flowers?'

'Yes, unbelievable, isn't it? Somebody's got the hots for you. There's no accounting for taste.' He smirks.

'Thanks a bunch, Robert,' she says lightly, but there's that feeling of apprehension again. Since when did something as innocent as a bunch of flowers make her belly twist so uneasily and her heart start beating so fast?

In the kitchen the flowers, pink carnations this time, have

been left in the sink in a pool of water. She sits at the kitchen table and reads the attached note. It's the same as before: 'Abigail with love', typed neatly on a small, white card.

She sighs, makes herself a cup of tea and checks her phone. There are a few unread messages. One from a teacher at work asking if she wants to go on a geography field trip next week, and one from Danny saying he feels better and asking how it went with Andrew Wilson. The third is from a number she doesn't recognize. She opens the message.

How about that date? Are you free tomorrow night? Do you fancy going to the cinema, eight o'clock? Alex.

Alex. *Of course.* He must have sent the flowers. She feels flattered and relieved, but she hesitates before replying. On the one hand, she doesn't need to make her life any more complicated than it already is, on the other, if she spends time with Alex, maybe she'll find out more about New Year's Eve.

'*Love to,*' she messages back. Then changes it to '*Okay x*'. After a moment's thought she deletes the kiss.

Chapter Ten

Abby's newly generous cleavage is spilling out all over the place, a web of blue veins over plump, pale skin. The short blue dress clings to her figure, clearly outlining a small but definite bulge. That won't do. She doesn't want Alex to know she's pregnant. Not yet. She takes it off and tosses it onto the bed. Then she pulls on a pair of stretchy tights and puts on a loose, lacy, black boho style dress over the top.

She examines herself critically in the mirror, scraping eyeliner over her eyelids and tucking her straight brown hair behind her ears. Her normally elfin face looks a bit puffier than usual and she definitely looks tired, but no one would guess she was pregnant, at least.

Rob whistles when she comes downstairs. 'What are you all tarted up for, Abby? Can you even walk in those heels?'

'Ignore him. You look very nice,' says Ellie. She's sitting on the sofa squashed up against the arm. Hector is taking up most of the space, sprawled across the cushions, his head lolling in her lap. 'Where are you off to?'

'Just to the cinema.' She hasn't told them about Alex. They'll only give her the third degree and she doesn't think she can face that right now.

Anyway, she tells herself, *it's not as if it's really a date. It's a fact-finding mission and that's all.*

'Bit dressed up for the cinema, aren't you?' says Rob. 'Who are you going with?'

She's saved by the doorbell.

'Gotta go!' Abby says, making a quick escape.

Alex is standing outside. He's wearing jeans and a green shirt, which is tight over his shoulders, and his hair is newly washed. She gets a whiff of musky shampoo.

'You look nice,' he says, smiling. Amused green eyes fix on hers and Abby feels heat rise in her cheeks. *Stay focused*, she thinks. *Remember this isn't really a date. Remember he could be a rapist.*

'What are we going to see?' she asks.

'Change of plan. There's nothing good on at the cinema, so I thought we could go to eat somewhere. Do you like Thai food?' he says as opens the gate for her.

'Love it.' Abby slides past, careful not to touch him.

'Good. Hope you don't mind walking. I thought it was a nice evening. Will you be alright in those heels?'

'No problem.' She smiles. She knows she probably should go back inside and change into flats, but she doesn't want to risk bringing Alex into the house and subjecting him to an interrogation by Rob and Ellie.

By the time they reach the centre of town, though, she's regretting her decision. Her feet are killing her. The heels are starting to rub and she's trying not to hobble.

'Here we are,' says Alex as they turn into a sort of open-air shopping arcade and stop outside an expensive-looking restaurant, boasting authentic Thai cuisine. Two large kneeling stone Buddhas flank the doorway. They are shown to a seat next to the window by a smiling waitress dressed in traditional Thai clothing. They order two green curries and, before she can stop him, Alex asks for a bottle of wine.

'This is great,' Abby says, looking around at the intricately carved wooden panels on the walls. 'I've lived here a year and a half already and I had no idea this was here.' She doesn't say that she probably wouldn't have come here even if she had – it's way outside her usual budget.

Alex shrugs but looks pleased. 'It's okay. Not up to London standards, I expect. This place must seem boring after living in London.'

Boring's the last thing it's been recently, Abby thinks.

'I like the peace and quiet,' she says out loud. 'This town must have been a great place to grow up.'

'Not really.' Alex stares morosely at his wine glass. 'There was nothing to do. I always had big plans to get out. Never thought I'd end up here.' He picks up his wine and drinks, and as he does, Abby notices a line of faded scars on the inside of his arm. She doesn't have much experience of drugs, but guesses they're track marks. *Danny wasn't kidding about him having a troubled past*, she thinks, feeling a little shocked. She wonders if he's really kicked the habit or if he's still using.

He puts down his drink and smiles at her, giving her one of those intense stares that makes the colour rush to her cheeks.

'So, Abigail Brooke, what made a girl like you move to a shithole like this?'

She laughs. 'Well, mainly work. I got a job at the school here, and then my sister lives here too.' She'd been in a mess after her break-up with Ben and had hated her job in London. Then Rob mentioned that there was a position at the school where he worked. Why not come and live with him and Ellie? It would do Ellie good, he said, to have Abby around. It would do them both good.

'Aren't there any schools in London?'

'Well, yes . . . But that wasn't the only reason. I'd split up with my boyfriend and I wanted a clean break.'

'Ben?' he says.

She stares at him surprised. 'Yes, but how do you know about Ben?'

He grins. 'You told me all about him New Year's Eve – what a bastard he was, how he shagged your best friend.'

Jesus. What else had she told him?

'I wish I could remember more about Danny's party,' Abby says. 'What else did I say?'

'You showed me your biopsy scar. Told me you were worried about breast cancer.' He leans towards her, his green eyes suddenly serious. 'You told me your mum had it, that she died when you were nineteen.'

98

'God, I'm sorry.' Abby cringes. 'It sounds like I told you my whole life story.'

A waitress brings their food. Abby is glad of the distraction because she can feel tears welling up at the thought of her mum. There's a short silence as she takes a forkful of green curry.

'That's something we've got in common,' he says once the waitress has gone. 'I lost my mother too . . . when I was eighteen.' His eyes darken.

'That sucks,' Abby says lamely. No age is a good age to lose a parent, but she knows from experience that when you're starting out, trying to make your own way in the world, it's particularly difficult. Was that why he'd gone so badly off the rails? She could have so easily gone off the rails herself if it hadn't been for Ellie. It was Ellie who'd really got Abby through that year after Mum died. Even though she was busy grieving herself, Ellie had been a constant visitor at uni, dragging Abby out on long walks in the countryside, making sure she wasn't drinking too much and, when she wasn't with her, skyping her every day to check she was okay.

'Yeah.' Alex waves his fork in the air. 'People think because you're an adult you should be able to cope. But I don't know if it makes it any easier.'

Abby nods. 'And there's all the things in your life they'll miss, like your graduation, your wedding . . .'

'Exactly.' Their eyes meet. Something like understanding passes between them.

His eyes are deep green and beautiful – especially now

they're full of emotion. He reaches out and touches her hand across the table. *Oh, crap.* She's always had a thing for bad boys. Now with this added connection between them she's in real danger of falling for this guy. This is not part of the plan. She mustn't let it cloud her judgement.

'So, it looks like I told you my whole life story on New Year's Eve,' she says, trying to bring the conversation back on track.

'Pretty much,' he says. If he's annoyed or surprised by the sudden switch in topic he doesn't show it.

Abby runs her finger over the edge of the wine glass. 'How long did we talk . . . ? I mean, I know I was talking to you on the stairs but after that I don't remember much.' She needs to fill in the gap between being on the stairs and winding up in Mark's room.

'Um, I don't know. For a long time. You went to the toilet and didn't come back. I looked for you for a bit, but I couldn't find you, so I just hung out in the living room. After that, I didn't see you until twelve o'clock when we all went outside to watch the fireworks.'

He shrugs. Again, she remembers lying on frosty grass, holding someone's hand. *Whose hand?*

'Who was I with? Outside?' she asks.

'I'm not sure . . . Why all the questions about New Year's?'

'No reason.' She flushes. 'I just don't like not remembering. That's all.'

'Is that why you're not drinking tonight?' He nods at her still full glass of wine. She hasn't touched it. 'You think I want to have my wicked way with you.'

'Maybe.' She tries to laugh, and takes a couple of sips so as not to arouse suspicion.

'Well, you're probably right.' He grins, reaching out and touching her hand.

'I didn't thank you,' she says as he pays the bill. 'For the flowers you sent. The carnations.'

'What carnations?'

Abby feels a twinge of unease. 'The flowers you sent the other day. They were beautiful.'

He gives her an odd look. 'I didn't send you any flowers.'

Chapter Eleven

They head outside into the chill night air.

'Where to now?' says Alex. 'The night is young.'

'I'd better get home. I've got work in the morning.'

'Really?' Alex puts his head on one side and smiles.

'Yes, really,' she says firmly.

Alex shrugs. 'Okay, if you insist, I'll walk you home.'

It starts to rain, a light drizzle, as they make their way back up the hill. The conversation flows surprisingly easily and soon Alex starts talking about Ben. 'What was he thinking of, your ex? He must have been crazy to cheat on a girl like you.'

'Well, I know. But there's no accounting for taste ...' Abby laughs, flattered but slightly embarrassed by the corny compliment.

'That's another thing we've got in common. My ex-wife cheated on me too.' Alex glares at the pavement. 'People kept telling me she was bad news, but I didn't listen.' He trips a bit and steadies himself by grabbing Abby's shoulder.

He's quite drunk, Abby realizes, and she wonders if he'd

been drinking before he picked her up. He didn't drink enough in the restaurant to be this drunk.

'Well then,' he says, outside her house. He looks down at her and smiles. Even drunk, his eyes are hypnotic, and Abby finds herself gazing back at him, unconsciously drawn towards him. He touches her cheek gently and then suddenly they're kissing. He tastes of wine and something else, something unfamiliar but not unpleasant.

This is probably a bad idea, she thinks, but it's been such a long time since she's kissed anyone and there's a pent-up longing inside her that she hadn't even known was there. Alex's hands snake around her waist and he pulls her against him. She tenses. Surely now he'll notice the tell-tale bump under her top, but if he notices he says nothing. He breaks away for breath and then kisses her again, harder this time, pushing his tongue in her mouth, his hand sliding downwards around her bum. She pulls away.

'Have we done this before?' she says.

He holds her at arm's length, smiling. 'You're kidding me, right?'

Abby tenses. 'What happened exactly at Danny's? We didn't . . .'

He laughs. 'No nothing like that. We kissed, that's all. Like this . . .' He kisses her again, softly. 'It was fucking lush, actually.'

Abby breaks away. 'Where did we kiss?'

'Just on the lips. Don't worry. Though I could kiss you somewhere else if you like.' He grins at her cheekily.

Abby smiles back uncertainly. 'No, I mean where were we?'

'On the stairs.'

Abby thinks she remembers the smell of his aftershave, the feel of his lips on her mouth.

Feeling suddenly like this is all a big mistake, she turns and fumbles with the key in the lock. 'Well, goodnight,' she says.

'Hold on a second. Can't I come in?' He sways drunkenly.

She shakes her head firmly. 'Not a good idea.'

'Why not?'

'Well for a start, I live with my sister and her husband.'

'So?' He pulls her back towards him, tugging gently at her coat. 'We're all adults. What do they care?'

'Get off me.' Abby pushes him sharply away and he falls back against a bush.

'Fuck me,' he says, pulling leaves from his hair. 'Okay, no funny business, I promise. I'll just come in for a drink.'

Abby shakes her head. 'No, sorry.'

His eyes darken for a second. Then he smiles. 'Okay,' he says. 'How about another date? Tomorrow?'

'I can't.'

'The day after, then.'

'Look, there's a lot going on in my life right now.'

'Your loss,' he slurs, stumbling backwards as she shuts the door in his face.

Abby switches on the light inside and tickles Hector behind the ears. She wonders how well Danny really knows

Alex. He said that there was no way Alex would have taken advantage of her when she was drunk and out of it, but he seemed pretty pushy just now, and if she hadn't been really clear, where would he have stopped?

'Please help yourself.' Jenny waddles in and deposits half a huge, cream-covered cake on the table in the staff room. 'Left over from our silver wedding anniversary.'

'How many years is that. Twenty-five? You get less for murder. Poor Jim,' Chris says.

Jenny laughs. 'Cheeky monkey,' she says, wagging a finger at him, then bustling back to the office.

It's the day after her date with Alex, and Abby is slumped in the corner of the room. She feels tired and slightly nauseous.

Danny cuts two large slices of cake and hands one to Abby.

'That's too big. I can't eat all that,' she protests, pushing the plate away.

'Why not? You're eating for two now, aren't you?'

'Shhh,' Abby hisses and looks around the staff room to see if anyone heard him, but no one's listening. Thea is giving a massage to Jess, a Biology teacher, and Chris is subjecting the new Maths teacher to a long monologue about his holiday in Italy last year.

'So how did it go with Alex?' Danny asks, mouth full of cake. 'What did you find out?'

Abby's face grows hot. 'Not much,' she admits.

'Oh my God. You're blushing. What happened? Go on, dish the dirt.'

'Nothing happened,' Abby lies. 'We had a meal, we talked. He told me about his mum, that's all.'

'You like him though, don't you? I can tell,' says Danny. 'Are you going to see him again?'

'No, I don't think so. I mean, it's not exactly a good time. My life is complicated enough.'

'It's probably for the best.' Danny nods.

'I thought you liked him?'

'I do. It's just, like I said before, I'm not sure Alex is relationship material. In any case, as far as I know he's still hung-up on his old girlfriend. Did he tell you he's got a kid?'

'No, he didn't.' Abby is astonished. 'How old . . . ?'

She breaks off because Thea, Jess and the new Maths teacher have gone back to their classrooms and so Chris comes over to talk to them.

'Don't you know it's rude to whisper?' he says. 'What are you two plotting?'

'Oh, nothing,' replies Danny smoothly. 'Abby went on a date last night, that's all.'

'A date. Abby? Really?' Chris's eyes widen. 'I thought you were celibate. Well, come on then, Abigail. Tell us all about it.'

Abby shrugs. 'It was nothing.'

'Oh, okay.' Chris grins. He looks around and leans forward. 'Anyway, while Thea's not here I'd like to invite you two to dinner for her birthday. I want it to be a surprise. I'm going to cook her some traditional Greek food. I don't need to invite this new bloke of yours, do I?'

'No.' Abby sighs impatiently. 'It was just a date, that's all. Nothing serious.'

'So, what's his name?'

But Abby is spared from more questions about Alex because the bell goes for lessons.

Outside it's raining, a steady downpour. Danny and Abby rush to the shelter of the nearest covered walkway.

'So, you didn't find out anything more about New Year's?' Danny asks as they skirt the inclusion building.

'Not really. He told me we kissed but apparently nothing else happened.'

'Well, this is me,' he says outside the large, grey, Stalinist English block. 'Wish me luck. I've got Nine Yellow.'

Abby smiles. 'Good luck,' she says, and heads for the Art Room. As she's walking through the door her phone beeps. *Alex*, she thinks. Despite what she said earlier, she feels a small thrill of excitement. It's been ages since she's been attracted to anyone. Even so, she's not sure how she will respond if he asks her out again. She opens the message.

It certainly isn't from Alex.

Abby reads it through twice to make sure she hasn't made a mistake. But the message is clear and simple. And it makes her blood run cold.

Stay away from Alex Taylor.

MAY

Your baby is about 170–200 grams now, and growing fast, which explains why you probably feel so hungry! Your baby's eyelids and eyelashes are now formed, and fine hair might start to grow on their head. The nervous system is already working, and they can yawn, stretch and even suck their thumb. This month you may start to feel your baby kick.

Chapter Twelve

The life inside Abby is growing by the day. It flutters inside her, making small stammering movements that constantly remind her of its presence. Her waist is thickening, and she's been forced to buy maternity clothes. Pretty soon it's going to be obvious to everyone that she's pregnant.

It's time to tell Ellie. She can't put it off any longer. But it's difficult to find the right moment. Rob is always around, or else Ellie is tired and stressed from work.

It's a week into May before Abby finally plucks up the courage. They're walking Hector in Ashridge Wood. The sun is shining through the leaves and a sea of bluebells covers the forest floor. Ellie is happier than she's been in a long while. Things are going well for her at work. It looks like she'll become a senior partner in the practice when Dr Samuels retires next year. Right now, she's striding along recounting an amusing story about a patient who mistook suppositories for pills.

She cracks up laughing, doubling over and clutching her belly. 'He didn't suffer any ill effects, thankfully,' she says.

Abby laughs too, and soon the two sisters are giggling away until there are tears streaming down their faces. It's a long time since Abby's heard Ellie laugh like that, and she wonders if she is finally on the road to real recovery. If you can ever recover from the loss of a baby, that is.

If there's ever going to be a good time to break the news, now is it.

'So, what's going on with you?' Ellie asks when they've stopped laughing and caught their breath. 'I feel like I hardly see you these days. Have you been avoiding me?'

'Course not,' Abby says. She stops in a clearing and takes a deep breath. 'But there is something . . . something I need to tell you . . .'

Ellie stops and gives her a searching look. 'What is it? Tell me. You're making me nervous.'

Abby's heart is racing. It'll be like ripping off a plaster, she tells herself. Quick and painless.

'I'm pregnant,' she says. And she strides ahead so that she won't have to look Ellie in the eye. For a second, Ellie looked so wounded that Abby wants to wrap her in her arms. But the look passes so quickly she might have imagined it. She hopes she imagined it.

'How many months?' Ellie catches up with her. Her voice is careful, as if she's measuring out gunpowder with a teaspoon.

'Over four already.'

Ellie digests this. 'And how long have you known?'

'Since March.'

There's a silence as they walk on out of the woods, past horses in fields, estate workers' cottages and the rusty shells of abandoned farm machinery.

'Is it Ben's?' asks Ellie eventually.

'No.'

'Oh, I thought maybe that time you went to London you might have hooked up again.'

'No.' It's true Abby went to London just before Christmas and she met up with Ben and Chloe for lunch, but nothing happened. She just sat there watching Ben and Chloe being smug, and trying to pretend she was completely over it all.

'So, whose is it?' Ellie says, stopping to pick up a stick for Hector and flinging it into the air.

Abby takes a deep breath. 'I don't know.'

'You don't know?' Ellie stops in her tracks, staring at Abby incredulously.

'It happened on New Year's, at Danny's party. I was so drunk that night I don't remember anything.'

Ellie shakes her head. 'Oh my God, Abby, that's awful. Are you alright?'

Abby's voice wobbles, and tears spring up in her eyes. 'Not really,' she manages to say. 'I think that my drink might have been spiked, that someone targeted me.'

Ellie takes her hand and squeezes it. 'Oh, Abby,' she says. 'I don't think you need to worry about that. Surely none of Danny's friends would do something like that? I mean, you probably just blacked out from drinking too much. It happens all the time. I saw it so many times when I was on rotation at the STD clinic, people who got wasted and couldn't remember if they had used protection or even who they went home with.' She frowns as another thought occurs to her. 'You should get yourself tested, Abby, just in case. I mean, I'm sure it will be okay, but it's better to be on the safe side.'

Abby wipes her eyes and nods. She knows she should do as Ellie says, but she just can't face going through a whole series of invasive tests right now. She's got enough going on. She's relieved, though, that Ellie doesn't think that it's likely she was drugged or raped. She respects Ellie's opinion and wants to believe that she's right. But there's still a nagging voice at the back of her head that won't allow her to completely discard the idea.

'But that's not all. Some weird stuff has been happening.' Abby walks on, shoving her hands in her pockets. 'I've been getting weird texts and all those flowers.'

'But I thought the flowers were from the guy you went to the cinema with?' Ellie keeps pace, glancing sideways at her.

'Alex. That's what I thought at first, but no. They're not from him.'

They've reached the old stone folly, and they sit on the cold metal seat inside, staring out at the ride. A man walks past with a red setter, and then a mother trailing children and dogs.

'I mean, I know it sounds crazy . . .' says Abby.

'It is strange,' Ellie agrees. She looks deep in thought.

'Then a few days ago I received this.' She takes her phone out of her back pocket and shows Ellie the message.

Ellie reads it, frowning. 'But I don't understand. Why would anyone want you to stay away from him?'

'I don't know.' Abby sighs. She hasn't put it all together in her head yet, but she feels there's something she's missing. Something at the back of her mind, just out of reach.

'Maybe it's from his ex?' Ellie suggests as they stand and continue their walk back down the main ride towards the car. 'You said he was married before, right?'

'Hmm, maybe,' Abby says, unconvinced.

They walk on for a while in silence, each lost in their own thoughts.

'You know, I used to come here a lot, after I lost the baby,' Ellie says, suddenly stopping under a chestnut tree by the fence with a sign that says KEEP OUT.

Abby stares at the sign, confused. 'But it's private property.'

'So? They never use it and it's the one place I knew I could be completely alone. It's really beautiful down there. There's a lake and an old ruined house.'

'Ellie, I know this must be hard for you—'

'Not at all,' Ellie interrupts, giving her a brittle smile. 'I knew there was something going on with you, but I never would have guessed ... that you were pregnant. I can't believe my little sister is going to have a baby.' Her voice cracks a little, and Abby glances at her anxiously. She takes Abby's hand and squeezes it. 'But I'm really happy. Why wouldn't I be? I'm going to be an aunt. How about you, are you okay with this? You're going to have a baby. I know it's not exactly the ideal circumstances, but is there a part of you that's excited, at least?'

'Sure,' Abby lies. Because how can she explain to Ellie, who wants nothing more than to be a mother, that the thought fills her with revulsion? She feels afraid, too. Not just of having the baby and being a mother but of something else. A feeling she hasn't quite put into words yet.

As they reach the gates, and Ellie calls Hector and puts him on the lead, Abby realizes what it is that's making her feel afraid.

The person who sent the message about Alex sent it the day after her date. They must have known she was with Alex that evening. They must have been watching her.

Chapter Thirteen

'If a pregnant woman is starving, guess who dies first, the woman or the unborn baby?' Thea throws this question out there, apropos of nothing.

It's Thea's birthday dinner, and Abby and Danny are at her house sitting round her large kitchen table. On the table is the detritus of a large Greek-themed meal Chris has cooked; a half-eaten moussaka, bowls of salad, hummus, tzatziki and roast potatoes. Thea is on her fifth glass of prosecco already and she's polished off the whole bottle pretty much by herself. She doesn't seem to have noticed that Abby isn't drinking.

'I don't know. Probably the woman?' Danny guesses.

'Yes!' Thea looks at Abby. Her eyes are glassy and she's slurring her words. 'We always get a shitty deal, even from nature. It's bad enough we have to deal with men and all their crap.'

Chris rolls his eyes. 'Haven't I just cooked you a lovely meal and organized this lovely dinner with your friends? What more do you want?'

Thea ignores him. 'First, you're sick and fat for nine

months,' she continues. 'Then you go through the worst pain you can imagine. And all for what? So, you can produce a shitting, screaming little being—'

'Hey, that's our son you're talking about!' Chris interrupts, but Thea is on a roll.

'Then they turn into this tyrannical dictator who expects you to indulge their every whim twenty-four seven.'

Abby looks at the photo of Oliver pinned to the fridge. He's in a bucket in Chris's arms grinning up at him. He looks pretty angelic to her.

'Do you know what he did today? The ungrateful little brat actually bit me.' Thea pulls up her sleeve and shows them a large bruise at the top of her arm. 'All because I refused to let him play with an electric socket. I'm telling you, Abby, don't ever get pregnant. Ever. It's the end of the road. The end of life as we know it.'

Abby takes a deep breath. 'It's a bit late for that.'

Now that Ellie knows, she doesn't see any reason why she shouldn't start telling other people. She told Rob after she and Ellie got back from their walk and was surprised by the calm, uncharacteristically sensitive way he reacted.

There's a stunned silence. Chris and Thea stare at her. Danny fiddles with his fork.

'What?' says Thea.

'I'm pregnant.' She pulls her top tight to show them her rounded belly. She's finally invested in some maternity trousers and her belly is straining at the elasticated waist. She's surprised they haven't noticed.

'You're kidding,' says Chris.

'What he means is, "That's great, Abby."' Thea stands up and staggers over, kissing her sloppily on the cheek. 'Congratulations. God, I feel awful now for what I was saying. I was just letting off steam. You know I don't mean it.'

'Who's the lucky fella?' asks Chris.

Thea kicks him as she sits back down. 'That's none of our business,' she hisses.

'Ow, sorry,' says Chris. 'I was only asking.'

'It's okay,' says Abby. She takes a deep breath. This is the difficult part. 'Actually, I'm not entirely sure.'

Thea giggles inappropriately, then covers her mouth and Chris's mouth falls open.

'What do you mean, you don't know?' he says.

'It happened at my party,' Danny explains. 'Abby doesn't remember. She drank a bit too much.'

Abby takes a sip of prosecco. She needs it right now. 'I was wondering, actually, if either of you saw me with anyone?'

Thea frowns. 'You were talking a lot with a dark, good-looking guy at the start of the evening. After that, I didn't see you for a while. Then, at twelve o'clock, we all went out to watch the fireworks.'

Lying on frosty grass staring up at the sky, holding someone's hand.

'It was you!' Abby realizes. 'We lay on the ground. Were we holding hands?'

'Yes, that's right. I think so. You were really pissed, kept telling me how much you loved me. But I went home after that. I needed to get back for the babysitter. But Chris might have seen more. You stayed until about two. Right, Chris?'

'Yeah.' Chris helps himself to a piece of baklava, cupping his hand underneath to stop the honey dripping. 'To be honest, I didn't see that much of you. The only time I saw you was just after Thea left. You were talking to some posh bloke in Mark's room. Tall, ginger, kind of weaselly-looking. You looked like you were arguing.'

'That'll be Hugo,' says Danny grimly. 'I told you he's a slimy piece of work.'

He scrolls through his phone and shows Abby a photo of a young man. Pale lashes, cigarette in one hand, holding his other hand out to the camera as if it's a paparazzi shot.

Abby examines the picture carefully and shivers in recognition. It's the man she remembers from Mark's room, sitting under the musket. 'I wonder what we were arguing about,' she says thoughtfully. 'I think I need to speak to him. Do you have his number, Danny?'

Danny shakes his head. 'Sorry, no. He's notoriously difficult to get hold of. He's travelling round the world at the moment. Last I heard, he was in Thailand. Maybe you could find him on Facebook or Instagram?'

'Do *you* know what we were arguing about?' Abby asks Chris.

Chris shrugs. 'I don't know. We left you to it, went to watch a boxset in Danny's room.'

'Who's we?'

'Me, Mark and Andy ...' Chris begins, but he breaks

off because a little boy appears in Minion pyjamas in the doorway.

'What are you doing out of bed, Ollie?'

'I'm thirsty,' he says, staring wide-eyed at Abby and Danny.

Chris sighs. 'Come on, then.' He stands up reluctantly and fills a plastic cup from the tap. 'There you go, young man,' he says, taking Ollie by the hand and disappearing upstairs.

'How are you coping?' Thea asks later, pouring herself another drink. Chris is settling Oliver upstairs and Danny has gone out into the garden to smoke. Thea and Abby have settled in the living room on the slightly sticky leather sofas.

'Not very well,' Abby admits. 'I feel invaded.' She struggles to explain. 'It's as if my body's not my own anymore, as if I've lost control of my own life.'

Thea picks up a cushion and hugs it to her chest. 'That's totally understandable. I mean, it can be hard enough being pregnant under normal circumstances. It's such a big change to your life, your body, but this . . .' She tails off.

'There's something else, too.' Abby voices the fear that's been gnawing away at the back of her mind. 'I don't know if I'm being paranoid, but I think someone may have spiked my drink.' Her voice lowers to a whisper. '*I think I was raped.*'

Thea's eyes widen. She drops the cushion and leans forward. 'I don't think that's such a crazy idea. It's more common than you think.' She hesitates. She seems to be trying to decide whether to say something. 'When I was at uni I went to this party . . .' She swallows. Whatever she wants to say, she's finding it difficult. 'Everything was fine. I was having a good time, drinking a bit, but not too much. Next thing I knew it was the morning, and I was halfway across Manchester in some random man's bed. He told me nothing had happened, but when I got home my friend persuaded me to go to the doctor's and I tested positive for Rohypnol.' For a second Thea's expression darkens, and she stares down at the carpet, deep in thought. Then she looks up at Abby.

'Oh my God, I had no idea,' says Abby, feeling shocked. 'That must have been horrible.'

'It's in the past. I try not to think about it.' Thea shakes her head and sighs. Then she looks up at Abby and takes her hand. 'How about you, though? I'm so sorry this has happened to you, Abs. You must feel really upset and angry.'

She does feel angry, furiously angry, Abby realizes, as well as violated, disgusted and ashamed. She can't shake off the idea that somehow this is all her fault, though she knows that if it were anyone else in her place, she would never believe that they were to blame.

'The worst is, I don't know who to be angry with,' she says. It's a relief to talk to someone who seems to understand. Danny doesn't really get it, and with Ellie, she feels like she has to pretend she's happy about this pregnancy.

'What are you going to do?'

'I really have no idea.' Tears are welling up in her eyes. 'It's just all a big mess.' Something about Thea's sympathy sets her off and she finds herself crying, big sobs that shake her belly and make the baby inside her flutter.

'Oh, Abby.' Thea moves to sit next to her on the sofa and puts her arm around her. 'Look, tell me to shut up if I'm out of order, but I know a great clinic. I can give you the number, if you decide on an abortion.'

'It's too late for that,' says Abby, wiping her eyes.

Thea stares at her. 'How far gone are you?'

'Five months.'

'Really? You don't look that big,' Thea takes a swig of wine. 'Anyway, I could take you there. We could try. Sometimes they can bend the rules in exceptional circumstances and I think your circumstances count as exceptional.'

'Thanks,' says Abby. 'But I'm going to be okay. I'm going to look into adoption.' It's a decision she made a while ago, but she hasn't told anybody yet.

'Are you sure? There was this girl I took to the clinic I'm talking about. She was twenty-seven weeks, but they went ahead with an abortion anyway because she was so young and for other reasons . . .' Thea breaks off. 'Shit, I really am too drunk. I shouldn't be telling you all this.'

Abby takes out a tissue and wipes her eyes. 'Who was the girl?' she asks.

'I shouldn't have told you. I promised. Just a girl from school. She didn't want her parents to know.'

Abby stares at her. 'Jesus. Really, Thea?' Thea could get into so much trouble. She's not supposed to divulge that kind of information. If a pupil tells a teacher anything like that, they're supposed to share it with the designated child protection officer, which in their school happens to be Rob.

She certainly shouldn't have been getting involved, taking her to an abortion clinic.

'What else could I do?' protests Thea. 'She was desperate, and she trusted me. Her parents are strict Muslims. They probably would have disowned her if they'd found out.'

Abby thinks about this. In this ethnically uniform town there's only one girl that Thea can be talking about.

'Tanseela Jamali?' she says, surprised.

Thea claps her hand over her mouth. 'Shit, yes. Jesus, I'm too drunk. You must promise you won't tell anyone, Abby. Promise me, please.'

Abby remembers teaching Tanseela last year. A quiet, well-behaved girl who was very good at drawing. She's the last person she could imagine getting into that kind of trouble. 'Jesus, she's so young. I just can't picture it, somehow. She's such a good girl. I find it hard to imagine her dating anyone, let alone having sex.'

'It's always the quiet ones, though, isn't it?' says Thea. She drains her wine glass. 'Though, it was kind of weird. At first, she refused to admit she'd even had sex.'

'And did you believe her?'

Thea laughs. 'Er, hello? You do know how babies are made, don't you? Of course I didn't believe her.'

'What if it's an issue of abuse? Someone older . . . or someone in her family? Don't you think you should tell someone?'

Thea puts her glass down and grabs Abby by the arm. 'No, and you mustn't either. She trusts me. Anyway, she's left the school now, so it's not our responsibility. Promise you won't tell anyone. I haven't even told Chris.'

'Told me what?' says Chris returning to the room carrying couple of coffee cups.

'Oh, nothing, women's stuff. You wouldn't be interested,' Thea says glibly.

Abby's still thinking about Tanseela as she and Danny walk home through the town centre. She can't help thinking that Thea has made a terrible mistake, and she doesn't know what she should do about it. She knows what she ought to do. She ought to tell the head teacher or Rob, but she doesn't want to get Thea into trouble and potentially cause a lot of unnecessary grief to Tanseela. Besides, Tanseela has left the school now.

She sighs as they head through the market square, the large church lit up orange from below, the gargoyles leering down at them. But it's not only that she's worried about Tanseela. There's something else bothering her. The similarity with her own situation is striking. What if Tanseela was telling the truth? *What if she really believed she hadn't had sex? Is it too much of a stretch to think there could be a connection?* She shakes her head. No, that can't be. What possible connection could there be?

'You're very quiet,' Danny says as they head down the main high street.

'Yes, sorry. I was just thinking about work.' She wants to ask Danny what he thinks, but she can't broach the subject

125

without betraying Thea. She needs some time to think and work out the best thing to do.

'Well, don't,' says Danny. 'Thinking about work is strictly forbidden on a Saturday night.'

'Sorry.' She grins.

They talk about Danny's sister, who is getting married in a couple of months, and her fiancé, who Danny doesn't like, until they reach the point where their two routes home diverge.

'I'll see you later,' he says. 'Unless you want me to walk you home?'

'Don't be daft. I'm fine. It's only a ten-minute walk.'

'Okay.' He shrugs and smiles. 'See you Monday then.'

But once Danny's gone, she immediately regrets not taking him up on the offer. It's dark and cold, and the streets are deserted apart from a group of women out on a hen night. They totter by, cackling with laughter, their heels ringing on the tarmac, heading towards the market square.

Stay away from Alex Taylor. Ever since she received that message she's been unable to shake the feeling that someone's watching her. And it's probably her imagination but she feels it strongly now. There's a tingling in the back of her neck and she thinks she can hear footsteps behind her. But when she looks back over her shoulder the street is empty. She's being paranoid, she tells herself. But Thea taking the idea of date rape seriously has left her feeling shaken and jumpy. It feels like a real possibility for the first time.

She turns down an alleyway between the café and the

betting shop, taking the short cut through the car park. It's almost completely empty. There are just a couple of cars at the far end near the recycling bins. All she can hear is the clip of her own shoes on the tarmac, the sound of her own breathing, and a faint rustling of the hedge that surrounds the bowls club. A cat or a small animal of some kind, she tells herself. Even so she jumps, and her heart starts racing, when one of the parked cars suddenly turns on its head-lights. She puts her head down and walks quickly towards the exit. The car's engine revs but doesn't move. What's the driver doing? She can't shake the feeling that he's watching her. She speeds up, her legs wobbling awkwardly. And the car begins moving. It crawls around the car park and parks again near the exit. *What the hell?*

She can't help thinking about the time Ellie was attacked. When Ellie was seventeen she was walking home from the pub one night when a car stopped alongside her, and a man tried to grab her and drag her into the car. She only escaped because she happened to be just outside their house and their dad heard her cry out. Abby was only eight at the time and didn't fully understand the implications, but she realizes now that it must have been terrifying. Ellie has never talked about it to her since, and Abby wonders why. Is it typical Ellie putting a brave face on things, or because she really has put it behind her?

Abby shivers. Why is she thinking about that now? There's nothing sinister about the car. It's probably just a couple. Maybe they're making out, or maybe they're having an argument. There could be any number of reasons why they've stopped.

All the same, Abby takes a small detour and leaves the car park by a different exit. She rounds the corner. But the car's engine revs up again. It follows her out of the car park, drives past, and then parks just in front of her. She crosses the road keeping as much distance between her and the car as possible.

Then there's the sound of a car door being opened behind her, and someone calls out and there's the sound of footsteps behind her. She's really panicking now, her heart hammering away, pummelling her ribs. She stumbles forward, diving into the alley that runs past their back garden, but the footsteps follow her. She speeds up, resisting the urge to run. *Don't let him know you're scared*, she thinks. She's nearly there. If she shouts out now, Rob or Ellie will hear. The footsteps get faster and faster. He's going to catch up any second. He's gaining on her.

Abby calls out. 'Ellie! Rob!' But her voice comes out as a frightened croak. Her heart is pounding out of her chest. She puts her hand on the gate but it's too late. Someone grabs her by the shoulder and she screams at the top of her lungs.

Chapter Fourteen

'Calm down, love,'

She's gibbering and shaking with fear. Her vision is clouded with panic, but she turns and makes out the face of an old man with a short grey beard. He's looking down at her with a concerned expression. 'Are you okay?' he says. 'I didn't mean to frighten you. I just wanted to give you this. You dropped it in the car park.' And he puts something small into her trembling hands. In the state she's in, it takes her a couple of seconds to register that it's her purse.

'Oh,' she says. 'Oh . . .'

And then the door flies open, and Rob bursts out in his dressing gown. He's wild-eyed and he's brandishing a large, sharp kitchen knife. 'What's going on?' he blusters. 'Are you alright, Abby?'

The old man looks alarmed and raises his hands in a gesture of surrender. 'She dropped her purse. I just wanted to give it back, that's all. I didn't mean to frighten her.'

'Is that right?' Rob looks suspiciously from the man to Abby, still gripping the knife.

Abby nods. Now the panic is subsiding, she realizes she's made a mistake and is starting to feel very embarrassed. 'Yes, it's true. Put the knife down, Rob.'

'I'm so sorry,' she mutters to the man as she hurries into the house. 'And thank you.'

'That's alright, now,' he says as she shuts the door. 'You take care of yourself.'

'What was all that about?' Rob asks, pouring her a cup of tea in the kitchen. 'With all that screaming, I thought you were being murdered. That poor man nearly had a heart attack when I came out with the knife.' He chuckles.

Abby shakes her head and manages a small smile. 'I don't know. I thought he was going to attack me.'

Rob stares. 'Why the hell would you think that?'

'I don't know. I suppose I'm just a bit on edge at the moment.'

'You can say that again.' Rob places a cup of tea in front of her on the kitchen table. 'You shouldn't be walking about late at night by yourself anyway, especially in your condition. Next time, why don't you give me a ring and I'll come and pick you up?'

Abby sips the sweet tea. Her hands are still shaking so much she nearly spills it. She feels she needs to explain what must seem like a massive overreaction. 'It's just I think someone might be following me.'

'What, like stalking you?' Rob raises his eyebrows.

'Yes. I've been receiving these weird messages lately. Did Ellie tell you?'

'No. What kind of messages?'

She tells him about the flowers, the text message warning her to stay away from Alex.

'Am I getting wound up over nothing?'

Rob frowns. 'I don't know, Abs. You think your boyfriend's ex is really that crazy?'

'What if it's not Alex's ex? What if it's someone that's jealous of Alex, not of me?' She groans and puts her head in her hands. 'I don't know. I feel like *I'm* going crazy.'

Rob laughs and ruffles her hair. 'What do you mean, *going* crazy? You always were crazy, Abigail, but that's why we love you.' He sits down opposite her at the kitchen table. As he sits, his leg accidentally brushes against hers and Abby shifts away a little, disconcerted. She wonders vaguely if he noticed. If he did, he gives no sign.

'I'm sorry I woke you up with my screaming,' she says. 'And thank you for coming to my rescue. You're my knight in shining armour.'

He grins. 'It's okay. I'm awake now. Did you have a good time?'

'Oh, yes ...' she'd almost forgotten about Thea's dinner party. 'It was nice.' She thinks about the revelation Thea made. If anyone knows anything about Tanseela, it'll be Rob.

'We were talking about Tanseela Jamali. You remember her? You gave her extra English lessons last year, right?' she says.

'Tansy? Uh-huh.' Rob stands up, takes a beer from the fridge and opens it. 'Yes, lovely girl.'

'What's she like? I mean, I taught her before, but I never really got to know her. She was so quiet.'

Rob takes a slug of beer and wipes the foam from his beard. 'Bright. Hard-working. Sweet. Why do you ask?'

'No reason. It's just Thea was talking about her tonight. What are her family like?'

'Um . . . nice, friendly. Her mum makes the best chapatis.'

'What about her dad?' Abby vaguely remembers a short, anxious-looking man at parents' evening. She can't imagine him as a child-abuser, but then again, how would she be able to tell?

'Didn't see him much. Seemed nice enough. Bit strict maybe.'

'I know her brother, Abdul. I taught him last year, and she's got an older brother too, right?'

'Yes, Javid. He's at university, studying Engineering, as far as I know.'

Abby rests her elbows on the table. She's thinking hard. 'Did she go out a lot partying?'

Rob stares at her. 'That's a strange question, Abigail. I have no idea. But I would be very surprised if she did.'

Abby nods. Tanseela certainly doesn't seem like the party type. If someone has slipped her a roofie, it's hard to know when it could have happened. But then maybe she wasn't abused or raped. Perhaps she lied to Thea after all. Perhaps it was a simple case of teenage sex with some spotty boy at school, and she just didn't want to admit it to Thea. It's the most likely explanation.

'Well, I'm going to head to bed,' says Rob, draining his beer. 'I don't know about you, but I'm knackered. Don't forget to turn off the lights when you come up.'

But Abby is still on edge, wired. There's no way she'll get to sleep now. She switches on the TV and tries to numb her mind. There's a programme on about people buying storage lockers in America, but she can't concentrate. Thoughts are whirling in her head, and the events of the evening replay in a jumble. The man with her purse, Thea and her offer to take her to a clinic, Tanseela, Chris and what he said about her talking to Danny's friend Hugo.

Hugo Langley.

Seized by a sudden conviction that Hugo Langley is important somehow, she takes out her phone and goes on Facebook. A quick search reveals five Hugo Langleys, none of whom seem like they could be the Hugo Langley she's looking for. She clicks on one that hasn't got a photo, just an anonymous white silhouette. But it's clearly not Danny's friend. He lives in Sweden for a start. Disheartened, she scrolls through her feed, takes a quiz: *What kind of Disney princess are you?* Apparently, she's Merida from *Brave*. Then, finally feeling sleepy, she climbs the stairs to bed.

As she reaches the top of the stairs her mobile vibrates in her pocket making her jump. Who the hell would be messaging her at this time of night? She waits until she's in her bedroom, the door firmly closed before reading the text.

It's from Alex.

How about dinner tomorrow night? Just as friends, no funny business.

Chapter Fifteen

The lights in the stairwell are on a timer and they turn themselves off just as Abby climbs the stairs to Alex's apartment. She fumbles for the light switch in the darkness, fighting a sudden irrational panic. She's never been scared of the dark before, but lately everything seems to frighten her. She runs up the next flight of stairs before the lights can go out again and is relieved when she reaches Alex's door. From inside she can hear music, Nick Cave's deep, strangled voice crooning away.

'Abby, come in,' says Alex, grinning as he opens the door. As she brushes past him, his eyes flick down to her belly and widen in shock. Now Ellie knows about her baby, she wants him to know too, and she's deliberately worn a tight dress that shows off her bump. She looks at him carefully, gauging his reaction. She's pretty sure his shock is genuine. Either that or he's a very good actor.

His flat is open plan, modern and masculine. The lounge area is dominated by a large flat screen TV and a black leather sofa. The kitchen and lounge are separated by a stainless-steel breakfast bar where Abby hoists herself up onto a stool, accepting Alex's offer of a glass of Coke.

'I'm guessing you're not drinking,' he says. He lifts a tea towel off a bowl and takes out a ball of dough. 'Hope you like pizza. My speciality. Perhaps I should have made more. I didn't know you were eating for two. How many months are you?'

'Five.'

Has he made the obvious connection? Abby wonders. Five months ago. New Year's Eve. If he has, he's not letting on.

'Boy or girl?' he asks casually.

'I don't know yet.' Abby sips her Coke, then puts it down. Is it her imagination or does it taste a little weird? *How easy would it be for him to slip something into her drink?* she thinks. She's alone in the flat with him and entirely at his mercy.

Alex spreads the tomato sauce on the dough, frowning. 'Is the father still in the picture? Should I be jealous?'

'Nope, and nope,' says Abby.

'Good.' He gives her a lopsided grin that completely disarms her. Of course he's not going to drug her. She's being paranoid. She picks up the Coke and gulps it down to prove to herself that she's not afraid.

'Does he know about the baby?' he asks, as he puts the pizza in the oven.

'No,' Abby says slowly, giving herself a chance to think. 'It was Ben. You know, the guy I told you about? We got together again around Christmas time. It was just that one time and I don't want him to be involved, not after the way he treated me.'

135

'Why didn't you tell me you were pregnant before?' he asks later, as they sit at a small table, eating the pizza. There's a rose at the centre of the table and candles. It's a pretty obvious attempt at seduction, but Abby can't help feeling touched at the effort he's gone to.

'I didn't think it was important. I didn't think I was going to see you again. Anyway,' she counters, 'why didn't you tell me you had a kid?'

'Oh . . . Danny told you about Dylan, huh?' Alex scrolls through his phone. 'This is him,' he says, showing her a picture of a dark-haired little boy, about two years old, holding a watering can and smiling shyly at the camera. 'He's a year older than that now, though.'

'He's gorgeous,' she says honestly.

'He's great,' he agrees. 'Best thing that ever happened to me. They change your life, kids. My life was a mess before Dylan. It was because of him I turned it around.'

Abby looks around at the flat. There's no sign of the domestic disorder that goes with a young kid – no toys, no high chair, no baby bouncer.

'Where is he at the moment?' she asks.

'He lives with my ex, Bethany.'

After they've eaten, they sit together on the squeaky leather sofa. Alex shuffles up close to her. 'You haven't changed your mind, have you, about what you said the other night?' he says. 'Cos I really like you, you know, Abigail.' He takes her hand and rubs the palm with his thumb. His touch sends a troubling sensation racing through her body. She extracts her hand carefully and shifts away a little. She knows where this could lead, and she also knows that it's probably not a good idea.

'Why did you break up, you and your ex?' she asks, trying to distract him.

Alex sighs and sits forward, the mood broken. 'It was her who broke it off. I was really angry when she cheated on me, but I would have taken her back, mug that I am.'

Abby absorbs this. If Bethany was the one who finished the relationship, why would she be jealous of Alex now he's seeing someone else?

'Does she know about me?'

Alex shrugs. 'I don't think so, why?'

She shows him the message on her phone.

'*Stay away from Alex Taylor,*' he reads out loud. 'Shit. Who sent you that?'

'That's what I want to know. Could Bethany have sent it, do you think?'

'No way,' he says. 'That's not her style. Anyway, it's not from her phone. Look.' He pulls his own phone out of his pocket and shows her Bethany's number.

'She could have used a different phone,' Abby says.

'Well, yeah. But like I said, it's not her style. Besides, she's moved on, got herself a new boyfriend.' His expression darkens. 'Anyway, I don't want to talk about Bethany. I want to talk about you and the other night.' He leans towards her, smiling. 'I really enjoyed kissing you.' Abby smiles back and feels the

137

heat in her face and neck. She can't help it. Even if she weren't in the situation she's in, he would be all wrong for her, she knows that, but there's something about him that's magnetic.

'Do you remember a tall man with red hair?' she says, moving away slightly. 'He was at Danny's New Year's Eve party. He's called Hugo, I think?'

'Christ. What is it with you and New Year's Eve? No, I don't . . . Wait, yeah, maybe there was some posh bloke – bit of a twat, if you ask me. He was asking where you were, after you left. He asked Danny for your phone number.'

Abby sits up. 'Danny didn't give it to him?'

Alex frowns. 'I don't remember. I didn't stay to find out. Why?'

'I just don't like not remembering things, that's all.'

Alex sits back and rests his arm on the back of the sofa. There's an awkward silence for a moment. 'How's the baby, anyway? Have you felt it kick yet?'

'It's kicking me right now.' Lately, the baby has been kicking her a lot, and the movements are getting stronger all the time, constantly reminding her of its presence.

'Can I have a feel?'

'Sure.'

He places a hand on her belly. The baby judders and Alex laughs. 'Fuck me, I think he just punched me. He's got quite an attitude, hasn't he?'

Abby laughs too. Then suddenly they stop laughing and they are staring into each other's eyes. Abby feels warmth flood through her body.

'The other day . . . when you said you had a lot going on in your life, I suppose you meant the baby . . .' he says.

'Well, yes, that and other things . . .'

His hand is still on her belly. The baby is perfectly still, as if it knows there's something afoot.

'Do you still feel the same way?' he says softly.

Abby doesn't answer, but touches the tattoos on his arm tracing the black pattern on his bicep. He makes a low moaning noise.

'God damn it, why are you so sexy?' And slowly, deliberately, he lifts her top and places a warm, rough hand on her bare midriff. He leans over and kisses her gently, and Abby kisses him back.

'Doesn't it put you off, me being pregnant?' she says, between kisses.

He grins. 'No, it's kind of sexy. I like a bit of curve. Pregnant or not, you do things to me.' He kisses her again and his hand snakes up under her top to her breast. *What the hell*, thinks Abby. *At least I can't get pregnant again.*

But the sex, when it comes, is disappointing, distressing even. There's an awkward fumbling when they take off their clothes and Abby tenses up as soon as he enters her and is suddenly flooded with anxiety. *Has this happened before?* she thinks. She can't shake the image – no, not an image exactly, more of a feeling – of someone pinning her down as she lies there helpless, unable to move. *Is she remembering or imagining what happened to her that night?*

139

Please, no, she begs in her head as he thrusts inside her, but the words don't come out.

Is this it? Is she ever going to enjoy sex again? she wonders as she lies next to him afterwards, tears rolling down her cheeks. Alex is already fast asleep, lying on his front, the covers pushed off and his limbs sprawled, his back rising and falling with his breath. He's really attractive and sweet, and she really thought she wanted this, but there's no getting round the fact that the experience was an ordeal.

She lies there for a long time, staring at the moonlight flooding through the curtains, washing his skin smooth and grey like a pebble. It seems like she's only just dropped off to sleep when her phone buzzes loudly in her jacket pocket on the floor. Alex grunts and rolls over but doesn't wake up. Abby stretches out an arm, picks up her jacket from the floor and, half asleep, she opens the message.

I know where you are, slut. I'm watching you. Are you trying to make me jealous? Is that it? I told you to stay away, Abigail. Why are you wasting your time on a loser like Alex Taylor?

Abby sits up in bed, suddenly fully awake, and reads the message again. She glances over at Alex, but he's still soundly asleep, snoring gently.

I'm watching you.

Abby shivers. *Is he here right now? Outside?* There's the sound of a car engine starting up. Is that him? She gets out of bed and rushes to the window. Heart hammering, she pulls the curtain back and peers out into the darkness. The street is empty, the black road gleaming in the moonlight. At the far end of the street a dark car pulls around the corner. She tries to make out the make and licence plate – but it's too dark, and she can't even be sure of the colour.

She lies back down in bed, but she's too wired to sleep. Angry and scared. She goes to the main room and turns on the light. The light feels stark and it's cold on the tiles in her bare feet. She shivers, and paces up and down, fuming. *How dare he?*

Are you trying to make me jealous?

Whoever it is, he's clearly delusional. Perhaps ringing him back will only add fuel to his delusion, but she needs to do something.

She writes back, '*Leave me alone, you freak.*' Then she stabs the SEND icon with her finger before she can change her mind. She sits and waits for a while, staring at the phone waiting for a reply, but nothing comes. So then she picks up the phone again and taps CALL. Her chest feels tight as the phone rings. She waits.

She has no idea what she'll say if he answers, but at least she'll hear his voice. Maybe she'll even recognize it. She's scared of what she'll find out, but it's better to know than deal with this uncertainty. But the phone rings and rings until she gets a recorded message saying the person she has called is unavailable: *'Please try again later.'* She switches the phone off and throws it down on the sofa in frustration.

'What are you doing?' Alex is at the door, eyes half closed, squinting in the light.

'Oh, it's nothing.' She picks up the phone but doesn't bother switching it back on again.

'Come back to bed.'

Abby lies on the bed unable to sleep, eyes wide open until the grey daylight crawls through a gap in the curtains and she hears the clanking of the rubbish truck outside.

She slips out of bed before Alex wakes up, pulls on her clothes and lets herself out of the house, closing the door softly behind her.

JUNE

Your baby now measures approximately 34–36 cm and weighs 660g. As their reflexes develop, they may react to loud noises by jumping or kicking. Their taste buds develop too, and they can taste the different flavours you eat. This is a special time in your pregnancy, as you and your baby begin to respond to each other.

Chapter Sixteen

Abby is dreaming – a series of strange, disturbing dreams. In one of them, the baby inside her has petrified, but even though it's stone, it keeps on growing and growing, weighing her down, until it's so massive her distended belly is scraping along the ground and she can barely walk. This dream segues into another. She's at a party, and someone – she can't see his face – offers her a drink, but as she lifts the glass to take a sip she realizes a snake is coiled around the stem, its head close to her lips, tongue flicking, poised ready to strike. She wakes up just as the snake is about to bite. Her heart is racing, and the baby is kicking her belly frantically.

Someone is knocking loudly on her bedroom door. Half awake, she stumbles out of bed and opens it. Ellie is standing there holding a cup of tea.

'You didn't forget, did you? You've got a doctor's appointment today. It's in an hour.'

Abby groans. *That's right.* Ellie insisted on making an appointment for her with Dr Rowe a few days ago.

'Okay, I'll be right down,' she mutters. She slurps her tea

and dresses quickly, pulling on a pair of leggings and a baggy T-shirt she's borrowed from Rob. She's beginning to regret involving Ellie in this pregnancy. After the initial shock, far from being upset or jealous, Ellie seems to have embraced it with a whole-hearted joy that is almost frightening. Last weekend she dragged Abby out shopping for baby stuff, and yesterday evening she climbed up in the loft and brought down the skeleton of the cot they bought when she was pregnant with the baby she lost. It's now sitting in the corner of Abby's room in pieces, a reproachful reminder that Abby needs to deal with this situation quickly before it gets out of hand.

'Somebody might as well use it,' Ellie said firmly when Abby told her she didn't want it.

Abby hasn't had the heart to tell her there will be no need of a cot. She's already decided she's going to give it up for adoption as soon as it's born.

Just under an hour later they are sitting in the waiting room at the doctor's. Ellie has bought a book of baby names and is reading aloud through the A's.

'Ada, Adelaide . . . ooh, *Ariana*'s nice.'

'We don't know yet if it's going to be a boy or a girl,' Abby says. 'What's the point in choosing a name?'

A pretty little girl with butterfly hairclips is playing with a wooden track in the corner of the room. The mother is preoccupied, on her phone. When the girl tugs at her arm, to get her attention, she shrugs her off. Abby watches Ellie watching them. She's staring at them steadily, her lips pressed together into a judgemental line. Abby can guess what she's thinking. That if she had a gorgeous little girl like that, she wouldn't waste one minute of her time with her.

'Didn't you find out the sex at your twenty-week scan?' she asks, not looking at Abby.

'I didn't have one.' Abby doesn't mention that she hasn't been for a check-up for ages, not since she went to talk to Dr Rowe about Aaron.

'You haven't had a scan?' Ellie tears her eyes away from the little girl and frowns at Abby. 'Why not? You have to get a scan. Scans can check for anomalies and give doctors information, so they can treat babies in the womb or after birth. It can be potentially life-saving.'

A nurse pops her head round the door and smiles at Ellie. 'Abigail. Dr Rowe will see you now.'

They make their way into the stuffy office. Dr Rowe is sitting at his desk tapping away at the computer. He jumps up when Abby and Ellie come in and pulls up seats for them.

'I hope you don't mind,' says Ellie. 'I thought I'd tag along.'

'Not at all.' He smiles. 'You must be excited to be an aunt.' He turns to Abby. 'Well, how's Mum doing?'

For a confused second Abby thinks he's asking about her own mother, then realizes he means her. 'Oh, um . . . fine,' she says.

'Good. I was a little worried, because you've missed a couple of appointments.' He looks at his notes.

Ellie sighs. 'Abby, you really should get regular check-ups – shouldn't she, Simon?'

Dr Rowe nods. 'Once a month at least, and after twenty-eight weeks once every two weeks.'

Ellie waits anxiously as the doctor measures Abby's blood pressure, weighs her, and takes a blood sample.

'Well, everything seems fine,' he says, smiling, at last. 'Your blood pressure is still a little high. You need to make sure you don't miss any more appointments. Have you been having any headaches, blurred vision?'

Abby shakes her head.

'Well, I expect it's nothing to worry about. And how are you feeling in yourself? Any concerns?'

Only that I think I might have been raped and I'm being stalked by some lunatic, Abby thinks, but she just shakes her head. She just wants to get out of there. She's finding it difficult to breathe, and the nausea which she hasn't felt for a long time is coming back. She feels trapped, and she can't bear the way Ellie and the doctor are looking at her – like this is a normal pregnancy, like she's a normal mother.

Ellie shuffles impatiently in her seat.

'We should book her in for an ultrasound, shouldn't we, Simon? She missed her twenty-week scan.'

Dr Rowe fiddles with his notes. 'Did you? Ah, yes. I'll make you an appointment at the hospital right away.'

'Do I have to?' says Abby.

'Well . . .' Dr Rowe clears his throat.

'You have to have a scan, Abby,' Ellie interrupts. 'Tell her, Simon.'

She's getting agitated, and Abby knows Ellie believes that

if she'd had more scans when she was pregnant, the problem with her baby might have been spotted. But this isn't true. The cord didn't become wrapped around the baby's neck until she was in labour, so no amount of ultrasounds would have made any difference. Logically, Ellie must know that too, but she doesn't think logically when it comes to the baby she lost.

'It really is a good idea to have at least one scan.' Dr Rowe nods. 'To check for any anomalies.'

'Okay.' Abby sighs.

'Good. I'll book you in for next week.'

Ellie goes back to her office to catch up on some paperwork, and Abby makes her way back out through the waiting room. It's filling up now – a couple of old ladies, a mother with two children, and two men: an old man and a younger man in a hoodie. The younger man raises his eyes and stares at her as she walks past, and she can still feel his eyes on her back as she exits through reception. Could he be her stalker? Could he have followed her here? She gives herself a mental shake. She's being ridiculous. She's never seen that man before in her life. What could he possibly have to do with her? But as she passes through reception, the feeling that someone is watching her intensifies.

She turns, but it's only a girl, about seventeen, pretty, dark-skinned.

'Hi, miss, I thought it was you,' she says, smiling.

It takes Abby a moment to work out who it is. She's changed so much since she last saw her. She's slimmer for a start. She's wearing make-up and her sleek black hair is coiled up in a bun, making her look older and more sophisticated. But it's not just that. It's something else. There's an aura about her. She was always such a shy girl, but now she seems confident, radiant almost.

'Remember me, miss?'

'Yes, of course, Tanseela.' Abby smiles warmly. 'How are you? You look great.'

'Thanks, miss. You too.' Her voice tails off unconvincingly. Abby is uncomfortably aware she looks anything but great. For a start, she's dressed in leggings and an old T-shirt of Rob's, and her hair hasn't been washed for a while.

Tanseela looks down at her belly and her eyes widen.

'Congratulations, miss. I didn't know you were pregnant.'

Abby places a hand on her belly and flushes slightly. 'Yes, nearly six months now.'

Outside they stop. 'Well it was nice to see you, again,' says Tanseela. 'Hope it all goes okay with the baby and everything.' She turns and heads away from town.

Abby watches her walk away, back straight, hips swaying gracefully. Then she considers what Thea told her at dinner the other day.

'Wait! Tanseela!' she calls out on impulse.

'Yes?' Tanseela stops and turns.

Abby's words come out in a breathless rush. 'Have you got a few minutes? I'd like to talk to you about something.'

'What, miss?'

'Not here. It's kind of personal. We could go for a coffee somewhere.'

Tanseela flushes slightly. 'Um, well . . .' She looks at her watch.

'Please, Tansy. It's kind of important and it will literally only take a few minutes, I promise.'

'Er . . . well, okay. I'm meeting my dad at eleven, but I've got a bit of time until then.'

Chapter Seventeen

Abby sits outside in the Swan Yard café sipping coffee. The sun has broken through the cloud and she turns her face towards it, trying to soak up its rays before it vanishes again. Tanseela has gone to the toilet and as she returns to her seat, weaving her way gracefully through the tables, Abby notices a couple of young men blatantly ogling her.

'There's something different about you,' Abby says when she sits down. 'I can't put my finger on it.'

Tanseela smiles and touches her cheek self-consciously. 'It's the mole, miss. I had it removed.'

That's it. She used to have a large, unsightly mole on her left cheek. Abby had become so used to it she'd barely noticed it, but now it's gone, there's not even a scar, and it's made a big difference to her overall looks.

'Well, you look great.' She smiles.

'Thanks, miss.'

'And how are you, Tansy? What have you been doing now since you left school?' Abby realizes she's stalling, trying to work up the courage to ask the questions she really wants to ask.

Tanseela wraps her hands round her mug. 'I'm doing a hairdressing course. I'm really enjoying it, so far.'

'You haven't thought about coming back to school, doing your A levels? You were so talented in Art.'

'Maybe . . .' Tanseela gives her a direct look. 'But that's not what you wanted to talk about, is it?'

'No,' Abby admits. She clasps her hands in front of her.

'I just . . . want to know . . . are you happy? I mean, in general? Is everything okay?'

Tanseela lifts one shoulder. 'Sure, why not?'

She does look happy. Radiant, even. Perhaps Abby's fears are unfounded. She's not sure she's wise stirring this up, but she needs to be certain that Tanseela is okay. And she needs to know for herself, too. She can't help feeling that Tanseela is connected to what's going on. She chooses her words carefully. She mustn't say anything too leading.

'There's nothing bothering you? No one? Nothing you want to talk about?'

'No, miss,' Tanseela's eyes widen. 'I'm fine, honestly.' She looks at her watch. 'Look, I've got to meet my dad in a minute. What's this all about?'

Abby takes a deep breath. 'It's just that I spoke to Mrs Baker the other day, and she happened to mention what happened last year . . .'

Tanseela's eyes widen. Then she flushes angrily. 'I'm sorry,

153

miss,' she says stiffly, 'but I don't see what that's got to do with you.'

Abby kicks herself. This isn't the way this was supposed to go. But she presses on regardless. 'She took you to the clinic, didn't she?'

Tanseela glares at her with big, hostile brown eyes. 'She had no right to tell you that. She promised she wouldn't tell anyone.'

Thea is going to kill me if she finds out, Abby thinks. 'No, well, she didn't actually tell me it was you,' she explains hurriedly. 'I ... guessed. I'm just concerned about you, that's all. I wanted to make sure you're okay.'

Tanseela stands up and slings her bag over her shoulder. 'Well, I don't mean to be rude, miss, but it's really not your business. You're not my teacher anymore. You've no right ...' She turns to go, then appears to think better of it and sits back down. She stares at Abby, chewing her finger. Suddenly there's a hint of the old Tanseela again – the timid little girl who sat in Abby's class last year. 'You haven't told anyone else, have you, miss?'

'No, Tansy, I haven't,' says Abby. 'And there's no reason why I would need to tell anyone. Not if it was consensual. I mean if you and your boyfriend both wanted to have sex ...'

A strand of hair falls over Tansy's face and she tucks it behind her ear. 'Like I told Mrs Baker, me and my boyfriend, we haven't had sex.'

Abby leans forward in her chair. 'Come on, Tanseela, you're an intelligent girl. You know it doesn't work like that.

154

People don't get pregnant without having sex. It's just not possible.'

Tanseela folds her arms. 'All I know is that it happened to me,' she says obstinately.

'Do you think someone could have spiked your drink, maybe at a party, or maybe you drank too much one night?'

'I don't drink, miss.' She clasps her hands in front of her. 'Please, please, promise you won't tell anyone. My dad'll kill me if he finds out.'

Abby hesitates. Tanseela is sixteen now. Crazy as it seems to Abby, she's old enough to legally have sex. But at the time it happened she was still underage. She's fairly sure she's supposed to tell someone. But Tanseela seems so happy now, and what good will it do, stirring everything up again?

'I promise,' she says. 'That is, as long as you're sure you're okay?'

'I am, miss, and thank you.'

After Tanseela is gone, Abby sits for a long time in the coffee shop, thinking. The funny thing is, she believes her. At least, Abby believes that Tansy believes she didn't have sex, and she feels somehow that this fact is important – that there is some connection between what happened to her and what happened to this sixteen-year-old girl. But what?

Abby walks up the hill towards her house, still deep in thought. All the strange things that have happened over the past few months run through her head on a loop. She searches for a pattern, for some kind of link. But really, she's no nearer to working it out. She sighs as she lets herself in through the back door and flings her keys on the kitchen counter. Maybe she would be happier if she forgot about the whole thing – forgot about trying to find the father of her baby and just accepted her situation. If Tanseela could get over this and move on, then so can she.

She makes herself a cup of tea and wanders into the living room. Rob is sitting with his feet up on the coffee table talking on the phone. 'Ah, yes, here she is now,' he says, beckoning to Abby. 'Do you want to speak to her? Yes . . . yes, it's terrible, I know.

'It's your dad,' he mouths, raising his eyebrows. There's never been much love lost between Rob and Dad, and since Sue arrived on the scene their relationship has been even colder.

'Hello, sweetheart,' Dad says as Abby takes the phone. 'I've got a meeting in Cheltenham Sunday afternoon. I thought I could come and visit you. Kill two birds with one stone.'

Shit. She knew this moment was coming. Even with the rift between them, she could hardly expect not to see her dad for nine months. There's no way she can disguise her baby bump now. Dad's going to get the shock of his life.

'That sounds lovely,' she says out loud.

'Great,' he says. 'I'll meet you at about one. I thought I could treat you and Ellie to a meal . . . and . . . Rob, if he wants to come.'

'I've got some news,' she says, taking a deep breath.

'Oh? Good or bad?'

'I'll explain when I see you.'

'Oh, okay, love . . . Well, take care and see you soon.'

'What did he want?' asks Rob when she hangs up.

'Lunch Sunday afternoon.' She wags a finger at him. 'So, you'd better be on your best behaviour.'

'What do you mean? I'm always on my best behaviour,' he protests in mock offence. 'Anyway, I think I'm busy Sunday. I've just remembered I said I'd go for a drink with Stu.'

'Yeah, right. That's convenient.' Abby smiles. She flings herself down on the sofa. She feels suddenly exhausted. Absent-mindedly, she checks her mobile. There are a couple of messages. One from Danny asking how her doctor's appointment went and inviting her to the cinema tomorrow night. And there's a voicemail.

It's Alex.

'Listen, I'd like to see you tomorrow. We could go to the park. The forecast is good and –' he clears his throat – *'there's someone I want you to meet.'*

Chapter Eighteen

The park is full of teenage kids playing Frisbee or sprawled on the grass soaking up the sun. Abby sits and waits on a bench by the old Roman wall, wondering if she should have come. She guesses that the 'someone' Alex wants her to meet is his son, Dylan, and although she's flattered, she's also worried. *Is it a sign he wants their relationship to get more serious?* She's not sure she's ready for that. Perhaps she should call things off with him, before they get too complicated. After all, she needs to get her own life sorted first, before she gets involved in anyone else's. And right now, her life is about as far from sorted as it could be.

She watches as an elderly couple shuffle past along the footpath that runs around the lake. There's a man fishing on the bank and a family with a toddler feeding the ducks. Nothing suspicious. Nothing to cause alarm. But, still, she can't shake the idea that she's being watched. Lately, everywhere she goes she feels like someone is observing her, monitoring her every move. What if they're watching her right now? She turns and looks around. Behind her are the woods that separate the park from the dual carriageway. Even on this bright day, they're dark and gloomy, and in Abby's current state of mind there's something sinister about them. *How easy would it be for someone to hide there in the shadows?*

'Hello,' says someone behind her, and she jumps and turns to see Alex, with an empty pushchair, a small, dark-haired boy clinging to his hand.

'Oh, you gave me a fright,' she says, trying to laugh off her reaction. 'You must be Dylan.' She smiles at the boy, and he smiles back shyly, hiding behind Alex.

'I'm sorry we're late.' Alex flings himself down on the bench next to her. 'Some wanker drove into the back of me at the roundabout, then drove off.'

'Oh my God. Were you hurt?'

'No, we're okay. Just a bit shaken up. But the rear lights are broken and there's a big dent in the back. I only just had it serviced, as well.'

'Did you see the licence plate?' Abby asks.

He shakes his head ruefully. 'No, I was too busy making sure Dylan was okay. It was an SUV, black, I think. That's all I noticed.'

'How annoying.'

'Yeah, you can say that again. Anyway. Never mind. It's just money.' He pulls Dylan round to the front of him, putting his hands on his shoulders. 'This little fella is Dylan, my son. Dylan, this is Abby, a friend of mine.'

Dylan gives her a long, assessing stare and tugs Alex's hand. 'I want to go on the swing, Daddy,' he says.

'Okay, mate.' Alex ruffles his hair. 'It'll take him a while to warm up to you,' he says apologetically to Abby as they head to the play park.

Abby smiles. She feels awkward with little kids. Teenagers she can handle, but small kids have always made her feel uncomfortable. That's one of the reasons why it's ridiculous to think she could ever be a mother.

In the play park Abby and Alex sit on a bench and watch as Dylan climbs to the top of the spider frame.

'Is he okay up there?' Abby asks, as he reaches the top and sits balancing precariously.

'Yeah, he'll be fine. He's like Spider-Man, that kid, always climbing. Anyway, how are you?' Alex moves closer to her, so their legs are touching. 'I had a good time the other night. Didn't you?'

'Not bad,' she says cautiously.

'Not bad?' He laughs. 'Just not bad? I must be losing my touch.'

This would be a good time to tell him she wants to break it off, but his eyes have caught the sunlight and he's looking at her with a half-amused, half-quizzical expression that weakens her resolve. She smiles back – she can't help it – and, encouraged, he takes her hand and leans in for a kiss.

'Not here,' she says, looking around over her shoulder.

Alex cups her chin in his hand, pulling her towards him. 'Why not?'

'People will see us.'

'So what? Let them watch.'

160

'But . . .' She breaks away. 'Somebody doesn't like us being together. Look, I want to show you something. Someone sent me this the other night when I was round at your house.' She takes out her phone and shows Alex the message she received.

He reads it, frowning. 'What do they mean, "a *loser* like Alex Taylor"? Who the hell sent you this?'

'I don't know. I thought maybe you might have some idea. Are you sure it's not from Bethany?'

'No, I told you, Bethany wouldn't do that. She's got a bit of a temper on her, but she's not into mind games. She'd be more likely to punch you in the face than send you hate mail. No, this must be from one of *your* exes . . . What about these flowers you've been getting? I think . . .'

But he doesn't finish what he's saying, because at that moment Dylan comes running up and starts whining, tugging at his arm.

'You're tired, mate. Why don't you have a kip?' says Alex, and he tries to strap Dylan in the pushchair, but the boy kicks and screams wildly, so he reaches into his bag and pulls out a packet of biscuits.

'If you get in your chair I'll give you a biscuit, alright?' He holds a biscuit above Dylan's head, as if he's a dog he's training, and eventually Dylan climbs into his pushchair, gnaws at the biscuit and then almost immediately drops off to sleep, clutching the soggy biscuit in his hand.

'He can be a little sod at times,' says Alex as they walk back around the lake.

'Mm, he's cute when he's asleep.'

He laughs. 'Yeah.'

Abby is trying to work out how to tell him she thinks they shouldn't see each other anymore, when he brings them to a stop on the other side of the lake in a patch of grass surrounded by trees.

'This is a good spot,' he says.

'For what?'

'For a picnic,' he says. Pulling a bag from under the push-chair, he spreads a blanket down on the grass and starts unpacking an impressive amount of food.

'Wow, you've thought of everything,' says Abby, lowering herself down onto the grass. She's touched by the effort he's put in. He's even made chocolate brownies. She's never had a date like this – certainly not with Ben, whose idea of romance was a couple of pints and a curry.

'The problem with Dylan is that his mum spoils him,' says Alex, opening a Tupperware box of sandwiches and glancing over at Dylan, who is still asleep. 'He used to be such a good boy, but lately . . . Christ, he can be a nightmare.'

'Isn't that normal for a kid his age? Isn't that why they call it the terrible twos?'

'Yeah, well, Dylan's three already.'

Abby props herself up on her side and tugs at a handful of grass. She thinks about Carla's twins. 'Yes, but I think it can go on into their threes. Not that I know much about parenting . . .'

'You'll know soon enough,' says Alex, shuffling closer

162

to her and placing his hand on her belly. He gazes into her eyes. 'Is this private enough for you? No one can see us here.'

'Well . . .' says Abby, weakening, and when he kisses her, she doesn't protest, and when he pushes her backwards onto the grass she twines her fingers in his hair, kissing him back eagerly, giving in to the pleasurable sensation of being in his arms.

She's not sure how long they're there, chatting, eating and making out. It doesn't feel like all that long before Alex stands up, shakes the grass off his clothes and looks at his watch. 'I said I'd get Dylan back to his mum by five and I've got to sort out my car. We'd better get going.'

His car is in a parking space by the road, just outside the park. Abby inspects the damage. The rear bumper is caved in and one light is cracked. 'You're lucky you and Dylan weren't hurt,' she says.

'Yeah, and I don't think the other bloke's car was damaged at all. The bastard.' He lifts Dylan from the pushchair and straps him into the car seat. 'After I drop off Dylan, I'm going to take it to the garage, see what they can do . . . But do you want to come round to mine tomorrow?'

'I can't,' says Abby, half relieved to have a genuine excuse and half wishing she could take him up on his offer. 'I'm meeting my dad for lunch.'

'Oh, alright.' He shrugs, looking disappointed, and gives her a peck on the lips. 'I'll call you, okay?'

*

Despite his bad-boy appearance, Alex is such a sweet, thoughtful guy, Abby thinks as she turns into her street. Maybe they could make a go of it after all. She envisions a scenario in which she keeps the baby, and she, Alex, Dylan and the baby become a family unit. She imagines the two of them strolling through the park, pushing a pram, Dylan trotting along beside them. But she knows in her heart that it would never work.

'Hey,' Abby calls out as she comes through the front door. She hears Rob grunt in acknowledgement from the living room. Abby dumps her bag in the hallway, goes into the living room and sits down opposite Rob. 'Is Ellie home?' she asks.

'She's out for dinner with Carla tonight,' Rob says, finally lifting his eyes from the TV to acknowledge Abby. Her eyes travel round the room and settle on the table by the TV. There's a heart-shaped cactus in a small brown pot that wasn't there before.

'What's that?' she asks.

'Your secret admirer again.' Rob fiddles with his phone.

'What?' she says, heart sinking. She picks up the pot and finds the envelope attached. '*Abigail*' is written on the envelope, typed neatly as before.

'Is it real?' she says. It looks plastic, but when she digs her nails into the flesh, a sticky substance oozes out.

'Hey, don't ruin it,' says Rob, looking up. 'Who's it from? That bloke you've been seeing?' *It could be from Alex.* She holds on to this idea. *Please God, let it be from Alex*, she prays, ripping open the envelope. But the attached message is unsigned and typewritten.

Abigail, you take my breath away.

She reads it twice, her heart in her mouth. *It must be a coincidence. It has to be.*

'Well?' Rob says, staring at her curiously. 'What does it say?'

'Nothing much.'

She shoves the note into her pocket and heads upstairs. In her room, she locks the door and then stands in front of the mirror, staring into her wide grey eyes, running her hand over the baby bump. Then she tugs at her leggings, yanking them down around her thighs, and runs her fingers over the small tattoo between her hip and the top of her thigh. She had it done three years ago when she and Ben were on holiday in Spain. They'd had a few drinks and Ben had suggested they get matching tattoos. It had seemed like a good idea at the time. Thank God, she hadn't gone ahead with the matching-tattoo idea. Instead she'd opted for a quote. A quote from her favourite poet, Maya Angelou: *Life is not measured by the number of breaths we take, but by the moments that take our breath away.*

It seemed like a good motto for her life at the time – to live life to the full. After all, life is short – her mum's death had taught her that. But now, with all the weird, crazy shit that's been happening, she's not so sure she wants to live a full life. *A normal, quiet life would be great, thank you very much.*

She pulls the note out of her pocket and reads it again, shaking her head. *No, it's a coincidence,* she tells herself. *It's a*

165

coincidence. It's got to be a coincidence. But the choice of words is disturbing. *'You take my breath away'.* It's almost as if the sender knows – as if they've seen the tattoo.

She shivers. The thought of someone seeing something so intimate without her knowledge makes her feel dirty, as if tiny bugs are crawling all over her skin. She has a sudden urge to wash. Heading for the bathroom, she strips off her clothes and steps into the shower. She turns it on at full power, letting the hot water sting, and she scrubs herself vigorously until her skin is pink.

By the time she gets out of the shower, Abby feels a little calmer. It's a common enough phrase after all – 'You take my breath away'. It's not necessarily a reference to the tattoo. She wraps herself in a towel, heads to her bedroom, locks the door again and gets dressed. She's pulling on a baggy T-shirt when her phone vibrates in the pocket of her jacket. *It's probably Danny*, she thinks vaguely, asking how her date went. Good. She wants to talk to him, ask him what he makes of the note. She takes the phone out and swipes the screen. But it's not Danny. It's another text, the number withheld.

Leave me alone, she thinks angrily. She hesitates, torn between curiosity and the urge to delete the message without opening it. Curiosity wins. She reads the first sentence and suddenly she can't breathe:

Life is not measured by the number of breaths we take, but by the moments that take our breath . . .

166

Abby tries to breathe in and out slowly, but her breath comes in short, shallow gasps. She feels dizzy and deeply afraid. She steadies herself by leaning against the wall and forces herself to read the rest of the message.

Life is not measured by the number of breaths we take, but by the moments that take our breath away. How true that is. And how precious those moments are. The first time I saw you, Abigail, you took my breath away. When I made love to you, I knew we were meant to be.

Her heart is racing and she sinks onto her bed, blackness curling at the edges of her mind. Her hands tremble as she scrolls through the message again. Alex was right. The texts are clearly not from Bethany. She's suspected as much for a while, but this is the first time she's been forced to fully acknowledge the truth. She presses her eyes shut. Everything is closing in on her. There can be no doubt now. The text messages and the flowers are from the same man.

The man who raped her.

Chapter Nineteen

Because he *did* rape her. She's certain of that now. This was no accidental drunken fling between consenting adults. Why else would he withhold his number? Why else would he be taunting her like this?

Revulsion and outrage twist inside her as she thinks of this man using her the way he did. She places a hand on her belly and the creature inside jabs savagely.

He put this parasite inside me, she thinks, feeling a wave of hatred. And just for a moment, she wants to tear it out with her bare hands. Suddenly furiously angry, she digs viciously into her skin with her nails, creating long red scratches. And as if in answer, the thing inside her wriggles frantically.

What are you doing, Abby? she reproaches herself, staring at her stomach appalled. *It's just a baby, an innocent baby.* And just as quickly as it appeared, the anger evaporates and a wave of despair and shame washes over her. She sinks to the floor and curls up, sobbing hopelessly.

She replays her memories of New Year's Eve again and again in her head – arriving at the party, drinking with Mark in the kitchen, talking to Alex on the stairs. She thinks about what she was wearing, that red dress, with the low-cut back. *Was she sending out the wrong signals?* According to both Danny and Alex, she was flirting a lot that night. *Has she brought this on herself?* Logically she knows this is nonsense. *Even if she was wearing a short dress, even if she was flirting, so what? Why shouldn't she? It's no excuse for what he's done.* But the shame spreads through her anyway, like poison in her veins.

It's already dark outside when Abby is finally all cried out, and she's stiff from being curled up on the floor. She wipes her nose, sniffs, and glances at the clock on her bedside table. It's eleven o'clock. She's been lying here for hours.

Get a grip, Abby, she tells herself sharply. *You're not helping anything by falling apart like this.* With an effort of will, she gets up shakily and picks up her phone. She needs to try to think about this whole thing calmly and rationally. She reads the message through again, the phone trembling in her hand.

When I made love to you . . .

Love had nothing to do with it, she thinks bitterly. Is it possible her stalker really believes it was an act of love in his twisted mind? Or maybe it's his way of letting her know he still has power over her?

. . . I knew we were meant to be.

He really is completely delusional. It's obvious he's got some kind of sick obsession with her. She shudders with fear as the full implications sink in. This man, whoever he is, is dangerously insane and it's clear that he's not going to leave her alone. Perhaps he'll even try to hurt her again.

At that moment a loud rap on the door makes her jump and her heart leap out of her chest.

But it's only Ellie. 'Abby? Rob said you never came down for dinner,' she calls. 'Are you alright?'

Shit. She can't face seeing anyone in this state. She sniffs and wipes her eyes, trying to make her voice sound as normal as possible.

'Um . . . I'm fine,' she manages. 'I'm just not feeling very well.'

'You sound awful. Can I come in?' Ellie rattles the door handle. 'Why've you locked the door? Are you okay?'

'I'll be okay in a bit.'

'Do you need anything before I go to bed? Some water? Painkillers?'

'No, I'm fine. I just need to be on my own for a while.'

There's a pause. Then Ellie sighs. 'Well, if you're sure.'

She listens to the sound of Ellie's footsteps on the stairs. Abby wishes she could call out to Ellie and confide in her. They used to be so close. They used to share everything, but ever since Abby found out she was pregnant there's a distance between them that seems impossible to bridge.

Abby pulls off her clothes and crawls into bed, burying her face in the pillow. She has never felt so alone.

Chapter Twenty

Abby is cold when she wakes up the next morning, still curled up in her towel on top of her covers, after only a couple of hours of troubled sleep. She swings her feet over the edge of the bed. As she does so, she catches sight of herself in the mirror. She looks terrible. Her mascara has run, her face is haggard, and her nose and eyes are red from crying. *This is not you,* she thinks angrily. *This is who he wants you to be. He wants you to be afraid because that makes him feel powerful.* She stands up, taking a deep, shuddering breath. Well, she's not going to let him make her afraid. She refuses to be a victim.

She stands in front of the mirror and brushes her hair, scraping it back tightly in a ponytail. Then she rubs off the mascara and squares her shoulders. *You're not going to let him get away with this, Abby Brooke,* she tells herself. *Tomorrow you're going to go to the police. But first you have to get through this meal with Dad.*

Dad is already waiting in a booth in the Little Chef when they get there. And Sue is sitting next to him. *Great.* Abby's heart sinks. That's all she needs. It's bad enough having to talk to Dad about this pregnancy, let alone Sue, who is practically a stranger. And not a stranger she particularly likes, from the little she knows of her.

Dad stands up and pats Ellie and Abby awkwardly on the arm. 'Good to see you both,' he says. 'It's been a long time.'

He turns to Abby, his eyes sliding down to her belly, and does a double take, but he says nothing. Then Sue stands up and pecks them on the cheeks. She steps back and stares blatantly at Abby's baby bump.

'Oh my God, Brian!' she says. 'You didn't tell me you were going to be a granddaddy! How exciting.'

Abby slides into the seat next to Ellie, being careful not to bump her belly against the edge of the table. She raises her chin defiantly. 'Yes, so . . . as you can see, I'm pregnant.'

Dad clears his throat. 'I suppose congratulations are in order,' he offers cautiously.

Congratulations. The word feels like a slap in the face, under the circumstances. Abby fights off a wave of nausea, the blackness encroaching. *Stay calm*, she tells herself. *Stay calm.*

'Thanks,' she manages to say.

'Are you okay?' Ellie asks, glancing at her anxiously. 'Abby wasn't feeling too well last night,' she explains to Dad and Sue.

'It's no walk in the park, is it, having a baby?' says Sue. 'I remember when I was pregnant with my first son I was sick as a dog all the time, morning, noon and night. They call it *morning* sickness, don't they? But I wasn't just sick in the morning. I was sick all day long.' She pats her short, blonde hair and pauses for breath.

'So, how . . . ?' Dad tries to interject. But Sue hasn't finished talking.

'And then there was the birth. Oh my God. Nothing can prepare you for that. It's the worst pain you'll ever feel in your life. My Max was a whopper too – ten pounds, five ounces, he was . . .'

Sue carries on her monologue as the food arrives and throughout the meal, sharing long stories of her first marriage, her children, and horrific tales of childbirth gone wrong. She's clearly forgotten that Ellie lost her own baby only a couple of years ago.

Abby glances over at Ellie a few times during the meal but her sister is staring down at her food, her lips pressed firmly together, as if she's trying to stop herself speaking. It's probably just as well, Abby reflects. Ellie has quite a temper, and if she lets Sue know what she really thinks, it won't be pretty. 'Of course, Maxwell's father wasn't a very nice man . . .' Sue says, chewing a mouthful of chicken. 'Not like your dad here.' She turns to Abby and gestures towards her belly. 'Where's the father of this wee one today? I hope you've chosen a better man than I did.'

Abby grips the table. For a moment she is unable to speak.

'Er . . . the father is not in the picture,' Ellie says quickly, glancing with concern at Abby.

Dad looks alarmed. 'But how will you—'

'So, you're going to be a single parent,' Sue interrupts.

173

'Well, it's more and more common nowadays, I suppose. I'm old-fashioned of course. But I do think a child is better off with a mother and a father.' She purses her lips. 'You know, I saw a programme the other day about how gay couples get sperm donors. It's not natural, if you ask me. Disgusting.' Ellie and Abby exchange a look. Abby is surprised that Ellie doesn't answer. She's usually not slow to stand up for what she believes, but she's clearly making a big effort to get along with Sue today.

The meal drags on for what seems like forever. Abby forces herself to eat one mouthful after another, trying not to gag as the food slides down her throat, trying to nod and smile politely at Sue and Dad. All the time she's fighting the urge to run back home and hide away. She feels so exposed, as if her skin has been ripped off. And she's tormented by the thought that her rapist might be in the room somewhere, watching her, enjoying her fear. The relief when the waitress finally comes and clears away their plates is intense.

'How are you going to manage for money, Abby?' Dad asks as he pays the bill. 'Childcare is expensive these days, you know.'

'I don't know . . .' Abby shrugs helplessly. She *won't* be needing childcare, of course. But they don't know that yet.

As they're leaving the restaurant, Dad reaches into his pocket and pulls out his wallet. He thrusts some notes into Abby's hand. 'That's just to tide you over, love,' he mutters. 'I'll put something in your bank account later.'

'It's okay – really,' protests Abby, but he won't take no for an answer, and she feels too weak and tired to argue, so she slips the money into her handbag. She'll give it back later when she tells them about the adoption.

'Are you sure you've got enough money, Brian?' Sue says as they're leaving, looking at Abby with narrowed eyes. 'You know we've still got to pay for that cruise.'

'Oh well, I suppose they're made for each other in a way,' Ellie says with a sigh, once Dad and Sue are gone and they're driving home. 'He never speaks, and she never stops talking.'

Abby smiles wanly. Sue is the least of her worries right now. All the shock and emotion of the last twenty-four hours is catching up with her, and she feels drained and exhausted. The thought of talking to the police tomorrow terrifies her. But she has to stay strong. She can't lose courage now.

Chapter Twenty-One

'So, how can I help you, Abigail?'

She's at the police station talking to a policeman who's introduced himself as PC David Whittaker. He's a chubby, middle-aged man with a large, round face and a facetious smile. He's made Abby wait for him while he finishes a pastry and he's currently sitting opposite her, brushing the crumbs from his uniform.

She takes a deep breath. 'I think someone is stalking me,' she says.

'You think someone is stalking you?' he repeats, raising his eyebrows. Abby guesses it's not the kind of problem he's used to encountering in this sleepy little police station. Probably the most he ever deals with is lost wallets, missing pets or confused pensioners.

'Yes,' she says firmly.

He looks her up and down sceptically, evidently trying to decide if she's a lunatic. Abby didn't sleep much last night, and she's suddenly aware that she forgot to brush her hair and that the T-shirt that she put on in a hurry this morning has dog hairs all over it.

'Okay then,' he says slowly. 'I'll have to log a report.' He pulls out a phone and taps the screen with a stylus.

Abby looks around. On the walls are various public information posters and an appeal for information about a spate of recent burglaries in Swindon.

'Bear with me a minute,' says PC Whittaker. 'Bloody thing's acting up again. It was easier when we had pen and paper.' He clears his throat. 'Ah yes, here we are. Now then, what exactly is the nature of this harassment?'

'Well, I keep getting flowers and weird text messages.'

PC Whittaker taps his phone. 'Did any message come with the flowers?'

'Yes, but I'm afraid I left them at home.'

'And the name of the offender? What's the name of the person sending you these?'

'I don't know.'

He puts down his stylus and stares at her. 'You don't know?'

'No. The messages and the gifts, they're all anonymous. The texts too.'

She opens the message she received at Alex's and hands him her phone. His eyes flick over the screen. 'Hmm,' he says thoughtfully. 'Who's Alex Taylor?'

'This guy I've been seeing. It's nothing serious. But each time I see him I get a message like that.'

'And you have no idea who this could be? Because this

sounds to me like they could come from a jealous lover, an ex-boyfriend maybe?'

Abby thinks of Ben and shakes her head. 'My ex lives in London. He couldn't know that I've been seeing Alex. Anyway, it was him who broke off our relationship, not the other way around.'

'Someone else then, someone who's asked you out and you've rejected?'

She shakes her head. 'No, he sent me another message last night claiming we had . . . *been* together.'

PC Whittaker sighs and flicks through her phone again. He reads the messages, slowly, aloud, pausing and reddening over, '*when I made love to you*'. Abby feels the heat rising in her cheeks, too, and she squirms uncomfortably in her chair.

'It certainly seems like this is a person you've been intimate with. Are you sure you don't know who it could be?'

Abby closes her eyes. She feels sick and dizzy. 'I'm sure,' she says, opening her eyes and looking directly at the police officer. 'There's something else I haven't told you yet.'

'Oh?'

She hesitates. She knows the story sounds bizarre, unbelievable even, and she badly needs him to take her seriously. But she also needs him to understand why she feels so threatened, and this is the only way to convince him.

'I think the person sending me the messages is the father of this baby.' She places a hand on her belly, feeling the taut skin. The baby inside stays very still.

PC Whittaker looks confused. 'I don't quite follow ... If he's the father, then ...'

Abby takes a deep breath. 'About three and a half months ago I discovered I was pregnant. The baby was conceived at a New Year's party, but I have no memory of the conception.'

PC Whittaker blushes slightly. 'You have no memory of having sex?'

'That's right. I think I might have been drugged.'

He clears his throat. 'So ... are you saying you've been raped?'

'Yes.' Abby wraps her arms around herself. Hearing the words out loud makes all those feelings of revulsion, shame and anger come flooding back, and she's fighting to maintain control.

PC Whittaker frowns in consternation. 'That's a very serious allegation, Abigail. Why didn't you report it at the time?'

'I didn't realize it had happened until I discovered I was pregnant two months later. By then, any trace of the drug would have disappeared.'

He scratches his head. 'I'm sorry to have to ask, but ... were you drinking at the party?'

'Yes,' Abby admits reluctantly. 'But I don't think I drank enough to black out like that.' It's a lie, but she worries she'll lose his sympathy and that he won't believe her if she tells him the whole truth.

'I see. Well, in any case, it would still be rape if you were unable to give your consent, but that might be difficult to prove unless there were witnesses.'

The phone rings and he picks it up. 'Yes, hiya, Steve. I'm in an interview at the moment.' He chuckles at something, 'I'll call you back in a minute, mate.'

He's still grinning as he hangs up. But he quickly wipes the grin from his face as he turns to Abby. 'Sorry about that. Now, where were we? Yes, so, Abigail, if you like, I can refer you to the Rape and Serious Sexual Offences Unit, where a detective can work on your case. They can give you an examination, though I have to tell you, without you actually having a suspect in mind, and given the time that's elapsed since the alleged offence, I think it might be problematic. In the meantime, about the harassment – there are some things we can do.' He picks up Abby's phone and scrolls through the messages. 'We may be able to trace the caller if they have a contract.'

'Good.' The thought of tracing her rapist and confronting him fills her with dread, but it's what needs to happen, she reminds herself. It's the reason she came here.

'Have you made it clear that you don't want him to contact you?'

'I did.' She shows him the message she sent when she was at Alex's flat.

'Good. That's good. Though I would avoid incendiary language like "freak", and getting into a conversation with him is a bad idea. He may take that as encouragement.' He sighs. 'So, the first thing I suggest is that you change your phone number. And then you give the new number back out, one person at a time, to the people closest to you first. Don't tell anyone why you're doing it, not even your closest friends. That way, when or if the messages start again, we'll be able to work out who your stalker is. The second thing you should do is keep anything you receive from this guy and keep a record of when and where you receive it. Okay?'

'Okay.' Abby nods.

He smiles kindly. 'So, do you want me to contact RASSO?'

'What?'

'Sorry, the Rape and Serious Sexual Offences Unit.'

Abby imagines a sceptical detective, lots of intrusive questions, and a terrifying physical examination. She can't bear the idea of someone prodding and poking her, asking her more questions, judging her. And, as PC Whittaker says, it will probably all be for nothing as it happened so long ago and there are no witnesses.

'No, thanks,' she says. 'I'd rather wait and see if we can find out who sent me the messages first.' When she finds her stalker, she'll have her rapist, and the police can do a DNA test to prove it.

PC Whittaker frowns. 'We can send someone round to your house if you don't feel comfortable going to the unit.'

'No, thanks,' Abby repeats firmly.

'Well, if you're sure . . . Would you like me to put you in contact with a counsellor?'

'No, I'm fine, thank you.' So now he thinks she's crazy. *Great.* He probably thinks she's making this whole thing up.

He sighs and hands her a card. 'Well, this is my number. Don't hesitate to contact me any time if you're worried or if you receive any more messages.' He stands up and ushers her out of the office, his hand resting lightly on her back. 'Leave it with me – I'll see what I can do.'

Abby walks out through the car park and onto the high street. She feels strangely discouraged by the whole interview. *PC Whittaker was polite and sympathetic, and he went through the motions because he has to*, she thinks, but she's not sure how seriously he took her about the rape. *He probably thinks she's some slut who got drunk and knocked up at a party.*

She heads through the town square. All the market stalls are set up and there are too many people milling around for Abby's liking. The thought that her stalker could be somewhere amongst them makes her feel dizzy with fear. She pushes her way through the jostling crowd and emerges on the other side as if she's coming up for air. At least PC Whittaker made a show of taking her seriously, she thinks. And his advice about only giving out her number to a few people wasn't such a bad one.

She stops at the corner. *There's no time like the present.* Turning around, she heads back towards the phone shop.

Chapter Twenty-Two

'I can't find any record of your previous scans . . .' The sonographer shuffles some papers, frowning. She looks flustered. A strand of her grey-brown hair has come loose from her ponytail and is falling across her face; her tanned weather-beaten cheeks are flushed.

'That's because I haven't had any,' says Abby.

It's been a week since she went to the police, and Abby has come with Ellie to the hospital. She's lying on the couch with her maternity trousers rolled down over her hips and her shirt lifted, her stomach protruding in the air like a mountain, while Ellie sits in a chair by her side, her hands clasped as if she's praying. Abby's hoping to get this over with quickly. The whole thing is making her very uncomfortable and filling her with a sense of unease she can't really articulate.

'Oh? Okay . . .' The sonographer looks surprised. 'Your doctor should have offered you a scan at fourteen weeks. Well, anyway, better late than never.' She tucks her hair behind her ear. 'This will feel a little cold,' she says. She rubs gel on Abby's stomach, then picks up her probe and runs it over Abby's round, taut skin. Like magic, a grainy black and white image appears on the monitor next to the bed. At first, it's hard to make out because the image shifts and morphs like a picture in the sand, but after a few seconds Abby can make out ribs and a hand, and Abby draws in her breath as the whole image comes into sharp focus.

'Wow,' says Ellie, clapping her hand to her mouth. 'That's your baby, Abby.' Tears are already welling up in her eyes and the sonographer laughs and hands her some tissues. 'It should be the mother crying, not her sister.'

For just a second, Abby feels the excitement too. It's hard not to be excited when confronted by the miracle of life. For a second she forgets everything, and she's a normal mother with a normal baby. Then the reality of her situation comes crashing back. This baby is an invader – a Trojan horse put there by her enemy. She doesn't want it. She turns away, tears welling up in her eyes.

'Now it's Mum's turn.' The sonographer smiles, misinterpreting the reason for her tears. 'It's an emotional moment, isn't it?'

She moves the probe around, pressing hard in places and clicking on the computer. 'Everything seems to be in order,' she says at last.

'Are you sure?' asks Ellie anxiously.

'Yes, as sure as I can be.' The sonographer smiles at Abby. 'Would you like to know the sex of your baby?'

'Why not?' Abby shrugs. What does it matter, boy or girl? It's all the same to her. She's not going to keep it.

The sonographer moves the probe around some more, then fixes it in one spot. 'Well,' she says. 'We can never be a hundred per cent sure, but I'm fairly certain you're expecting a baby girl.'

Ellie squeezes Abby's hand. 'A baby girl,' she whispers. 'A perfect little baby girl – a little Abigail.'

Abby tries to smile for Ellie's sake, but inside she feels numb.

'Girls are great,' says the sonographer. 'I should know – I've had three of them. Though they can be a nightmare when they're teenagers.

'There's one other thing,' she says as Abby pulls down her top and sits up. 'Your due date is the twenty-third of September, right?'

'Er . . . yes.' Abby has memorized the date of her delivery. It's her delivery in more ways than one. The date she will finally be free again.

'How sure are you about that date?'

'Fairly sure,' Abby says, surprised. 'Why?'

'From the size and development of the baby, I would have estimated a bit earlier.' The sonographer laughs and shrugs. 'But that doesn't necessarily mean anything. Scans in the third trimester are not that accurate for dating. And besides, only five per cent of women actually give birth on their due date.'

'I didn't know that,' says Abby. She stands up and picks up her bag. Ellie and the sonographer are both beaming at her as if she's just won the lottery or run a marathon, and all she wants to do is scream.

*

'A girl!' exclaims Ellie as they drive back from the hospital. 'Now we can begin some serious shopping. Let's stop off in town. There's a cute little baby boutique just opened next to the coffee shop.'

'I can't afford a baby boutique,' says Abby. 'Let's just go home.'

'I'll treat you,' says Ellie. 'Please let me, Abby.'

Abby hasn't seen Ellie this happy in a long time, and she finds herself agreeing, even though she's never going to need baby clothes.

Little Me is a small boutique at the far end of town, the kind of shop Abby normally avoids: small, and ridiculously expensive, with overzealous shop assistants who watch you like a hawk. But Ellie is on a mission and Abby finds herself in there, unfolding Babygros and pretending to examine them while Ellie happily rifles through racks of tiny dresses.

Afterwards, they go for a coffee in the Swan Yard and sit outside at wooden tables in the sunshine. The café is full of people, and the tables haven't been cleaned. Abby waits at the one free table while Ellie goes to the counter and orders them coffee. She looks around self-consciously. She's become suspicious of crowds. The messages have stopped since she changed her phone number and she hasn't received any flowers, but she can't shake the feeling that he's still there, somewhere, watching her.

'I got you a latte – hope that's okay,' says Ellie plonking down the tray on the table. She picks up the dress she has bought out of the paper bag. It's wrapped in tissue paper

– cream-coloured silk with pink and green embroidered flowers around the collar.

'Isn't this adorable?'

Abby smiles faintly.

'You know, Abby, I've been thinking about your situation,' says Ellie, with forced brightness. She folds the dress reverently and places it back in the bag. 'I know it's not going to be easy for you to manage by yourself, but we're here for you. I don't want you to worry about anything. If you want to have a break from work to look after the baby, that will be fine. Rob and I will support you financially, and with the money from Dad . . .'

'That's very kind of you but—'

'We can redo the spare room, make it into a nursery, or you can move in there and we can use your room as a nursery . . . We can . . .'

Ellie carries on, tripping over her words in her enthusiasm. Each word seems like a strand in a web that's going to trap Abby inside. She can't let Ellie carry on talking. She can't stand it anymore. She has to let her know the truth.

'I'm not keeping the baby,' she blurts.

Ellie doesn't answer immediately. Her hand freezes on the coffee cup just before it reaches her lips.

'What?'

'I'm going to give it up for adoption.'

Ellie takes a slow, careful sip of coffee. Her expression is suddenly watchful, as if Abby is a wild creature she mustn't startle. 'What? Why?'

Abby sighs and picks up her coffee cup. 'Isn't it obvious? I'm just not ready to look after a baby. I've only just learned how to look after myself. I mean, I didn't ask for this baby. I don't want it. I don't even know who the father is. He raped me. It makes me feel sick just to think about it.'

'Abby, you don't seriously think you were raped, do you? You didn't even know you'd had sex, so how could you possibly know that you've been raped?'

'I know but . . .'

Ellie smiles. She's not really listening to Abby. 'You'll change your mind, I know you will, as soon as you see her sweet little face . . .'

Abby doesn't answer, swallowing her annoyance. How can she tell her that she hates the baby – that she feels nothing but resentment for this little parasite inside her?

Chapter Twenty-Three

It doesn't matter what Ellie says, Abby is not going to change her mind about giving the baby up for adoption. To prove this to herself, she's booked an appointment with an adoption counsellor, and she arranges for her to come to the house on a Saturday when Rob and Ellie are out, visiting Rob's family in Devon. They'll have to know about it sooner or later of course, but right now Abby can do without having to explain her decision.

All morning it's been dark and stormy, and Abby stands by the window watching the lightning and the driving rain as the counsellor pulls into the driveway in a small red Mini. She stands shaking her umbrella and laughing loudly on the doorstep as Abby opens the door.

'Oh, Lordy what a day! Hi, you must be Abigail. My name is Christine, but you can call me Chrissie.' She steps out of the rain and hands Abby her coat. She's comfortably plump and dark-skinned, with wiry greying hair, an easy, professional warmth and a loud belly laugh that Abby finds disarming.

'You look well,' she says with a chuckle as Abby shows her into the living room. 'When I was pregnant I looked like a whale, but you've got a neat little bump.'

'Thank you.' Abby doesn't feel 'neat' – she feels heavy and cumbersome – but it's nice of Chrissie to say so. 'Can I get you something to drink?'

'So, Abigail, you're interested in adoption?' says Chrissie, after Abby has brought her a cup of herbal tea. She perches on the edge of the sofa, smoothing her skirt.

'Yes,' Abby says firmly. 'I'm not just interested, I know that it's what I want.'

'Do you mind me asking why?'

Abby does mind her asking, but can't very well say so. 'The father is out of the picture,' she says. 'And I'm not really in a position to look after a baby.'

'I see.' Chrissie nods, and gives her a sympathetic but shrewd look which makes Abby wonder if the laughter and bustle is all a bit of an act.

'So where do we start?' she asks, impatient to get on. 'Do I have to sign any papers?'

Chrissie laughs. 'Not yet,' she says. 'Slow down. You have several different options to consider. Perhaps it's best I run through the process and all your different options first.' She starts to outline the procedure, which seems surprisingly complicated. Abby listens impatiently at first but then drifts off, staring out the window at the rain until something Chrissie says catches her attention.

'You can choose to have some contact with the child or none at all . . .'

'Oh, I don't want any contact,' Abby says quickly. Too quickly. Chrissie gives a little sharp look.

'I see,' she says evenly. 'Then there's the adoptive family. You can usually have a say about the type of family that adopts your baby.'

Abby hasn't even considered this. 'What do you mean exactly?'

'Well . . . religion, race, education, hobbies. That kind of thing. Usually people want the adoptive family to be as similar to them as possible.'

Abby shrugs. She hasn't even thought beyond handing the baby over. 'I don't really care. I just want a family that's loving and kind. That's all.'

Chrissie smiles. 'Good answer. That's the most important thing, isn't it? You can rest assured, all the families on our books have gone through a rigorous screening process. The vast majority have an awful lot of love to give. When you're ready, we can send you video profiles of families we think are suitable.'

'I'm ready now,' says Abby. 'Can you show me some profiles now?'

Chrissie hesitates. 'Well, I suppose there's no harm in taking a look.' She takes a tablet out of her bag, switches it on and clicks on the first clip. It's entitled 'Joel and Maria' and shows a happy-looking couple walking hand-in-hand up a garden path into an elegant-looking house. It shows Maria cooking with her six-year-old nephew, and then Joel and Maria walking hand-in-hand through autumn leaves. They talk about their sadness at not being able to share their life with a child of their own. The overall impression is of a wholesome, loving couple. But for Abby, their trump card is that they live in Yorkshire. Far enough away to make bumping into them once the baby is born unlikely.

'I like them,' says Abby, when the clip is finished. 'I want them to adopt my baby.'

Chrissie seems taken aback. 'Well . . . Joel and Maria are a lovely couple, but don't you want to look at some of the other profiles before you make a decision?'

'No, they're perfect,' Abby insists. She just wants to get the whole thing over with as quickly as possible.

'Well . . .' Chrissie looks doubtful. 'I suppose a meeting can be arranged. Nothing you decide now is final. You can change your mind after the baby is born, and up until it has lived with its adoptive parents for up to thirteen weeks.'

'I'm not going to change my mind,' Abby says firmly. 'I already know I want to give it away. Can't we sort this out now?'

Chrissie smiles. 'That's not the way it works, I'm afraid.'

She carries on talking in her easy, comfortable way, and Abby listens, feeling increasingly frustrated. It seems as if the whole process is set up to discourage her from giving up her baby.

'I can put you in touch with someone who's been through

it all, if you like,' Chrissie says as she's leaving. She scribbles down a name and number on the back of her card. 'And don't forget you can call me if you have any questions.'

Abby stands in the doorway watching Chrissie drive off. She'd hoped to get this sorted, but it's clearly going to be a long process.

It's only when she's out of sight that Abby realizes Chrissie has left her umbrella.

She's reading through some of the information leaflets Chrissie has left her when the doorbell rings. Thinking it's Chrissie back again for the umbrella she opens the door.

'You forgot your . . .'

But it's not Chrissie.

'Alex!' exclaims Abby. 'What are you doing here?'

He's standing on the doorstep, swaying. His beautiful green eyes are bloodshot and unfocused, and he looks even more dishevelled than usual, his black hair is wet and plastered to his scalp. Abby wonders if he's been drinking or taking drugs.

'Well, that's nice, I must say,' he slurs. 'Do I need a reason to visit my girlfriend?'

Abby winces slightly at the word 'girlfriend'. *Whoever said she was his girlfriend?* But she lets it go. He looks in the mood for an argument and she doesn't want to start one. 'Of course not,' she says evenly, taking his coat. 'Come in.'

As he brushes past her into the living room, she catches a definite whiff of alcohol. 'Have you been drinking?' she asks.

'I may have. What of it?' He looks around the room and

193

picks up a photograph of Ellie and Rob on their wedding day. 'This your sister?' he asks. 'She doesn't look much like you, does she?'

Abby glances at the photo, swallowing back emotion. Ellie looks so much like Mum in that picture. The determination and optimism in her blue eyes as she smiles at Rob makes Abby's heart ache. This is the Ellie before she lost her baby. Unstoppable Ellie.

'No,' she says to Alex. 'She takes after my mother, and I look like my dad's side. Like my—'

'Have you been avoiding me, Abigail?' he interrupts, replacing the photo on the mantelpiece.

Abby is taken aback. 'No. Why?'

'It's just I've been trying to get you on the phone all week. How come you didn't answer? If you're not interested any-more, you just have to tell me, and I'll back off.'

This would be a good time to tell him that they should break it off. She really doesn't need the complication of a relationship right now, but he looks suddenly so wounded she feels sorry for him, and flattered that he cares. Besides, even drunk at eleven o'clock in the morning, there's some-thing very attractive about him.

'It's not that,' she finds herself saying. 'I got a new phone. I . . . er . . . lost the old one and I've a new number.' She's only given the new number to Ellie, Rob and Danny, with strict instructions for them not to give it to anyone else. And so far, it's working. She hasn't received any more messages from her stalker.

'Why didn't you tell me?' Alex takes a step towards her.

'I've just been so busy with work lately, and this pregnancy and everything . . .' She tails off lamely. She can tell Alex doesn't believe her. If only he knew, that's not even half of it.

'Here – I'll message you now,' she says, fishing out her phone. 'Then you can save the new number to your phone.'

'Okay.' His expression softens a little, and he sits down on the sofa, taking out his mobile. 'I don't understand, though. Why didn't you just keep your old number when you changed your phone?'

She perches on the edge of the sofa next to him. 'Some kids at school got hold of it and they've been calling me . . . You know, prank calls. It's very annoying.'

She doesn't believe that Alex could be her stalker. Why would he send her messages warning her off himself? It would make no sense. And it would have been impossible for him to send her the message she received when she was at his house because he was fast asleep. But she's sticking to the plan anyway, and she doesn't tell him the reason she's changed her phone number. 'So, you can't give this number to anyone else, alright? Just in case it gets back to one of the kids again?'

'Alright.' Alex shrugs. He looks around, out of the window at the rain lashing against the pane. 'It's quiet here, huh? Where's your sister and her husband?'

'They're in Devon, visiting relatives.'

'So, we've got this place to ourselves then.' He grins.

She finds herself grinning back. 'I suppose so.'

'I've missed you,' he says, and he moves closer towards

195

her, tugging at her jacket, pulling her to him and kissing her softly. 'I've missed this,' he whispers. There's a taste of alcohol and something else she can't identify. She pulls back slightly, and he places a warm hand on her belly.

'How's your little mini-me?'

'Fine. I had a scan the other day.'

She shows him the picture she's saved to her phone and he looks at it politely, even though he can't possibly see anything other than a blurry image. 'I've still got Dylan's ultrasound,' he says. 'It's magic, isn't it? The first time you see them.'

Abby shrugs. 'Where's Dylan today?'

'With Bethany.' His expression darkens. 'And the new boyfriend. I don't like the guy at all. I don't like Dylan being around him, but what can I do? Anyway –' he leans towards her – 'I don't want to talk about Bethany. Where were we?'

They are kissing again and, despite her reservations, Abby feels herself responding, kissing him back, tilting her head, giving herself up to pure sensation, forgetting, as his hand reaches up the outside of her thigh under her dress.

'Life isn't measured by the number of breaths you take . . .' he murmurs as he reaches the tattoo.

She pulls away sharply.

'What did you say?'

'It's a quote, isn't it? Your tattoo. Where does it come from?' He pulls her back towards him, nuzzles her neck. She shoves him backwards, hard.

'How do you know about that?'

'I saw it the night you came over to mine of course. What's the problem?

Abigail is thinking frantically. *It was dark that night when she took her clothes off. He couldn't have seen her tattoo.*

'How could you see it? The lights were out.'

He shrugs. 'I woke up in the night to go for a piss. I turned on the light. You were asleep. You'd kicked off the covers and ... Jesus. What does it matter? I just thought it was a cool tattoo, that's all.'

'Of course ... I'm sorry.'

'Have you got any other tattoos?' He tugs at her jumper and pulls it over her head, kissing her and running his hand over her bra. She lets him kiss her, but something inside her has switched itself off, and she feels nauseous as he pushes her back against the cushions and she feels his erection press against her belly and smells his sweet, stale breath. She's suddenly aware she's all on her own with him. She's suddenly afraid.

'Wait. This is a mistake,' she murmurs. 'I'm sorry.'

But, maybe he doesn't hear because he carries on kissing her. For a second Abby can't move. She's pinned down by his weight. For a second of pure panic she thinks he's going to force himself on her. Then she wrenches herself away.

'Stop!' she shouts.

'Jesus, alright. Calm down,' he says. For just a fraction of a second, he looks furiously angry. Then he gives a short laugh.

'Fucking hell, Abby. Make up your mind. I've never known anyone to blow so hot and cold.'

Abby stands up, pulling on her top. She suddenly sees what a mistake she's making continuing to see Alex. 'I have made up my mind,' she says. 'I don't think we should see each other anymore. There's just too much going on in my life right now.'

He looks at her, anger and disbelief stamped on his face. 'Are you sure?'

She nods firmly. Her heart is pounding. She just wants him out.

He gives a short, bitter laugh. 'Well, you've certainly got great timing, Abigail.' He picks up his jacket and heads to the door. Abby follows him, a horrible suspicion nudging its way to the forefront of her mind.

'Are you sure you didn't see the tattoo before?' she asks as he opens the door.

He turns and stares at her.

'What are you talking about?'

'At Danny's, on New Year's, you put something in my drink, didn't you?' She's shaking but she carries on. 'Then you took me to a bedroom and we had sex . . . You're the father of this baby . . .'

He stares at her. 'You're fucking insane,' he says. 'I have no idea what you're talking about, Abby. I'm not the father of that baby and the only time I ever fucked you, which by the way I'm beginning to regret, was the night when you came around to my house.' He opens the door and steps out into the rain, just as a streak of lightning cracks the sky.

'Would you take a DNA test to prove it?' she asks.

'*Jesus.* Are you serious? No, I would not,' he says, slamming the door behind him.

Abby turns the key in the lock and sits down on the floor with her back to the door. Then she looks down at her shaking hand. In her palm she has a strand of black hair, Alex's hair. She must have pulled it out while they were on the sofa. She closes her hand around it.

You never know. It might come in useful.

Chapter Twenty-Four

'Don't forget to feed Hector. And water the plants.'

'I won't.'

'And you've got a check-up on Thursday. You won't forget?'

'*Jesus*. No. Just go.'

It's summer half-term and Rob and Ellie are going to Crete for a week. Their taxi is waiting outside, the engine idling. Rob is helping the driver put the suitcases in the boot and Ellie is fretting about leaving Abby on her own. For her part, Abby can't wait to see the back of them. It'll be a relief to have the place to herself for a change and not have Ellie worrying and fussing over every little thing she does.

'See you later, Abs,' says Rob, kissing her lightly on the cheek. 'Don't do anything I wouldn't do.'

'That gives me quite a lot of leeway,' she says with a laugh.

Ellie hugs her and rests a hand lightly on her belly. 'Bye, you two. Look after yourself and the little one, won't you?'

Abby watches the taxi drive down the road and disappear around the corner. A whole week to herself stretches out in front of her. She has no work and she can do whatever she likes. What she really wants to do is curl up in bed for a week and forget about everything: about work, about the fact that she's pregnant and that there's a sick pervert stalking her. But that's not an option. She needs to face this thing head-on and find the bastard who's been sending her those messages – the bastard who raped her.

She starts off by switching on the computer and googling DNA tests. Maybe she can use the hair she got from Alex. But a brief search reveals that prenatal DNA tests are complicated and require blood from the mother as well as a mouth swab from the father. Also, she would need written permission from the suspected father. She snaps her laptop shut, feeling frustrated. She's wasting her time anyway. The man she's looking for is not Alex. She knows logically that it can't be him. He was with her when she received that text at his house. So why did she accuse him? She wasn't thinking straight, she supposes. The sheer panic she felt when he was on top of her must have clouded her judgement. She flushes with embarrassment as she remembers the things she said. He must think she's completely crazy.

She's still sitting there, wondering whether she should call Alex and apologize, when the phone rings.

'Miss Brooke, it's PC Whittaker here,' he says. 'How are you?'

'I'm okay,' she says, surprised. She hadn't expected to hear from him again.

'Just calling to give you an update on your case.' He clears his throat. 'Unfortunately, we haven't been able to trace the phones used to contact you. It seems he used several different SIMs and then disposed of them.'

'Oh.' Abigail swallows her disappointment.

'Have you received any more gifts or communications since you last saw me?'

'Well, no, but . . .'

'Good. So, it looks like he's got the message.'

'Yes, I suppose so.'

There's a pause. 'Have you thought any more about talking to a detective? We could send someone round to your house?'

Abby thinks about it. She's fairly sure her stalker watches every move she makes. If he saw a police officer at her house, who knows how he might react? 'No, thanks,' she says.

'Well, if you're sure. Let me know if you hear from him again.'

'Okay, thanks.'

Abby hangs up. She's grateful for PC Whittaker's concern, but she's not sure how much he can do as there is no proof, only her word, that she was raped.

She's tired of thinking about the whole thing, tired of feeling scared all the time. She feels like she's going round and round in circles getting nowhere closer to working out who did this to her.

She stands up and heads to the door. Perhaps what she needs is some fresh air. She needs bread and milk anyway. A trip to the shops might clear her head. She grabs her handbag and keys and slips out of the house. But as soon as she steps outside, she's immediately on edge. Something doesn't feel right. It feels as though someone's watching her. She opens the gate and scans the street but there's nothing to raise alarm – a mother with a pushchair, one of her neighbours parking in front of their house. She breathes in deeply, trying to steady her nerves. It's just a short walk to the supermarket. It's broad daylight. It will be fine. She turns into the alleyway next to her house. *One step in front of the other. It's okay,* she soothes herself, *it's okay.*

In the car park the feeling of being watched intensifies.

I'm just imagining it, she thinks, and dives into the supermarket, heading straight for the dairy section. But as she's putting the milk in her basket she notices someone out of the corner of her eye – a man at the end of the aisle. She gets the distinct impression that he's staring at her. But when she turns to look, he slips away out of sight before she can tell who it is. She has the feeling, though, that it was someone she knows. There was a glimpse of broad shoulders, a grey suit. Her heart pounding, she runs to the end of the aisle and looks down the next, but he's disappeared. And she just stands there for a moment, confused and scared. *Did she imagine him? Is she losing her grip on reality?*

She needs to get out of this place as soon as possible, get home and shut herself inside, so she can breathe again. She heads to the checkout and joins the shortest queue.

She's paying for the milk when she sees him again, just in front of her, heading out of the door – the man in the grey suit – the one who was staring at her before. The hairs on the back of her neck stand up on end. He's not carrying any shopping, she notices with a chill. *Why come to the supermarket and buy nothing? Unless . . . unless he's been following her? Unless he's the man who's been watching her all along? Is this him? Is this her rapist?*

Outside the door he turns, and she sees his face in profile through the window. For a moment she can hardly breathe. *Andrew Wilson.*

She fumbles with her debit card, trying to slot it back in her purse, her hand is shaking so much. She's thinking rapidly, adding up facts: the lift home on New Year's Eve, the instinctive fear she felt in his car. And she's seized by a sudden certainty. Grabbing the milk, she rushes out of the door after him. She can still see him ahead of her, sauntering across the car park towards the main shopping street. There's a spring in his step as if he's happy, enjoying the summer sunshine. *You bastard. How dare you?* she thinks, anger surging through her, and without thinking she runs to catch up with him. She's so angry in that moment that she doesn't care if she's putting herself in danger. All she wants to do is make him pay for what he's done.

'I need to speak to you,' she says, grabbing his arm and gasping for breath as she catches up with him.

He turns, mild surprise in his bland, brown eyes.

'Oh hi, Abigail,' he says. 'I'm afraid the flat you looked at has been rented out. But I'm sure we can find you something else. We've got some great new properties. I'm on my lunch break now, but I'll be back in the office in about forty minutes.'

Her heart is racing out of control, fear surging through her. *What the hell is she doing?* But there's no backing out now.

'It's not about the flat,' she manages. 'It's a personal matter.'

He stares at her. 'I don't see . . .'

'It's very important. Please. It will only take a few minutes.'

He glances at his watch. 'Um . . . well, okay. I was going to get a bite to eat in a café near here. You can join me, if you don't mind watching me eat.'

They head to the café, where he buys a Cornish pasty and a bottle of water. Abby orders a coffee and they sit upstairs by the window looking down on the street. Andrew Wilson places his phone on the table in front of them and takes a bite of his pasty, crumbs showering all over the table. 'So, what did you want to talk about?' he asks cautiously. 'Is it something to do with Mark?'

'No . . .' Abby hesitates. Her heart is still racing a million miles a second and she's trying to keep her hands steady as she sips her coffee, but she ploughs on. 'Actually, it's about this.' She places her hands either side of her swollen belly and as if in answer the baby kicks, a short, sharp jolt just under the ribs.

Andrew's eyes widen.

'It was conceived at Danny's New Year's Eve party.' As she speaks, she observes his reaction carefully. He looks confused and wary. But that doesn't necessarily mean anything. Confusion and wariness are both normal under the circumstances. 'The thing is I don't remember how . . . or who the father is . . .' She pauses meaningfully, letting this sink in.

A red flush creeps up from his neck. He looks seriously rattled now.

'What's that got to do with me?' he blusters.

'Well I know you gave me a lift. I know that you didn't come into the house with me, but did we have sex in the car on the way back?' Abby deliberately doesn't use the word rape. He's hardly likely to admit to rape, and if he's as dangerous as she thinks he is, she needs to tread carefully and avoid provoking him. Let him think she believes it was consensual.

He freezes, holding his pasty just short of his mouth. 'What the . . . ? Look, I already told you we didn't. I'm a married man – happily married. I've got two kids.'

'Are you sure?'

'Of course I'm sure.' Andrew puts his pasty down. There's something condescending about his tone, and the furious anger Abby felt earlier returns with a vengeance.

'Have you been sending me flowers?' she blurts.

'What?'

'Have you been messaging me?' She lurches across the table, grabs his phone and tries to switch it on.

'What the hell do you think you're doing?' Andrew prizes the phone out of her hand. 'Look, I don't know what your deal is. Maybe you think I've got money, or maybe you're just plain crazy, but I didn't have sex with you, period. It's not my problem if you sleep with so many people you can't remember who the father is.' He stands up brushing crumbs from his shirt, his face is bright red. 'Now, if you don't mind, I'm going to get back to work.'

'Wait, please!' Abby says desperately, running to catch up with him as he strides down the stairs towards the exit. 'Would you be willing to take a DNA test to prove that you're not the father?'

He stops in his tracks; swerves round angrily. 'What?' His voice rises until he's almost shouting. 'No! Look, I'm telling you nothing happened that night. Read my lips. We did not have sex. Now leave me alone.' Everyone in the café is staring at them now; even the guy behind the counter has stopped taking orders and is watching them in shock. *It probably seems like an episode of* The Jeremy Kyle Show *to them*, Abby thinks, but she's really past caring.

'Wait,' she says, grabbing Andrew's arm. 'It's really easy. All you need to do is sign a form and give me a swab. Your wife need never know.'

He shakes his arm free. 'I said, no.'

She runs to the door, blocking his exit. 'You won't do it because you know the result will be positive. You're the father of this baby.'

'Get out of my way,' he raises his voice, shouting now. 'Leave me alone or I'll call the police. This is harassment. You're insane.'

Abby reluctantly moves aside, and he marches out, leaving Abby standing in the café. A customer stares at her.

'Are you okay?' he asks.

'Yes, fine,' she says.

It's the second time in a short space of time she's been called insane. Perhaps she really is going crazy.

But she's not. Abby knows that in her heart, and she's now sure that Andrew Wilson is the man who's been tormenting her. She's determined to make him stop – to make him face justice if she can. So, before she can change her mind, she heads across town to the police station.

'Andrew Wilson,' she says as she marches up to the glass screen in reception.

'What?' PC Whittaker blinks in surprise.

'That's the name of my stalker and rapist. He works at Brown and Lowe's. He's an estate agent.' Abby is still shaking from her encounter with Andrew Wilson but she tries to speak clearly and calmly. She needs to convince PC Whittaker, at least, that she's not insane.

'Hold on,' he says. 'How do you know?'

'He's been following me and he's the only one who could have done it. He gave me a lift home that night – the night I was raped.'

'Do you know if he came into your house?'

'No, he didn't,' she admits. 'But I remember him stopping somewhere on the way.'

'I see,' PC Whittaker says. 'I suppose we could check the CCTV. Do you know the registration of his car?'

'No, but he drives a black BMW and he would have been

leaving Queen's Street at about two o'clock on New Year's Eve and driving towards the Chesterton estate.'

'Okay, leave it with me. We'll have a word with him. In the meantime, I suggest you get some rest. It's not good for you to be stressing yourself in your condition.'

Chapter Twenty-Five

The confrontation with Andrew Wilson has taken it out of her and by the time she gets home Abby is drained emotionally and physically. She runs herself a bath and lies in the water, her belly floating above the bubbles like an iceberg. The water is warm and relaxing, but she can't switch off her thoughts. They swarm in her head like angry insects. Andrew Wilson's outraged face keeps surfacing in her mind. *What if she's made a mistake? What if it wasn't him?* She was so sure, but now all her certainty seems to be slipping away. She pulls the plug and watches the water get sucked down the plughole. Then she heaves herself out. She's sick and tired of thinking about the whole thing.

She needs to clear her mind, so she does what she often does when she needs to relax. She takes out her easel and sketch pad and begins a drawing of Hector, but she can't get him to sit still long enough to get a good likeness, so she takes some photos on her phone and then flicks back through. As she's scrolling through images, she stops, arrested by the picture of the ultrasound she saved to her phone. She gazes at it, fascinated. The grainy image, the ethereal light, the sense of other-worldliness. This is what she wants to draw, she realizes, scrabbling in her box for a charcoal pencil.

She draws for hours, losing track of the time, totally absorbed, trying to capture the translucent quality of the skin, the ribs, the sense of isolation and mystery. At last it's finished and she steps away from her work. It's very good, she thinks, some of the best she's ever done. It almost seems to be breathing, it's so real. But there's a disturbing quality that has crept in unintentionally. It seems almost as if it's trapped, trying to claw its way out. The face is distorted, and the eyes are dark, menacing smudges of charcoal.

She turns the picture to face the wall and wanders into the kitchen. She heats up a packet of noodles, feeling defiant. It's liberating without Ellie breathing down her neck, trying to force-feed her carefully balanced meals. One meal full of E-numbers and additives is not going to kill it.

She eats in front of the TV, feet up on the coffee table, and flicks through the channels. She's watching the news when she hears the front gate squeaking. Hector pricks up his ears and growls softly. Abby looks at her watch. It's just past ten o'clock and it's getting dark.

Who could be calling at this time in the evening?

She waits for the doorbell to ring but nothing happens. Just a faint rustle, then the sound of receding footsteps. *Somebody dropping off a flyer?* But it's late in the evening for that. She swallows a feeling of unease, and goes to the door and looks out. There's no one there. The sky is dark blue, a pale crescent moon peeping out between the roofs of the house opposite.

The front gate is open. She's sure she shut it earlier. She walks up the path and shuts it in case Hector decides to run off. Then she looks up and down the street. It's empty. She must have imagined the footsteps. What's wrong with her? Maybe Andrew Wilson is right. Maybe she's losing her mind.

But as she walks back down the path she notices the flowers wrapped in cellophane to the side of the doorstep. Roses this time. Red and pink roses. There's a note attached.

Moments that take your breath away: The first time I saw you naked. That mole on your right shoulder. The first time you smiled at me. I knew then that we were meant for each other.

She stops reading, snatches up the flowers and slams the door, locking it and bolting it behind her. Then she rushes around the house checking all the doors and windows are locked. In the kitchen, she pauses at the window and looks out at the garden, half swallowed by creeping shadows. There's something moving underneath the apple tree. Just a cat, she tells herself firmly, and closes the blinds, breathing deeply, trying to control her racing heart.

Then she sits at the kitchen table and snaps the stems of the flowers, one by one, and shoves them in the bin.

How long has he been outside watching her? She shudders, thinking about the way she was drawing with the light on, the curtains open – so exposed. Was he watching the house this morning? Did he see Rob and Ellie leave? Does he know she's here on her own? She picks up her phone and tries to ring Danny, but he doesn't answer. Then she tries Thea, but her phone is switched off. *Jesus, does nobody answer their phone?* She just needs to talk to someone, to quell the rising panic.

The boiler gurgles, upstairs a floorboard creaks. *It's an old house*, she tells herself. *It always makes these noises. There's no one in the house. It's not possible.* But anyway, she shuts herself in the living room and turns the TV up loud, watching old comedy re-runs and panel shows. She curls up on the sofa clutching a cushion.

She must have dropped off, because the next thing she knows, she's jolted awake by the sound of the phone ringing in the hallway. It's the landline. As she stumbles sleepily to her feet and out into the hall she wonders vaguely who it could be. Only a handful of people have the number, mostly family members. It's 11.30. Could it be Ellie phoning to say they've arrived? Or maybe Dad – though it seems very late for him to call.

Abby grabs the phone. 'Hello?'

Silence.

'Hello, Ellie? . . . Dad, is that you?' There's a long, empty pause, a ragged breath, then the click of the phone at the other end.

Just a wrong number, Abby tells herself. But why did they take so long to hang up? She switches off the TV in the living room, turns off the Wi-Fi, double-checks the doors and windows. Hector is asleep in his basket. He opens his eyes and wags his tail listlessly as she pats him. Then he rolls over onto his back, feet in the air, to have his tummy tickled. He's useless as a guard dog, she thinks, friendly to everyone, scared even of cats. But would he protect her if push came to shove? She doubts it very much.

'Well, goodnight then, Hector,' she says, climbing the stairs to her room. In her bedroom she can hear the clack of heels and the cackle of drunken laughter outside. People walking back from the pub. Then the footsteps recede and there's silence.

She's brushing her teeth when the phone rings again. Loud and shrill. Her first instinct is to ignore it. But what if it's Ellie? She runs downstairs.

'Yes, hello?'

Silence. This time there's definite breathing, the soft smack of lips.

She slams down the phone, takes it off the hook. Then she heads back upstairs and curls up in bed. She lies there for a while, her nerves on edge, before she finally drifts into an uneasy sleep.

Chapter Twenty-Six

'You don't look too good, Abby.'

'Well, thanks a lot, Danny.' Abby smiles weakly.

It's the next day, a bright sunny afternoon, and they're sitting in the garden, sipping iced coffee, their faces turned to the sun. Everything is quiet and peaceful. The only sounds are the low hum of a bumblebee in the flowerbed, the chatter of birds and the drone of a distant aeroplane flying overhead. The fear of last night seems far away and unreal.

Danny laughs. 'I mean, you look lovely as ever, but you're a bit pale and you've got dark rings under your eyes. I thought pregnant women were supposed to glow. Are you sickening for something?'

'No, I just didn't sleep well last night.' She does feel awful – dizzy and foggy headed. She must have only slept about three hours, altogether. She kept waking up in a panic, convinced *he* was in the house. When she did finally get to sleep the baby kicked her so hard that she woke up again.

'Why didn't you sleep?'

'He's started again.' Abby grips the side of her chair, remembering how frightened she was last night.

Danny stares at her. 'Who has?'

'My stalker. Only it's worse this time.'

Danny takes a sip of coffee. 'I thought all that stopped when you changed your phone number.'

'The texts have stopped, but he's started sending flowers again, and last night . . .' Abby pauses to steady her breathing. Talking about it is bringing it all back, the feeling of terror and helplessness. 'Last night he was outside my house. I heard him. He left flowers on the doorstep. Then later he phoned me on the landline.'

'Did you recognize his voice?'

She shakes her head. 'He didn't speak. I could just hear him breathing.'

Danny sips his coffee and frowns. 'How do you know it was him if he didn't speak? It could've just been a wrong number.'

'I just know, alright?' Abby puts her face in her hands, rubs her eyes. 'I'm so scared, Danny. I don't know what to do.'

Danny sighs and pats her hand. 'Oh, sweetheart. I don't think you need to be scared. A few flowers, a couple of messages, that's all. He's probably harmless. I mean he's an annoying creep, sure, but I doubt he's really dangerous. I don't think this could be the guy you slept with.'

Abby shakes her head. 'Danny, I know you don't think it's likely, but someone raped me, and it's him, I know it.' She pulls the note that came with the flowers from her

216

back pocket and hands it to Danny. 'This came with the flowers.'

Danny shields his eyes from the sun, examining the note. 'It's pretty creepy,' he admits. *That mole on your right shoulder . . .*' he reads out loud thoughtfully. 'Have you got a mole on your right shoulder?'

'Yes.' She shivers. 'That's what makes it so frightening. And I got a text quoting my tattoo. *Word for word*. How could he know what it says? He must have seen me naked. He wants me to know, he's taunting me.' She takes a deep, shuddering breath. 'With Ellie and Rob away, I feel so vulnerable all alone here in the house.'

Danny presses her hand gently. 'I could come over tonight if you like,' he says. 'I mean, I can't stay all night, I'm afraid. I've got to leave early in the morning.'

It's his sister's wedding in Liverpool. Danny is going up a couple of days early to help with all the preparations. Abby had completely forgotten.

'But I can stay until one or two o'clock . . . Would that help?'

'That would be great,' says Abby gratefully. 'You're a star, Danny.'

She sits back and shuts her eyes, feeling the warmth of the sun on her face. Perhaps everything will be okay after all. With Danny here, she feels safe and if the stalker tries to contact her again, Danny will be a witness. She'll know that she's not going crazy.

They chat for a while about school and about a new man

called Will who Danny has met. He makes her laugh when he describes their first date; how he was so nervous he spilt wine all over his shirt and then knocked the glass off the table as he was trying to mop it up. Danny has a way of telling a story that is hilarious, and by the time he leaves at four o'clock to sort some things at home and pack his bag for Liverpool, Abby is in a much better mood. He'll be back soon, and in the meantime, she tidies the house, with a new burst of energy and hopefulness. For the first time in a while she doesn't feel so afraid.

Good as his word, Danny turns up two hours later with pizza and a bottle of wine. 'I know you can't drink this –' he grins – 'so I'll just have to do the decent thing and drink it myself.'

'How selfless of you.' Abby chuckles.

They eat the pizza on the sofa in front of an old black-and-white movie Abby has never seen before. She tries to concentrate, but the movie is slow, and Abby is exhausted. She drops off to sleep halfway through and wakes up just as the credits are rolling.

'Sorry,' she says. 'I'm not much company, am I?'

Danny purses his lips. 'You missed the ending. It's a classic.'

Abby sits up and looks at her watch. It's nine o'clock already. 'Did anyone ring?'

'Nope. It's been quiet as a church. I'm beginning to think you must have imagined the whole thing.'

Abby is fully awake now and she turns on him angrily. 'What? What about the note then, do you think I imagined that?'

218

'I was just kidding, Abby, calm down. Of course I believe you.' He's slurring his words and Abby realizes he's getting drunk. The bottle of wine he bought is empty and he's started on another.

He catches her looking at it. 'I took another bottle from your kitchen cupboard, hope that's okay? I got a bit bored while you were asleep.'

'I'm sure it's fine. I'm sorry. I'll try to stay awake.'

Danny pours himself another drink, Abby makes herself a cup of tea, and they are just starting another movie, when the phone rings, loud and shrill in the quiet night.

They look at each other. Abby's heart is beating out of her chest. At least now Danny will know she hasn't been making it up.

'Do you want me to answer?' he slurs.

She nods and follows him into the hallway where he picks up the phone.

'Hello, Abigail Brooke's residence.' He winks at Abby. 'Hello?' He's silent for a second or two, and then he puts the receiver down. 'He hung up on me, the bastard.'

'Did he say anything?'

'Nope. Are you sure it isn't just someone getting a wrong number? I used to get loads of calls for the cinema when I lived in my old flat.'

'I just know it's him.' She thinks of the feeling she got when he phoned last night, the way the hairs on the back of her neck stood up, the way her throat got dry.

They have just settled back in the living room when the phone rings again.

'This is starting to piss me off,' says Danny, and he strides out to the hallway. Abby can hear him from the living room.

'Fuck off, you pervert, and leave her alone!' he shouts.

There's a pause, and then he slams down the phone. 'That told him,' he says triumphantly as he comes back and flings himself on the sofa.

But Abby feels uneasy. Danny shouting at the caller has probably wound him up and she doesn't want to think about what he might do if he's angry. But it does seem to do the trick. There are no more phone calls for the next hour and a half. They watch the rest of the movie uninterrupted and then start a boxset until, at about half past two, Danny staggers to his feet.

'I've got to go home now, Abs,' he says. 'I don't think that idiot will be bothering you again, not tonight at least.'

Abby wishes she could be so sure.

'Just make sure all the doors are locked. I'll keep my mobile on. Call me if there's a problem, okay?'

Abby nods. She's far from okay. But she doesn't want to be the needy friend who is always taking and never giving. 'Have a good time in Liverpool,' she says.

'See you later,' he says, kissing her sloppily on the cheek.

As she watches him lurch down the pathway she realizes that he's even drunker than she thought. Maybe she should have called a taxi for him. But she doesn't have enough mental energy to worry about Danny. She's got enough on her plate.

She locks the door, slides the chain into place and heads to bed. Lying in bed, her head buried under the covers, she tells herself everything is okay. *Everything is okay.* She repeats it over and over like a mantra until she falls asleep.

She's jolted awake by the phone ringing. She rolls over and looks at her alarm clock. It's five in the morning. *Jesus. Not again.* Anger surges through her body. She stomps down the stairs and snatches up the phone.

'Why don't you just fuck off and leave me alone?' she snarls.

There's an embarrassed cough on the other end.

'Uh, Abby . . . it's Mark.'

'Shit, sorry, Mark. I've been getting these nuisance calls.'

'Yeah, Danny told me. Look, I'm sorry to ring you so early but I thought you'd want to know right away . . . It's Danny.'

The way he says it she immediately knows it's bad. The blood leaves her heart. *Danny. No, not Danny. Let him be okay.*

'He's okay, right?' she says. Her voice wobbles. Tears are already stinging at the back of her eyes.

'Um, yes, he's going to be alright. They're just keeping him in for observation.'

'Who's keeping him?' It's as she feared: something has happened to Danny.

Mark's voice on the other end is calm. How can he be so calm? 'The hospital. He's at Cheltenham General.'

'Oh my God. What happened?' Abby pictures him being hit by a car or falling down somewhere, drunk. She should never have let him walk home alone in the state he was in.

'I'm going to visit him this morning,' says Mark. 'Do you want to come?'

'Yes, sure.'

'Okay then, I'll pick you up at eight thirty, alright?'

Chapter Twenty-Seven

Mark's Honda pulls up outside the house at eight thirty precisely. He stands outside the house twirling a black umbrella and he holds it over Abby's head as they make a dash for the car in the pummelling rain.

'So, how is he?' she asks, getting into the passenger seat and brushing the rain drops off her skirt.

'Um . . . okay.' Mark starts the engine and heads into town.

'What exactly happened?'

Mark doesn't answer for a moment. His face is grim as he weaves through the traffic in the town centre.

'He was attacked last night on his way home.'

'What?' Abby's stomach clenches in shock. Whatever she was expecting, it wasn't that. 'But he's okay, right?'

Mark presses on the pedal as they reach the main road out of town towards Cheltenham. He glances sideways at Abby. 'I think so. He's just got a few cuts and bruises and his wrist is broken. At least that's what they told me.'

'Thank God for that.'

Abby relaxes a little. The knot of anxiety in her stomach

is gradually unwinding. At least Danny is not seriously hurt, but she still can't quite believe that it's happened at all.

'Why . . . Who . . . ? I mean, did he get into an argument? Was he mugged?' It seems unlikely. Mugging's the kind of crime that happens in London, not in this sleepy little town where half the population is over sixty.

Mark stares straight ahead out of the windscreen. His eyes are glued to the road, his expression impassive as always.

'I don't know much. I guess we'll find out when we get there.'

They slip into silence. Abby gazes out of the window at sheep grazing in green fields. Through the trees she glimpses a silver river roping through the valley and the large, expensive private school building that perches on top of the hill. Even in the driving rain, this is idyllic countryside. It's hard to imagine any kind of crime taking place here, let alone a violent crime. But now she's been personally affected by two violent crimes in the space of a few months.

She feels a lurch of guilt. *Has this got something to do with her?* If she hadn't made Danny come around and got him involved in all her shit, then this wouldn't have happened. At least she should have made sure he got home okay. He was so drunk last night. She shouldn't have let him leave by himself. She should have insisted he call a taxi. But how was she supposed to know this would happen? She's walked home alone from Danny's house countless times and nothing has ever happened before.

'How are you, anyway?' Mark asks, breaking into her thoughts. 'Is the baby kicking you yet?'

'All the time.' It kicks her constantly. It's kicking her now, a steady insistent strike. Sometimes it feels like it's angry with her, or that it's trying to tell her something. Sometimes she can see the movement of her skin as it writhes beneath, like something stirring in a primordial mud pool. She runs her hands over her belly and pulls out the seat belt, so it doesn't feel so tight.

'It's a big change in your life, I suppose. You're not too stressed by the whole thing?' He takes a deep breath. He seems to be deciding whether to say something. 'Because my friend Andy Wilson called round last night . . .'

'Oh.' Abby has almost forgotten about her confrontation with Andrew, with all the other things that have been happening. She grips the seat as Mark swerves around the corner, thinking rapidly. How much does Mark know? How much should she tell him?

'He said you spoke to him the other day.'

Abby holds her breath. 'Did he say what we talked about?'

Mark squirms uncomfortably and clears his throat. 'He said you accused him of rape and that the police have been to interview him.' Mark glances at Abby. 'He was understandably quite upset.'

'Oh.'

'You really think Andy is the father of your baby?' he says slowly. 'You think he could have raped you at the New Year's Eve party?'

225

'Yes, I . . .'

But Mark doesn't give her a chance to answer. 'Because I have to tell you I find that hard to believe. He's a good guy, you know, and anyway he was with me most of the night and the rest of the time, when I wasn't with Andy, I was with you. So, I don't see how he could have, just purely from a logistical point of view.'

Abby shrugs. 'I don't think it happened at the party. He gave me a lift home that night. I think it must have happened then.'

Mark shakes his head. 'But how do you know? Do you have any reason to believe it's him, apart from the fact he gave you a lift?'

'No,' Abby admits slowly. 'But I don't see who else it could have been, and you've got to admit it's strange. What was a middle-aged married man doing at a party like that? Why wasn't his wife there with him, for a start?'

Mark flushes. He looks annoyed, or about as close to annoyed as Mark ever gets.

'He was there because I invited him, okay? He's a good friend of mine. And his wife wasn't there because she was working that night. She's a paramedic. Jesus, Abby, you can't just go about throwing around accusations like that. It could have serious consequences. You could seriously fuck up his life.'

He turns a corner and they drive over the top of a hill, looking down at Cheltenham spread out in front of them. The rain has stopped, and a weak sun is shining through the clouds. The rooftops are gleaming.

'If you're looking for someone to blame, what about that ginger bloke you were arguing with?' he says.

'What?'

'After the fireworks we went to my room to watch the boxset, but you were in there, shouting at a tall bloke with red hair. He looked like a slimy piece of work to me.'

Hugo Langley, again, Abby thinks. 'What were we arguing about?'

He shrugs. 'I don't know. We left you to it and went to Danny's room instead.'

Could it be Hugo? Abby turns this idea over in her head as they crawl through the town centre, caught up in the rush-hour traffic. *No, Hugo's in Thailand, so he can't have been stalking her. But perhaps she was wrong about Andrew Wilson, too. After all, she has no proof. She was so sure the other day, but now, talking to Mark, her certainty is dissolving. What if he's right and Andrew Wilson is innocent?*

'I'm sorry. I didn't want to upset you,' says Mark as they pull into the hospital car park. 'I know this whole thing must be very difficult for you, but Andy's my mate, you know, and I just think you're barking up the wrong tree.'

'It's okay, I'm not upset,' Abby lies. 'Let's talk about something else.'

On their way in, they stop at the hospital shop to buy some snacks and magazines for Danny. The volunteer on the desk informs them Danny is in Jenner Ward and they navigate their way through the labyrinth of corridors.

He's sitting up in bed next to the window. He has a bandage

around his head and a splint on his wrist. He looks pale and thin, his dark eyes glittering. Apart from that he looks okay, and Abby feels a rush of relief and affection.

'Danny,' she exclaims, giving him a hug. 'We've been so worried about you.'

Mark stands by the window, a slight smile hovering on his lips. 'How are you doing, mate?'

'I've been better, to tell you the truth,' Danny says wryly. 'But the doctor tells me there's no permanent damage.'

'Do you remember what happened?' Abby asks.

'It's a bit of a blur.' Danny presses his head gingerly with his good hand. 'It was just after I left your house. I was taking the short cut, through the park, you know.'

Abby nods. She often goes that way herself.

'I'd just crossed the bridge,' Danny continues, 'when I heard someone rush up behind me, and there was like this sudden pain in my head. Then nothing. Next thing I knew I was in an ambulance. Apparently, a couple found me lying unconscious in the mud.' He laughs. 'I mean it was worse than my sixth-form leavers' party where I fell face first into the mud. Do you remember, Mark?'

Mark shrugs and smiles. 'It's burned into my memory.'

'So you didn't see who attacked you?' Abby persists.

'Not really . . . I mean . . . no. I had the impression it was a man. He was wearing a hat I think.'

'What kind of hat?'

Danny shakes his head ruefully. 'I don't know.'

'Did they take anything?' asks Mark.

'That's the weird thing. My wallet was still in my pocket when I got to the hospital.'

'Well, at least you're okay. That's the main thing,' says Abby.

'Yes, it's been quite exciting actually. The police have been round to take a statement. I felt like I was in an episode of *Line of Duty*.' He grins.

Abby grins back. He's enjoying the drama, she realizes, and she's relieved that he's okay, but there is an idea scuttling about in her head like a bug and a knot of unease in her belly. She has a feeling that this attack wasn't random.

'Do the police have any idea who it was?' asks Mark.

Danny shakes his head. 'I don't think so. But I got into an argument with some homophobic arsehole two nights ago in the pub when I was with Will. He threatened to "smash my faggot face". Charming eh?'

'Did you tell the police?'

'Yes. They're looking into it.'

'What about CCTV?' says Abby. 'They must have CCTV.'

'Apparently, there's no CCTV in that part of the park, and the cameras that cover the main gates show that no one went in, apart from me and that couple who found me.'

'There are other ways into the park. Have they checked them out?'

'I'm sure the police know what they're doing, Abby,' Mark interjects.

'Hmm, I suppose so.' Abby stares out of the window at the small park with the damp rose bushes and empty benches.

The idea that has been troubling her ever since she heard Danny was attacked bubbles to the surface.

'Do you think it could have been the guy on the phone?' she says.

'What guy?' Danny is fiddling with the splint on his wrist.

'Whoever called the house last night. You shouted at him, remember? Told him to fuck off. Maybe that made him angry ... or jealous. I told you he was outside the house the night before. Perhaps he was watching the house again last night.' She shivers at the thought. 'Did you see anyone following you when you left?'

Danny sighs. 'No. I'm sure no one was following me. I would have noticed.'

Not necessarily, given how drunk he was, Abby thinks privately, but says nothing. She can tell Danny believes the idea is nonsense and she doesn't want to get into an argument with him right now.

But as she's driving home with Mark, another idea slithers into her mind. The car that hit Alex's car just before she met him in the park. What if that hadn't been an accident? What if someone had deliberately run into him, someone who was jealous of his relationship with her?

If she's right, and Danny's assailant is her stalker, then she's dealing with someone even more dangerous than she previously thought.

Over the next few days she keeps returning to the idea, like a dog gnawing at a bone. She runs the chain of events through her head over and over. And the more she thinks about it the more plausible it seems. It's too much of a coincidence to believe that the two things – the phone call and the attack so soon after – aren't connected.

It's nearly a week after the assault and she has finally built up the courage to phone the police to inform them of her suspicions when Danny calls her and tells her they've arrested the guy from the pub.

'Apparently, they have him on CCTV heading towards the park at the right time,' he says. 'The bastard, I knew it had to be him.'

Abby is surprised and confused. 'Are they sure they've got the right man?'

'Yes, it's him alright,' he says. 'No doubt about it.'

'Oh, well, that's good. It must be a relief,' she says.

But any relief Abby feels is short-lived. Even though her stalker has gone quiet for a while, she knows in her heart that he's still out there, watching her. Waiting.

JULY

Your baby is now roughly 40 cm long and weighs about 1.3 kg. It can open and close its eyes and if you shine a bright torch at your belly you might feel it respond to the light by turning its head.

Chapter Twenty-Eight

Every day Abby goes through the motions. She works, eats and sleeps. But she's stopped going out unless she needs to, and she's constantly on edge. When she does go out she's always looking over her shoulder; at home she jumps whenever the phone rings and stands in her room peering out from behind drawn curtains to see if she can catch him loitering outside. But she never sees anyone. And there are no more nuisance calls to her landline or her mobile. Weeks pass, and gradually she tries to convince herself that he's gone away, forgotten about her.

But he's there in her dreams, always there, just out of sight, in the shadows, watching her, taunting her. She has a recurring dream where he steps out of the gloom for a second and she catches a brief, tantalizing glimpse of his face. But before she can make out his features, he withdraws and is swallowed in darkness again. She has another dream where he's on top of her, pinning her down, and she is powerless to move and furiously angry. In her dream, she tries to make out his face but there's a bright light glaring in her eyes, blinding her. That's when she wakes up to the shrill ring of her alarm and she lies there for a second, the baby kicking her frantically. Then, exhausted, she climbs out of bed and gets herself ready for another day at work.

It's a week before the end of term. The kids have gone home, and Abby is tidying the Art Room, doing an inventory of all the art materials, trying to decide what needs to be ordered for next year, when Jenny pops her head around the door.

'Oh, Abigail, I'm glad you're still here. Gina wants to talk to you. She says could you come to her office and see her asap.'

Abby sighs and looks at her watch. It's already six o'clock. Now God knows what time she'll be finished. 'What about?'

Jenny shrugs. 'Not sure. Something about your maternity leave, I think.'

Abby crosses the quadrangle to the main school building and knocks on the door to Gina's office. She can never quite shake the idea that she's a schoolkid in trouble when the head summons her.

Inside Gina Watson is sitting behind her desk, talking to a young man with long brown hair tied back in a ponytail.

'Ah, this is Abigail now,' she says with the false, bright smile she reserves for parents and new members of staff. 'Abigail. This is Tom Marsden. He's going to cover for you next term while you're on maternity leave, and longer if you need it.'

Tom stands up, holding out his hand and giving Abby a pitch-perfect smile.

Abby frowns and shakes his hand. 'But I'll be back at work by the beginning of October,' she says quickly.

Gina laughs merrily and wags her finger. 'You say that now. But you'll probably change your mind. I've seen it happen countless times. Anyway, there's really no rush, Abigail. You take all the time you need. Enjoy the time with your baby. It's really very special.'

'But I won't need it,' Abby insists. 'I told you, I'm giving the baby up for adoption.' She's sure she's told Gina this before, but clearly she's forgotten, or more likely, knowing Gina, didn't listen in the first place.

Gina raises her eyebrows. There's a glint in her eye. She doesn't like being argued with. 'Let's wait and see, shall we, Abigail?' she says, smiling icily. 'Anyway, I thought you could show Tom around tomorrow. Let him observe a couple of your lessons. Get him up to speed with your plans for next year. I'm assuming you've written them all?'

Abby nods. She's barely started, but there's no point in telling Gina that. It's always safest to tell Gina what she wants to hear.

'Great. Well, you can introduce Tom to the staff now, if there's anyone still around.' She smiles at Tom. 'Generally, you'll find we're a friendly bunch. Thank you so much, Abigail,' she adds, picking up the phone, and Abby realizes they've been dismissed.

Great. Now Abby's never going to get home.

'I'm sorry if Gina gave you the impression that you'll be

here for a whole term,' she says as they head for the staff room, 'but it really will only be a month at the most.'

Tom smiles a charming smile. 'Whatever. I'm flexible.'

'But wouldn't a longer post be better for you?'

'Of course, but it's hard to find in this area. Anyway, I don't intend to stay supply teaching very long. Hopefully a permanent post will come up soon.' Abby gives him a side-long glance. He's handsome and personable and she can't help feeling threatened. What if he's better at her job than her? What if the kids like him more than her?

The staff room is virtually empty. Only Chris and Danny and one of the Chemistry teachers are left. Danny is marking a stack of books and Chris is on the computer, writing reports. She makes Tom a cup of tea and introduces him to Danny.

'So, you're Abby's replacement,' Danny says. He shuffles up so that Tom can sit next to him. This week is his first week back at school since the attack and he still has a cast on his wrist. 'Not that Abby could be replaced of course,' he says hurriedly, catching Abby's expression.

'Yes, well it's only going to be for a month,' she says firmly. 'My due date is the twenty-third and I'll be back at school within a week.'

'I wouldn't rush back if I were you,' says Danny. 'I'd have thought you'd have jumped at the chance to have a break from this dump. Paid as well. I know I've enjoyed mine. Though it was a bit of a drastic way of getting time off.' He waves his cast in the air.

Abby might have agreed with him not so long ago, but now

that it comes down to it she realizes how much she values her job, how big a part of her identity it's become. With this pregnancy, she feels trapped in a role she hasn't asked for, the baby weighing her down, literally and figuratively.

'What happened to your hand?' Tom asks, looking at Danny's cast.

'Ah well, that's a long story,' says Danny.

'Go on, tell me, I'm interested.'

So Danny launches into an involved and slightly exaggerated version of his ordeal while Tom listens with what looks like genuine interest.

'Oh my God,' he says suitably impressed. 'And have they arrested anyone yet?'

'Not yet.' Danny frowns.

'Oh, I thought they had?' says Abby, taken aback. 'I thought they arrested that man who threatened you in the pub.'

Danny shakes his head. 'He was seen in the area and they brought him in for questioning. I'm pretty sure he did it, but apparently there's not enough evidence to make anything stick.'

'What?' Abby shivers. She feels suddenly cold despite the bright sun streaming in through the large windows. What if she was right all along? If the man in the pub didn't attack Danny, then it could have been *him* – it could have been her stalker.

'Aren't you scared?' Tom asks Danny.

Danny smiles bravely, clearly revelling in the attention. 'Well, yeah, I'm scared, of course, but what can you do?

Anyway, I've signed up for self-defence classes – maybe you should come along with me, Abby. What do you think?'

'What?' Abby isn't really listening. Her thoughts are spiralling, swarming like angry insects. She's dimly aware that Danny and Tom have gone on to discuss self-defence tips they've seen on YouTube videos.

'Do you know if someone tapes your hands you're supposed to raise them above your head and bring them down very quickly, like this,' Tom is saying. He lifts his arms above his head and mimes bringing them down sharply.

'That is if you want to escape in the first place,' says Danny, giving Tom an arch look. Tom laughs and pats Danny on the arm.

'Well, I'd better go,' he says, still grinning at Danny. 'I'll see you tomorrow, Abigail.'

'Sure,' she says, absent-mindedly. 'See you later.'

'Well, he seems nice,' says Danny once Tom is out of earshot.

'Uh-huh,' Abby says. She's not thinking about Tom. 'I didn't know they'd let that guy go without charge.'

Danny frowns and stacks his books awkwardly with his one good hand. 'Really? I'm sure I told you.'

'So, if it wasn't him I could have been right. It could have been the man on the phone.' The fear that is constantly below the surface these days is rising in her throat.

Danny sighs. 'I don't know, Abs. I didn't say it wasn't him, just that they couldn't prove it.'

Abby shakes her head. 'It must have been the same person. I've just got this feeling. I mean it's too much of a coincidence, isn't it?'

'Well,' Danny says. 'You could be right. If you feel so sure, maybe we should tell the police.'

'I want to be completely sure before I go to the police. You know I as good as accused Andrew Wilson of rape.'

'Yes, Mark told me.' Danny sips his coffee and gives her a look of concern. 'So, you think that was a mistake?'

'Yes ... no. I don't know.' She doesn't know what to believe anymore. 'After the fireworks Mark said he saw me in his room, arguing with Hugo Langley. But Hugo couldn't be the one who sent me those flowers and messages, not if he's in Thailand.'

Danny presses his hand to his lips. 'Ah, shit, didn't I tell you? He's back from Thailand. Sorry, Abby, I've been so preoccupied with the assault and my wrist and everything, I forgot to tell you.'

The hairs on the back of Abby's neck stand on end. 'How long has he been back?'

'I'm not sure, a few weeks I think. I could arrange a meeting if you like.'

Abby thinks. Even if Hugo has been back for a few weeks it still would be impossible for him to have been sending her all the flowers and messages, but he's the one person that was there that night that she hasn't spoken to yet.

'Okay. That's a good idea, but I don't want him to know why I want to speak to him.'

241

'I could say you're interested in moving to Thailand, that you want to pick his brains about what it's like to live there.'

Abby considers this. She can't think of a better plan.

'Okay,' she says standing up. 'Thanks Danny.'

She's still thinking about Hugo in the car as Rob drives her home.

'You're quiet, today,' Rob observes, turning onto the dual carriageway.

'I'm just tired, that's all.' Abby rests her head against the window and rubs her forehead. She really doesn't want to discuss this with Rob.

'Not too tired to go out this evening I hope?'

'No. Why?'

'Oh, didn't Ellie tell you? We're taking you out for a meal. Our treat. There's something we'd like to talk about.'

Abby can guess what they want to discuss and she's not looking forward to it at all, but there's really no avoiding it any longer. 'Okay, where are we going?' She sighs.

'I booked us a table at the Three Compasses.'

'The Three Compasses, really?' Great. That's all she needs. It's a Monday night and Alex will almost certainly be there. She hasn't seen him since he came to her house and she as good as accused him of rape. She's mortified now about the way she acted, and she doesn't relish the idea of bumping into him again.

'Why? Is there a problem?' Rob asks, glancing over at her curiously.

'No, it's fine.' It's a small town. She's bound to see him sooner or later. It might as well be sooner.

She's hoping the pub will be crowded but it's a Monday night and of course, sod's law, it's virtually empty. There's nowhere to hide. Alex is talking to an old man sitting at the bar and laughing. When he sees Abby, he stops laughing abruptly and starts wiping down the bar, his mouth forming a grim line.

She can't very well ignore him, so after they've ordered their food, she tells Ellie and Rob she'll catch up with them and heads to the bar to get some drinks.

'What can I get you?' Alex asks coldly, avoiding her eyes.

'A pint and a glass of white wine, please. Oh, and a Diet Coke.' She watches him as he pulls the pint. 'How are you, Alex?' she asks awkwardly as he slops the beer onto the bar.

'I'm okay.' He shrugs and frowns. 'I'm surprised to see you in here though. After what you said the other day I shouldn't have thought you'd want to see me ever again.'

Abby hoists herself up onto a bar stool. 'I'm sorry about that. I was in a bad place that day. I don't really believe all the things I said. Can we be friends?'

Alex frowns for a moment then his face relaxes into a smile. 'Why not?' He pours the wine and the Coke swiftly and expertly into glasses. 'You probably did me a favour anyway. I'm back with Bethany. We're going to give it another shot.'

'Oh, that's good,' says Abby, swallowing an irrational twinge of jealousy. 'But I thought you said she was seeing some other bloke.'

'Didn't work out.' He takes her money and opens the till. 'She realized what an arsehole he was.' He rests his elbows on the bar. 'Anyway, how about you? How are you? How's Danny? I heard he was mugged or something?'

'Yeah, he's okay. He broke his wrist but otherwise he's okay.'

'Did they get the guy?'

'Not yet.' Again, there's that uneasy curling in her stomach.

'Well, give him my regards,' Alex says, handing her the change.

It would never have worked long term with Alex, anyway, she reflects as she carries the drinks to the dining area. They really weren't all that compatible. But she can't help feeling sad that it's over. In her mind it was more than just a fling. She isn't just attracted to him, but has become genuinely fond of him as well, and it isn't so easy to just switch off those feelings.

Oh well, she thinks. *It just wasn't meant to be.*

Ellie and Rob are sitting at a corner table, deep in conversation. They stop abruptly when Abby comes back.

'Who's that you were talking to at the bar?' Ellie asks, sipping her wine.

'Alex,' Abby says, sitting opposite Ellie and Rob, pushing back the chair so there's room for her belly.

'Oh, so *that's* Alex.' Ellie stares over. Her eyes widen, and she grins. 'I see why you liked him. What happened between you two? I thought you were really into him.'

'He got back together with his ex.' Abby shrugs.

'Well, I think you're well shot of him. Looks like a bit of a loser to me,' says Rob, tipping his chair back and grinning.

Abby looks at him sharply. 'What makes you say that?'

'Well, if he prefers another woman to you, he must be a loser, mustn't he?'

Their food arrives, and they talk about other things: Ellie's work, which has been manic lately because Dr Rowe is away on holiday and Dr Samuel has been off sick. They talk about the half-marathon that Rob has started training for, and they talk about Hector who cut his paw on some glass this morning. It isn't until they've finished their first course and they are halfway through their second that Ellie finally broaches the subject they've brought her here to discuss.

'So, I suppose you've guessed why we're here.' She pushes her plate away, the death-by-chocolate half finished.

Abby shakes her head. 'You wanted to tell me something?'

Ellie and Rob are both staring at her intently. She feels the weight of their expectation and it's making her uncomfortable.

'Not tell, ask. We've been talking and . . .' Ellie's eyes are shining. She looks at Rob and he nods encouragingly. 'We know you don't feel ready to look after a baby. We know you're looking for adoptive parents and . . .' Tears well up in her eyes and her voice starts shaking. She flaps her hands in front of her face. 'Sorry, don't know why I'm getting so emotional about this.'

Rob steps in. 'What Ellie's trying to say is that we'd like to adopt your baby.'

Abby puts down her spoon. She knew this was coming but, now it has, she's completely lost her appetite.

'But I already found a couple who want to adopt.' She fiddles in her bag, trying to find the details that Chrissie, the adoption counsellor has given her. 'They're called Joel and Maria.'

Ellie sighs. 'Why would you give your baby away to strangers when you could give her to us, who you know would love and care for her? If we adopted your baby, you could always stay in contact, be a part of her life.'

But I don't want to stay in contact. That's the whole point, Abby thinks. She can't believe that Ellie, who's usually so sensitive, should be so oblivious to her feelings about this. How can Ellie not see that the baby will just be a constant reminder of her father – of the sick, perverted way she came into the world? But perhaps Ellie is so desperate to have this child it's blinded her to everything else. And Abby knows Ellie doesn't believe that she was really raped. If she did, she would never be asking her to do this.

Abby opens her mouth to tell them about the message he sent, the one that proves that she was raped. But she can't speak. Those same feelings of shame and fear that she felt when she first got the note wash over her and the words won't come. She stabs at the banoffee pie which suddenly looks like a pile of slime.

'Just promise us you'll think about it,' says Ellie.

Abby sighs. There's no way she is ever going to agree to them adopting this baby, but right now she really wants to drop the subject. 'Okay, I'll think about it.'

When they arrive home, Abby heads straight up to her room. She doesn't want to talk. She needs to be by herself.

Opening the bedroom door, she's met by a rush of cool air and she's suddenly on her guard. The curtains twitch uneasily in the breeze. *That's weird. The window is wide open.* She's sure it was only a tiny bit ajar when she left.

She goes to the window and closes it. Then she looks around. Her skin is prickling. *Something isn't right.* The bed is made, but the bedspread is slightly rumpled as if someone's been sitting on it. And tucked under the covers, its head just peeking out on the pillow, is a teddy bear.

What the . . . ?

She pulls back the covers rapidly as if the bear were a snake or a poisonous spider and scrabbles around checking for a note. But there's nothing. Just the bear, staring at her with blank, black eyes. It's brown with a red satin heart tucked under its arm. *How the hell has it got there? Could he have put it there?* She shivers at the thought. But maybe it's just Ellie or Rob, buttering her up. Maybe they assumed she'd agree to the adoption and this is their thank-you present. Even though she doesn't like the idea, it's better than the alternative.

Downstairs in the kitchen Ellie is pouring herself another glass of wine and Rob is on his laptop with his headphones on.

'You didn't put this in my room, did you?' Abby says.

Ellie stares at the bear in confusion. 'No.'

'Rob?'

Rob pulls the headphones off. 'What?'

'Did you give this to me?'

He looks at the bear and laughs. 'You know we love you, Abs, but not that much.'

Abby feels sick. She places the bear on the kitchen table and eyes it warily like it might make a sudden movement. 'Someone's been in my room,' she says.

Her heart is hammering out of her chest. If she can't feel safe in her own bedroom, then where can she?

'What do you mean?' asks Rob, closing his laptop.

'Someone's been in my room. The bed is messed up and someone put this on my pillow.'

'No way, that's crazy.' Ellie gawps at her in disbelief. 'All the doors were locked. I locked them myself before we went out.'

'Well, where else has it come from? Tell me that. Look, I'll show you.'

She runs back upstairs with Ellie following close behind and together they inspect the room.

'He must have climbed in through the window,' says Abby. 'It was open when I came in just now and I didn't leave it like that.'

Ellie examines the window. 'Are you sure?'

'Yes. I left it just a tiny bit open. I left it like this and when I came in just now it was like this.' Abby pulls the sash window up and down to show Ellie what she means.

248

Someone has been in here. She's sure of it. Her nightshirt is still on the floor where she tossed it this morning and a stray sock has drifted under the bed. She picks up the sock and shoves it in the washing basket, then places her nightshirt under the pillow. There's such a jumble of objects on her dresser that it's hard to tell if anything's been moved. But she has the strong feeling that something is missing. She does a quick mental inventory. Her make-up bag, make-up spilling out, her moisturizer, hairbrush, a used razor, a couple of postcards she bought ages ago at the Tate. Suddenly, she realizes what it is.

'The photo of Mum,' she says. 'It's gone.' It's the photo of her mother – the photo taken in Skye the year before she died. Abby's most precious possession.

Bastard.

'Are you sure it hasn't just fallen behind?' Ellie pulls out the dresser, but there's nothing there but a lot of dust and an old comb with missing teeth.

He's taken the photo. She feels certain it's him – her stalker.

She looks out of the window. Her room is above the extension roof. With a ladder it would be quite easy to climb up and then in through the window. Abby has done it a few times herself when she's forgotten her key.

'Where are you going?' says Ellie, following behind as Abby runs down the stairs.

Abby doesn't answer. She takes out a torch from the kitchen cupboard and tests that it works. Her heart is pummelling in her chest, anger fuelling her.

'What are you doing?' asks Ellie as Abby opens the back door. 'Abby?!'

'I want to check something,' Abby says. Then, before Ellie can argue, she steps out into the chill night air and picks her way in the darkness, down the garden path.

The shed doesn't have anything valuable in it, and so they never bother locking it. The padlock is hanging open as she guessed it would be. The wooden door creaks as she opens it and she inhales the smell of creosote and dust. She shines the torch on a rusty old bike that never gets used and the lawnmower and a ladder. The ladder is lying on its side where it's kept but when she crouches down and shines the torch on the base she notices it's covered in mud. She runs her finger along the wood. The mud is damp. Someone has used the ladder very recently.

Chapter Twenty-Nine

Abby has hardly slept. Each time she gets to sleep she wakes up in a panic, thinking he's broken into her room. A couple of times she's woken convinced he's standing at the end of her bed.

Sitting here in the living room, she's tired beyond belief and she's having trouble focusing. PC Whittaker's head is swimming in front of her eyes like a mirage. Another police officer has come with him this time, a woman with short blonde hair who's introduced herself as PC Harmon. She takes a sip of the coffee Abby's brought her and looks at her notes.

'Let me see if I've got this right,' she says. 'You're saying that Andrew Wilson broke into your house?'

'Yes. No. Someone did.'

'Was anything taken?'

'A photo of my mother, there was a teddy bear and the ladder, the ladder was covered in mud and the window, the window was open . . .'

She's not making any sense. She sounds like she's raving,

she knows, but her head is throbbing, and her thoughts are muddled. PC Harmon and PC Whittaker exchange a glance. PC Whittaker's look clearly communicates 'Here we go again'.

'Hold on, slow down, Abigail,' he says with exaggerated patience. 'He took a teddy bear, a photo and a ladder?'

'No. He didn't *take* the bear. He left it on my pillow.' Abby rubs her eyes. She needs to calm down and focus if she wants them to take her seriously. 'I can show you.' She goes to the kitchen and finds the bear still sitting on the table. She brings it into the living room and shows it to the police officers.

PC Harmon puts on some white plastic gloves and places the bear gingerly in a clear plastic bag. 'Was there a note with it?' she asks.

'Not this time,' says Abby.

'What about the others?' PC Whittaker asks. 'You mentioned some other notes at the police station.'

Abby fetches the notes from the drawer where she's kept them, and gives them to PC Harmon, who leafs through them, a worried frown on her face. She hands them to PC Whittaker without comment.

'I'm scared,' Abby says. 'You need to do something before he does something really crazy.'

'Was there any sign of a break-in?' asks PC Whittaker. 'How did he get into the house?'

'I told you,' Abby snaps impatiently. 'Through the bedroom window.'

'Can you show us?'

They follow Abby upstairs to her room and examine the window carefully.

'Was it forced open?' asks PC Harmon running her fingers along the window frame.

'No,' Abby admits. 'I must have left it unlocked.'

'So, how can you be sure that he was in the house?'

'I already told you, because of the bear and the ladder. Look, I don't understand why you're not doing your jobs.' There's a hysterical note in her voice. She swipes her hand in a gesture of frustration and knocks the tub of moisturizer onto the floor. It lands on PC Harmon's foot; the lid comes off and white lotion spills onto the carpet and PC Harmon's shoe.

'We're doing everything we can,' PC Whittaker says calmly, but there is an edge to his voice. 'We brought Mr Wilson in for questioning after you made your initial claim. We even checked the CCTV footage for that night. We have him leaving Queen's Street at two o'clock, stopping at the garage on Gloucester Road to buy some petrol. He only stopped there for about two minutes and then he dropped you off at quarter past two outside your house. You entered the house alone. He's on camera the whole time. We can show you the footage if you want.'

Abby digests this. It confirms what she's been thinking since her conversation with Mark. Andrew Wilson isn't the man they're looking for. 'No, it's okay,' she says. 'I believe you.'

PC Whittaker clears his throat. 'In fact, I have to tell you, Mr Wilson made some counterclaims, which did check out. He said that it's not him that's been harassing you but the other way around.'

'What?' Abby gawps.

'Apparently you accosted him in a coffee shop in town, is that right?'

'No. Yes. Well. I just wanted him to tell me the truth . . .'

'Has it occurred to you that he may have been telling you the truth already?'

Abby puts her head in her hands. It is the truth. She knows that now. The CCTV footage proves that it couldn't have been Andrew Wilson and she's mortified when she thinks about the way she behaved in the café.

'Look,' says PC Harmon gently. 'If you're worried about a break-in, there are some simple steps you can take. With this type of window, you can instal a pin halfway up to stop it opening more than a few inches. We can send someone round to help with your home security if you like. Also, we'll have a word with the neighbours. See if they saw anything that night. You never know. Are they in now?'

Abby nods. 'Probably.' Being on a corner they have only one neighbour, an elderly lady called Barbara. As far as she can tell, Barbara's almost always in.

'Good. Well, we'll be off then. Call us if you're worried or if you think of anything else. And I suggest you go to bed and have some rest. You look all done in.'

It's true, Abigail doesn't feel well. They go downstairs,

and she watches out of the window as PC Harmon and PC Whittaker walk down the garden path and ring on her neighbour's door. She doesn't know what to think. It looks like she's cocked it up again. She sinks down onto the sofa, feeling dizzy. The room seems to be swaying, lurching like a boat on the water, but she forces herself to concentrate.

Think, Abby, think.

If the police are right, then Andrew Wilson couldn't have raped her. The only people that were alone with her that night were Alex and Hugo. She's already ruled out Alex because he couldn't have sent the messages. So that leaves Hugo.

She'd believed he was in Thailand when all the flowers and messages arrived. But Danny told her the other day that he's back. Maybe he's been back longer than Danny thought or maybe he never left at all.

She picks up her phone and calls Danny.

'Danny, I need you to arrange that meeting with Hugo Langley.'

Danny calls her back a few minutes later. 'He's staying at his parents' house and he's invited us over tomorrow afternoon. I'll pick you up at two.'

AUGUST

Your baby is still growing this month, but slower and it's getting a bit tight inside your womb, so you may well feel less movement. Babies born at thirty-four weeks can survive and thrive outside the womb. By now your baby will be able to recognize your voice and may even remember songs you sing now after they are born.

Chapter Thirty

This is one big, fuck-off mansion, Abby thinks as they step over the threshold. The hallway alone is bigger than the entire ground floor of Rob and Ellie's house. There's even a suit of armour just by the front door and a coat of arms hanging on the wall. It's not the kind of house Abby has ever been inside, apart from as a tourist. But she refuses to be intimidated.

Hugo Langley greets them at the door. He's dressed casually but expensively, his red hair swept up in a fashionable peak. He's taller and thinner than she realized from Danny's photo.

'Danny, long time no see, and Abigail, how lovely to see you again.' He kisses her on both cheeks. His smile is friendly and his manner's suave but there's something shifty about his eyes, Abby thinks. She has the impression of someone playing a part, the part of a gracious host. She tries to steady her breathing, fighting off a sudden swelling fear. *You can do this*, she thinks. *We can nail the bastard.* She grabs Danny's hand for reassurance as Hugo shows them to what he calls the 'Blue Room'.

The Blue Room is relatively small and, strangely enough, the only blue thing in the room is a large Chinese vase, one of many undoubtedly priceless antiques scattered artfully around.

Hugo watches Abby as she lowers herself into a chair.

'I suppose congratulations are in order,' he says. 'I must say I had no idea you were expecting.'

Abby runs a hand over her swollen belly. 'Thank you,' she says cautiously.

Hugo stretches and yawns languidly. 'And when's D-Day? When are you due?'

'On the twenty-third of September,' she says. 'Just over a month to go now.'

She observes him carefully to see if he realizes the significance of the date but he's giving nothing away. He gives her a shrewd look through sandy lashes. 'I don't suppose you want a whisky?'

'No thanks.' Abby sits very still.

'Danny?'

'It's a bit early for me,' says Danny, smiling blandly.

'I hope you don't mind if I do.'

'Knock yourself out.'

Hugo opens a dark wood cabinet, takes out a decanter and pours a drink. His hand is shaking slightly, Abby notices.

Hugo sits opposite Abby and Danny and takes a gulp of whisky. 'Well, it's been a while, Danny. How are you, my old friend?' he says.

'I'm fine.' Danny sits forward. His voice is neutral, but his leg is tapping away, betraying his nervous energy. 'How are you? I had no idea you were even in the UK. You didn't let anyone know. How long have you been back?'

'Oh, quite a while. I only stayed in Bangkok about three months. The whole thing was a complete shambles and the Director of Studies was an idiot.'

Abby is calculating rapidly. If he's been back since March, then he could have sent her the messages and flowers. A knot of fear tightens in her stomach as she realizes she could be sitting opposite her attacker.

Hugo crosses his legs and pulls out a packet of cigarettes. 'Do you mind?' he says, lighting one.

Abby shakes her head mutely.

'The school was a cowboy outfit but Bangkok itself is a fascinating place. Danny tells me you're thinking of doing a bit of travelling, getting a job yourself. I can't recommend Queen's College but, as a qualified teacher, I suppose you could get a job at one of the international schools. Though I don't know much about maternity services out there.'

Abby takes a deep breath. 'Actually, I'm not going to Thailand. There was something else I wanted to talk to you about.'

'Oh?' Is it her imagination or does he suddenly look wary, like a cat trying to decide whether to run or pounce.

'I want to talk about the baby. My due date is the twenty-third of September, which means this baby was conceived on New Year's Eve. The thing is, I don't remember anything about that night and I have no idea who the father is.'

There's a long silence. Hugo looks to Danny and back to Abigail, a slight sardonic smile playing on his lips.

'Is this a joke? Come on, admit it, Danny's set you up to this, hasn't he?'

'No joke,' says Abby.

Danny shakes his head. 'It's deadly serious. We actually think that Abby was raped.'

'Crikey.' Hugo sits back with his hands behind his head. 'Well it has nothing to do with me, I can assure you.'

'No,' Abby says hastily. 'We're not suggesting that.' There's no point in getting his back up – she's not going to make the same mistake she made with Andrew Wilson. 'But I've been talking to everyone who was at the party that night and I'd be interested to know what you remember. For example, did you see me on my own with anyone?'

Hugo takes a drag of his cigarette and blows the smoke out slowly.

'Well, I arrived about ten. And that was the first time I saw you. You were sitting on the stairs, snogging some chap. He had dark hair, tattoos. The next time I saw you wasn't until quite a bit later. We were in Danny's room just hanging. Playing Truth or Dare.'

'Who's we?'

'Oh, me and a couple of girls, Joss and Rebecca. You came in holding hands with some skinny chap, glasses . . .'

Mark, she thinks surprised. 'We were holding hands, are you sure?'

'Uh-huh. You said you wanted to join in the game.'

Again, that sense of déjà vu. The woman with the corkscrew curls, the musket on the wall. Abby was sitting with her back to the wall and she can see Hugo's face clearly now as he takes a drag of a cigarette.

'Was I acting strangely?' she asks. If she had been drugged, maybe the drug would have already taken effect by then. If it had, surely it would have been obvious to everyone.

Hugo shrugs. 'Not that I remember. You were a bit embarrassed I think when that chap you were with declared his undying love.'

'What?'

'Joss asked him if he fancied anyone playing the game, and do you remember what his answer was?'

'No,' Abby says warily.

'He said he fancied you and always had. It was quite touching actually.'

Abby absorbs this piece of information. Perhaps she has always half known that Mark had a thing about her but has chosen to ignore it.

'What did I say when he said that?' she asks.

He shrugs. 'You just laughed and said you should just stay friends. Poor chap. He seemed a bit crushed, actually.' She has an image of Mark's face, his eyes dark and wounded. Is she imagining or remembering? She thinks about what PC Whittaker said about the stalker possibly being someone she'd rejected. For a second she considers this idea, then she dismisses it. It couldn't be Mark – gentle, nerdy Mark. No way. In any case, if everyone's telling the truth about that night, then he wasn't alone with her at any point apart from the beginning of the party in the kitchen, and she remembers that.

More than likely Hugo is making it up to stir up trouble or deflect suspicion. She's not sure she would believe anything he said. He's a snaky, slimy piece of work.

'Everyone went down to watch the fireworks at twelve o'clock,' he continues. 'You were talking to some woman with dark hair.'

'And after that?'

'We went back upstairs.'

Abby holds her breath. 'Just you and me?'

'No, we were with my friend, Joss.' Mark didn't mention Joss. Abby strains to remember. She can't recall exactly what Mark said, but she had the impression that she was on her own with Hugo.

'And?'

'We just talked.'

'I was told we had an argument. And there was broken glass.'

Hugo smiles. 'Yes, well, you were very drunk. You got very angry and threw a bottle across the room.'

Abby cringes with embarrassment. Much as she instinctively dislikes Hugo, what he says has the ring of truth. She remembers the glass smashing, shards jumping in the air seemingly in slow motion. Now she thinks about it, she can remember the bottle in her hand, the feeling of anger, but in her memory, she didn't throw the bottle deliberately. It was almost as if someone else had done it.

264

'Why was I angry?' she asks.

He shrugs and smiles. 'Apparently I said something objectionable. I don't remember what. I think it might have had something to do with gender politics. Don't worry, I often have that effect on people.'

'So, what happened then?'

'You left in disgust. I think you said you were going home.'

'That's it?' Abby stares at him, trying to work out if he's lying or not.

Hugo meets her eyes with a faintly amused defiance. As if he thinks it's all a big joke. 'Yes. Sorry I can't be more helpful.'

'If we speak to Joss will she confirm what you've said?' says Abby.

His eyes narrow. 'Sure, if you don't believe me.' He picks up his phone. Abby types the number into her phone as he reads it out.

'Well, it's been lovely . . .' Hugo stands up. 'But if you don't mind, I've got to get ready to go out. I've got an appointment.' He walks them to the door.

'Do call me, Danny, when you're next in London. I hope everything goes well for you, Abigail. I'm sorry I couldn't be of more help.'

'What did you think?' Abby asks as Danny drives her home along winding country roads.

Danny wipes condensation off the windscreen frowning. 'I don't know. He couldn't wait to get rid of us, could he?'

'No, and did you notice his hands were shaking?'

'That's probably withdrawal. I've got a feeling he's a bit of an alcoholic.'

'Hmm, yes, the several glasses of whisky might have been a clue,' Abby says sardonically. 'Do you know this girl, Joss, he was talking about?'

'Not very well. You should ring her, find out if he's telling the truth.'

'Who's that?' says Danny as he drops her off outside the house.

There's a silver SUV Abby has never seen before parked in the driveway. For a moment she's confused. Then she remembers.

'Shit, I forgot. The adoption people are coming today.'

She waves goodbye to Danny and walks up the garden path, steeling herself for what she's about to encounter. She knows it's not going to be pretty.

'You could have warned us,' Rob hisses as he opens the door.

Ellie is sitting in the living room with a man and woman that Abby recognizes, from the photos Chrissie gave her, as Maria and Joel. The atmosphere in the room is frosty. Ellie, straight backed, looks furious, and Maria and Joel look very uncomfortable.

Maria's face breaks into an anxious smile as Abby walks in.

'You must be Abigail,' she says, wrapping her arms around Abby as if she's a long-lost friend. 'I'm Maria, and this is

Joel.' Joel, who is about forty, with grey hair and a handsome tanned face, stands up and shakes her hand.

'Lovely to meet you, Abigail,' he says.

Ellie stands up. 'Excuse me,' she says. 'I'll leave you to it.' She looks pale and Abby can feel her agitation from across the room. It's emanating from her like steam. What a mess. She should have made sure Ellie and Rob were out before Maria and Joel came.

There's an awkward silence after Ellie leaves. Maria perches at the edge of her seat watching Abby as if she's a rare, wild creature that might startle and bolt at any second.

'Well, you look very well,' Maria says at last. 'Is everything going okay?'

'Yes, everything's fine.' *Apart from the small matter of the rape and stalking*, Abby thinks. But she doesn't want Maria and Joel to know anything about that – as far as they're concerned, this is a normal pregnancy. Then, because she doesn't know what else to say, she shows them the ultrasound picture on her phone.

'Look, Joel, our baby,' Maria breathes. She cradles the phone in her hand. Her eyes are wide with awe, as if she's gazing at a holy relic or witnessing a miracle. Joel comes and looks over her shoulder and clasps her hand.

'She's beautiful,' he says. 'Would you mind?' he asks Abby. 'Would it be okay . . . Could you send us a copy?'

'Sure.' Abby messages them the picture and then they make small talk for a while. They ask Abby questions about her life and she gives them heavily censored answers. In return they talk about themselves. Abby has the feeling that they are trying to present themselves in the best light, dropping in mentions of the charity work they do and what a great area they live in, how many parks there are, how perfect it is for small children.

'Are there any questions you'd like to ask us?' Maria asks finally. 'You can ask anything you like.'

'Not really . . .' Abby shakes her head. They seem like nice enough people and if she's honest she couldn't care less about anything else. All she wants is to get rid of this baby. She's counting down the days now until it will be out of her life and she can hand it over to Joel and Maria. Everything will be back to normal and she can forget the whole thing ever happened.

'And you're due on the twenty-third of September, is that right?'

'That's right.'

'Not long now then.' Maria beams and reaches for Joel's hand.

'No.'

Maria looks at Joel. 'We'd like to be present at the birth, if possible. I mean, if that's okay with you?'

A couple of strangers watching me push a watermelon-sized object out of my vagina. Fantastic, thinks Abby. On the other hand, if Maria is there, she can take the baby straight away. The baby will be Maria's, and there will be no attempts to get Abby to bond with it. 'That's okay.' She nods. 'I'll let you know when I go into labour.'

Maria beams. 'What kind of birth were you thinking of? Have you made a birth plan yet?'

Abby stares at her in confusion.

'I mean, are you planning to have a hospital birth, a home birth, or a water birth? What kind of pain relief are you willing to use . . . ?'

'As much pain relief as possible,' says Abby. 'If I had my way I'd have it under general anaesthetic!' She laughs. 'I had a biopsy last year and I had to be knocked out. I just couldn't stomach the thought of doing it under just the local anaesthetic.'

Maria doesn't smile. 'Biopsy?'

'For cancer, but it came back negative.'

'Oh.' Maria sits back, looking relieved. 'Anything you can tell us about any health issues in your family or in the father's family would be welcome. Just so we can provide the best possible care for the little one.'

'Well, my mum died of breast cancer five years ago but apart from that we're pretty healthy.' The fact that the baby's father might be a delusional rapist and stalker she thinks best not to mention.

Joel and Maria stay a little longer than Abby would like. They're friendly and kind, but Abby feels the weight of their longing and she's relieved when they finally decide to leave.

'Before we go . . . We got a little something for you,' says Maria as Abby heads for the door. She rummages in her bag and hands Abby a parcel wrapped in tissue paper. On a card with a picture of flowers she's written, '*To Abigail with all our love and gratitude*'.

Inside the box is a beautiful necklace with what Abby is fairly sure is a real diamond pendant. Abby gapes at it. She's never owned a piece of jewellery like this.

'It's too much,' she mumbles, embarrassed.

'Not compared to what you're giving us.'

After Joel and Maria have left, Abby goes up to her room. Ellie's door is firmly closed, and she can hear Rob and Ellie murmuring behind it. She sighs. She'll have to deal with Ellie later. She has problems enough of her own right now. Sitting on her bed with her knees pressed against her chest, she takes out her phone and calls Joss.

Joss answers after a couple of rings. 'Hello?' Her accent is plummy, and she sounds slightly breathless.

'Hi, is that Joss?'

'Yes?'

'You probably don't remember me, but my name is Abigail Brooke. We met at Danny's New Year's Eve party.'

'Oh, Abby, yes, of course I remember. Hi. How are you?'

'I'm okay, thanks. You?'

'I'm fine.' There's a short silence as Joss waits for Abby to explain why she's calling, and Abby chews her nail wondering how to broach the subject. 'I was just wondering if you could clear something up for me,' she says at last. 'It's about that night.'

'Oh?'

'Do you remember much of the evening?'

'Yes. Well, it's quite a while ago now. What do you want to know?'

'It's to settle an argument. Mark and I can't agree. I wonder if you could tell me what we did. I know we were up in Mark's room. But I don't remember many details. I'd had quite a lot to drink.'

Joss chuckles, a deep throaty laugh. 'Yes, you were completely wasted. Don't worry, though, you were quite a charming drunk.'

'What were we doing?'

'Just chilling. Oh, and we played Truth or Dare.'

'Who's we?'

'Me, you, Hugo, my friend Rebecca and that guy, Mark. We went down to watch the fireworks for a bit at twelve o'clock and after that we went up to the bedroom again and just talked. You got into an argument with Hugo . . .'

Abby remembers, or thinks she remembers, his smug face smirking at her, a feeling of rage and then the glass shattering. 'What was the argument about?' she asks tentatively.

'I don't really remember. I think he said something sexist. He likes winding people up, does our Hugo.'

'I remember some glass smashing . . .' Abby holds her breath.

'Yeah, you threw a bottle at Hugo, but don't worry, you missed, and I don't think you were actually aiming at him.' She laughs. 'Unless, that is, you've got a very bad aim. Besides, he probably had it coming to him.'

It ties in with her memory and what Hugo told her. She could have thrown it. Abby considers all Joss has told her. As far as she can tell, it confirms everything Hugo said. It looks like he was telling the truth after all.

'You were there in the room, the whole time?' she asks.

'Yes . . . Why? What's this all about?'

'Nothing,' Abby says. 'Thanks a lot. You've been very helpful.'

'And look, I know you and Hugo didn't hit it off and I know he can come across as, well –' Joss laughs again – 'a bit of a twat, to be frank, but he's a good guy at heart.'

Everyone is a good guy, it seems. According to Danny, Alex is a good guy. According to Mark, Andy is a good guy. Nobody is the kind of person who would drug or rape her, but someone did. This creature inside her is a constant reminder of that. Abby sits on her bed and rubs her hand over her belly. The baby is sitting in an awkward position on her pelvis and she feels uncomfortable and suddenly very tired. She lies flat on the bed staring up at the ceiling. She's just drifting off to sleep when the doorbell rings.

She's tempted to ignore it, but it could be Maria and Joel back again for some reason. It would be awkward if Ellie or Rob answered, so she races downstairs to get there before them.

But when Abby opens the door there's no one there, just an orchid sitting on the doormat, wobbling in the breeze, its bright pink petals obscenely splayed, the lower petal protruding like a flickering tongue.

272

She shudders. *Him again. But where the fuck is he?*

Pure rage surges through her, blotting out fear. She sprints down the path and stops at the gate, looking up and down the road. But it's empty. There's just one old woman shuffling along in her direction at the far end of the street. Determined, Abby opens the gate and runs around the corner but again the street is empty. Where the hell did he go?

Bastard. She sighs and heads back into the house, picking up the orchid on the way. Its cloying scent makes her want to vomit. She's never liked orchids. Right now, she positively hates them. She carries it upstairs and places it on the floor in the corner as far away from her as possible. Then she takes a deep breath and opens the attached note.

Moments that take your breath away. The first time I knew you were carrying my child. I knew we were meant to be. You must have known it too.

Chapter Thirty-One

'I'm sick and tired of this,' says Abby, banging the orchid down in the middle of the table at breakfast next morning, making Rob jump and spill the coffee he's holding down his shirt.

Ellie looks up from her toast and juice. She hasn't spoken to Abby since Joel and Maria turned up yesterday, but this shocks her out of her silence. 'Again?' she says, the colour draining from her face. 'What the hell's going on with this guy? He didn't break in again, did he?' She looks over her shoulder nervously as if he might be in the room with them right now.

Abby shakes her head. 'It was outside on the doorstep yesterday evening. He rang the bell but when I got there he was gone.'

'Jesus.' Ellie shakes her head. 'What a creep. I don't understand why the police aren't doing more. He has been in our house, what else does he need to do before they take this seriously?'

'There was a message with it, too.' Abby hands the envelope

to Ellie. 'He makes it completely clear this time that he's the father of this baby.'

Ellie reads the note, and shows it to Rob, her expression increasingly grim. 'Yes,' she says slowly. 'It does look that way. Or if he isn't, he certainly *thinks* he's the father of your baby. "*I knew we were meant to be*",' she reads aloud. 'Jesus, Abs, he's obviously completely delusional . . .' She picks up the pot and turns it slowly, lost in thought. 'You know, I've seen orchids like this in the florist's in town – the one near the bank,' she says. 'What's it called?'

'Flower Power,' Rob chips in.

'That's the one. They were in that same blue pot outside, on special offer. I'll bet he got them there.'

'Hmm, maybe.' Abby puts her head in her hands. She feels exhausted, defeated by the whole thing. Nothing she's done has worked. She's no nearer to discovering who did this to her than she was five months ago when she first found out she was pregnant.

'Listen, I've got an idea,' says Ellie. 'Maybe they'll remember who bought it in the shop. They can't have sold that many, not in a town this size.'

Abby lifts her head and smiles at Ellie. 'You're a genius,' she says, standing up and kissing her on the cheek.

'Wait. Where are you going? Aren't you going to have something to eat?' Ellie says as Abby heads for the door.

'I'm going to the florist's, of course.'

'Hold on a minute. Can't you wait till later? I've got to work today but I could go with you tomorrow.'

'No.' Abby shakes her head vehemently. 'I need to do this now.' She's tired of being frightened all the time, tired of feeling that *he's* the one in control.

'At least stay and eat something. You need to eat for your baby.'

'I'm not hungry.'

Abby rushes out of the room before Ellie can protest any-more. She flings her bag over her shoulder and opens the front door.

Halfway down the garden path, she takes her phone out. 'Danny?' she says when he answers. 'Are you busy?'

They're in the middle of a heatwave and the lilies outside the florist's are wilting in the heat, their stems drooping sadly. Even though it's still early in the morning, Abby feels as if she's wilting herself and although she's only wearing a light, cotton maternity dress, she can't seem to get cool – the baby inside her seems to act like a heater, making her hotter. She stops in a patch of shade and rests her head against the cool glass window.

'Where are the orchids?' says Danny. 'Are you sure this is the right place?'

'Yes, they must have sold out. They were definitely here a few days ago. Ellie saw them. Shall we go in and ask?'

Danny looks at his watch. 'Okay, Abs, but I can't be too long.' He has an appointment at the hospital to have his splint removed. 'I don't want to be late.'

The scent of frangipani and orange blossom hits their

nostrils as they enter the shop. A bell tinkles and the florist emerges from a back room, wearing rubber gloves and holding a pair of secateurs. 'How can I help?' She smiles. She's young and fresh faced, with long brown hair and a slight limp.

'Um . . . We wanted to buy an orchid. I noticed there were some in the window the other day,' says Abby. 'In pots? But they aren't there now.'

The florist nods. 'Yes, I'm afraid the last one sold yesterday. They were very popular. We've got some beautiful lilies on special offer now.'

'It was really an orchid we wanted.' Abby pauses. 'Do you remember who bought the last one?' She runs her fingers over the tips of a large tub of cornflowers.

The florist is taken aback. 'Um . . . Can I ask why you want to know?'

Abby is lost for words. But Danny comes to her rescue.

'I suppose it seems like a strange question, Sadie,' he says smoothly, reading her name badge, 'but my friend here received an orchid from your shop the other day. Whoever sent it didn't sign his name. She has an idea who he might be, but she wants to make sure. If you told us, you'd be helping the course of true love.'

Sadie laughs. 'I see. Well I'd really like to help but I wasn't here yesterday. I don't work on a Wednesday, you see.'

'Oh, that's a shame,' says Danny. 'If you weren't here yesterday, who was?'

'Um, Rachel, that's my boss. She'll be in later this

afternoon. If you came back at about three, you could speak to her then.'

'Okay, thank you.' Danny turns to the door. 'We'll come back this afternoon.' It seems there is nothing more to be gleaned from Sadie, and Abby is about to follow him out of the shop when she notices the camera in the corner of the room.

'You have CCTV?' she asks.

'Sure.'

'Could we take a look?'

'Oh ...' Sadie looks flustered. 'I'm not sure if that's allowed ...'

'Please,' says Danny with his most charming smile. 'She wants to know if it's the guy she likes. It could be the start of a beautiful romance. Right, Abs?'

Abby nods mutely.

Sadie hesitates. 'Can't you just ask him?' she says to Abby.

'It's complicated.' Abby clasps her hands together. 'Please ...' she begs.

Sadie blushes a little. 'Alright then, it can't hurt, can it?'

'Who said romance is dead?' says Danny, winking at Abby.

The florist takes them into the back room, switches on a TV screen, and starts rewinding the footage.

'Here we are. This is yesterday,' she says, stopping the recording and pressing FAST FORWARD.

Abby and Danny peer at the screen as people jerk in and out of the shop like an old black-and-white comedy sketch until Sadie freezes it at 2.15 in the afternoon.

'There,' she says. The screen shows a young, blonde girl approaching the counter carrying an orchid.

'I don't think she can be your secret admirer,' Danny comments.

Abby nods, though there is something strangely familiar about her. An uneasy feeling stirs inside. A thought nudges at the back of her mind but it slips away before she can grasp it.

'I feel like I've seen her before somewhere. Do you recognize her?'

Danny shakes his head. 'I don't think so. It's a small town. You've probably just seen her around.'

They trawl through the rest of the day's footage until the shop closes at 5.30 but no one else buys an orchid.

'Can we look at the footage from the day before?' asks Abby.

Just then the bell tinkles as someone enters the shop.

'Okay, just excuse me a minute.' The florist shows them how to operate the machine and goes out to the front of the shop to serve the customer.

They fast-forward through footage from the day before yesterday, watching intently as people enter and leave the shop. Quite a few men come in but none of them buy orchids.

'Wait. Stop. What about him?' exclaims Danny excitedly as they're approaching the end of the day. The clock in the corner of the screen says 5.20.

Abby rewinds to a middle-aged man in a long raincoat, who approaches the counter carrying an orchid. He has greying hair and a receding hairline. He puts the orchid on the table and seems to engage the florist in a long conversation. Abby's heart sinks as she watches him pay cash for the flower.

'Do you recognize him?'

Abby shakes her head. She looks closely at the screen. She's certain she's never seen him before in her life.

'Do you think he could be your stalker?' asks Danny.

'I don't think he could be. I've never even seen him before, so how he would know about my tattoo?'

She takes a photo of the frozen screen on her phone, just in case. Then they fast-forward through the last few minutes of the day.

'Did you find what you were looking for?' the assistant asks, coming back to the table with the CCTV monitor.

'I don't think so,' says Abby, disappointed. She'd been so sure this was her breakthrough.

'Oh, that's a shame. I hope it works out for you . . . with this guy.'

'Thank you.' Abby smiles politely.

'Well, it was worth a try,' says Danny outside the shop. 'I've got to dash. I'll see you later.'

'Mm,' Abby sighs. 'Thanks, Danny.' She waves him off, then walks back towards the house. She feels deflated. This has been yet another wild goose chase.

SEPTEMBER

Your baby is almost due now, though remember only roughly 5 per cent of babies arrive on their actual due date. You'll probably be feeling tired and clumsy and it might be difficult to get comfortable this month. On the bright side, the baby will drop lower in your pelvis, taking the pressure off your lungs and making it easier to breathe. Try to eat well and get plenty of rest.

Chapter Thirty-Two

The summer holidays are over, it's the start of a new term and Abby is stuck at home growing fat. Her weight has ballooned. She's put on almost two stone and can't see her feet anymore. Putting on shoes has become problematic. Most mornings she goes swimming because water is the only place where she doesn't feel like a beached whale. She feels as if she's in a kind of limbo waiting for the delivery, waiting to get rid of this unwelcome parasite inside her and become a single person again.

September doesn't bring any relief from the hot weather, just days and days of bright, dry sunshine and Abby finds herself struggling to keep cool. She can't walk far without getting a stich-like pain in her lower back, and a feeling of immense pressure on her pelvis. At the weekend, after only twenty minutes walking with Ellie and Hector in Ashridge Park, she has to stop. They sit in the café and order iced lemonade while Hector flops down, panting in the shade under the table. The café is crowded, mostly with young families. Abby looks around to see if anyone is watching her. It's become second nature to her now – the constant vigilance – the constant looking over her shoulder.

Ellie leans over and scratches Hector's neck. 'Have you thought any more about what we said?' she asks.

Abby is confused. She's still thinking about her stalker. 'About what?'

'About us adopting your baby. Rob and me.'

Abby takes a deep breath. This moment has been coming for a long time. She's been trying to delay it, but she knows it can't be avoided for much longer. In a way, she's glad Ellie has brought up the subject, so she doesn't have to.

'I'm going to go ahead with Joel and Maria – the couple that came to the house. I promised them I'd give them the baby.'

Ellie's body tenses like she's been stabbed in the gut. When she speaks, her voice is cold. 'So . . . you'd rather give up your baby to complete strangers than to me and Rob, is that it?'

'No.' *How can she explain it?* 'I know you would be a great mum and Rob would be a great dad. It's just I don't want to have anything to do with it when it's born. I want to forget this whole thing ever happened.'

'*Her.* You don't want anything to do with *her.*'

'Okay, with her. I don't want to be reminded of how she came to be.'

'That's pretty cold.'

'You don't understand. When I think about the father of this baby, I feel sick.'

'That's a bit overdramatic, Abby. I mean you don't even know who the father is. How can he make you feel sick?'

'Is it? I was raped, for Christ's sake, Ellie.' Abby's voice is shaking with rage. How can Ellie not see this? 'What do I say to her when she grows up and asks about her dad? Daddy's a creep who raped me and then stalked me.'

'How do you know you were raped? You don't even remember.' Ellie takes a deep, shuddering breath. 'You know what I think? I think you got drunk and slept with someone at the party. And you've made up this whole story to justify what happened.' Ellie pauses and flushes a little. 'I mean, I don't think you're consciously lying. I know you've convinced yourself it's true . . . but really, what proof do you have?'

Abby stares at her. She knew Ellie had doubts, but she can't believe what she's hearing. Not from Ellie – Ellie, who's always been her ally, her best friend.

'You really think that?' Abby says at last, feeling tears prick her eyes. 'What about the letters? The flowers. You think I made them up too? You think I wrote them to myself?'

Ellie shrugs. 'No, of course not. I think some kid in school has got a weird crush on you . . . I mean, whoever it is clearly has psychological problems, but I don't think they're dangerous and I don't think they're the father of your baby.' Ellie folds her hands in her lap. Her lips form a hard line. 'It's not just you anymore, Abby. You've got to think about what's best for the baby. You don't know anything about this couple. They could be child abusers, for all you know.'

'They seem like very nice people . . .'

But Ellie isn't listening. She doesn't want to hear anything positive about Joel and Maria. 'Whatever the father did or didn't do, that little person inside you has done nothing to you. She's half of you. How can you abandon her? It's not natural. It's selfish.'

This is too much. Abby is shaking with rage. *How dare she call her selfish?*

'*Me* selfish?' she raises her voice. 'Perhaps, you'd better take a look at yourself, Ellie. You're the selfish one here. You're not thinking about me at all. All you want is a baby for yourself. You don't care how you get it or give a fuck about what I'm going through. Just because you lost your baby doesn't give you the right to decide what everyone else does with theirs.'

Before Ellie has the chance to respond, Abby stands up and storms away down the footpath back toward town.

Chapter Thirty-Three

Abby shoves her clothes in the locker and slips the key on a red plastic band over her wrist. The swimming pool smells of chlorine and the air's warm and fuggy. A large, orange flume dominates one end of the pool and children are hurtling down, their shrieks of laughter echoing around the vaulted ceiling. She lowers herself into a lane and strikes out with determined strokes, enjoying the buoyancy of the water and trying to empty her mind through sheer physical exertion. But that's easier said than done. There's so much on her mind. She keeps returning to the argument with Ellie yesterday. She's already regretting the things she said. Okay, Ellie was out of order, but she really went too far, bringing up the baby she lost. It was cruel, and she's never been a cruel person. Maybe Ellie's right. Maybe she is being selfish.

Ellie has always been there for her and has done so much for her, a million small kindnesses over the years. Not to mention the way she and Rob have let her live in their home. This is the one time Ellie's ever asked Abby for anything and Abby has refused her. No wonder she's angry.

By the time she's finished ten lengths Abby has come to a decision. She's going to let Ellie adopt the baby. *It won't be so bad.* The baby need never know that Abby's her biological mother, and if it all gets too much, well, then she can always leave, go abroad, travel. Maybe that teaching-English-in-Thailand idea isn't such a bad one. She's always wanted to see a bit of the world.

It feels like a weight has lifted from her shoulders. She pictures Ellie's face when she tells her. How happy she's going to be. It feels good to be able to give Ellie the one thing she can't have, the one thing she wants more than anything.

Abby must be grinning because an old lady in a swimming cap smiles at her. 'Keep going,' she says, and it feels like profound advice. *Keep going.* That's all she can do, after all. As she gets out of the swimming pool and heads to the changing rooms she pictures Rob and Ellie in the park together pushing a toddler – a little curly-haired girl – in a swing, a child with the best start in life, because where could you find a better mother than Ellie?

Once she's dry and changed Abby finds her phone at the back of her locker. There are three missed calls, all from Ellie. Abby calls her straight back. She can't wait to tell Ellie her decision. But the phone just rings and rings until the recording says that *Elizabeth Campbell is not available, please try again later.* Abby switches off her phone. She's probably with a patient. It'll be better to wait and give her the news in person anyway.

On her way home Abby stops off at Mothercare and looks

at the bewildering array of baby products. She wants to buy something to symbolize her commitment to this decision, so she buys a pack of nappies, a couple of tiny white baby vests and sleepsuits and a new nightshirt for the hospital. At the supermarket she stops off and gets some food, the ingredients for lasagne, Ellie's favourite meal. Abby hates cooking, and Ellie and Rob are always teasing her about what a bad cook she is, but it will be a gesture, at least, a sign of how sorry she is for hurting Ellie and how committed she is to this decision.

For the first time in a long time, she feels properly happy and at peace. The sun is shining and just a couple of fluffy white clouds float by in the sky. Everything is going to be okay.

Even Rob notices the change in her. He's outside in the garden clipping the hedge and talking to their elderly neighbour.

'You look good, Abby. She's positively glowing, isn't she, Barbara? Still, not as sexy as you, though.'

'Oh, go on with you . . .' says Barbara. 'Isn't he an idiot?' She nods and smiles at Abby. 'You look about ready to pop.'

'Only another three weeks to go,' says Abby. She wants to tell Rob about her decision, but not before Ellie, so she says nothing. She'll wait until Ellie gets home from work. She'll tell them together over dinner. She pictures their faces when she tells them, as she stirs the cheese sauce for the lasagne. It feels good to be giving – to be thinking about something else for a change, instead of obsessing over her stalker. She wants to make this as special as possible, so she places a candle on the table. She even picks a flower from the garden and puts it in a vase in the centre of the table.

'Is it a special occasion?' says Rob, coming in and washing his muddy hands in the sink. 'You didn't need to go to all this effort for me, Abigail.'

'Not exactly . . .' Abby looks at the clock. Ellie is still not back. She should be home by now. She's usually back by seven o'clock at the latest.

'Well, I'm starving. What are we waiting for?' says Rob.

'Ellie, of course. Where's she got to?'

'Oh!' Rob slaps his head. 'Didn't you know? She's out with Carla for dinner this evening.'

Abby is gutted. All that effort wasted. 'Did she say what time she'd be back?'

Rob shrugs. 'I don't think she'll be late. She's got work early in the morning. She was a bit upset last night. What happened between you two?'

'It doesn't matter. We argued about something. But it's all sorted now.' Abby sighs. 'Anyway, it would be a shame to let this food go to waste.'

They sit and eat the lasagne in front of the TV. Then, after Rob has gone to bed, Abby waits up for Ellie, watching a police drama to pass the time. But when Ellie is still not home at twelve o'clock she starts to worry. She looks out of the window. The weather has turned. The stars and moon are obscured by dark clouds and there's an ominous rumble of thunder. It's not like Ellie to stay out so late on a week night, but maybe she's decided to wait for the storm to pass.

At one o'clock, when Abby goes to bed, Ellie is still not home. She guesses that Ellie hasn't forgiven her for the argument they had yesterday and is staying out late to avoid seeing her. She'll have to wait until tomorrow to tell her the good news.

Chapter Thirty-Four

There's the sound of heavy rain lashing against the window-pane and someone is banging on her door.

'Abby!' Rob puts his head round the door. 'Wake up!'

She rolls over, prizes open her eyes and looks at her alarm clock. It's 6.30 in the morning.

'What is it?' she says groggily as Rob comes in. He's dressed for work in a shirt and tie, but he, too, looks tired and bleary eyed.

'Shit, Rob. What kind of time is this?' she says. 'Get out of my room.'

'She's not back. She hasn't come back yet.'

Abby is immediately wide awake. It's worse than she thought. Ellie must be really angry with her. She sits up, clutching the sheet to her chest. Since it's been so hot, she's taken to sleeping in the nude. 'Okay, give me a minute. I'll be right down.'

Once Rob has gone she grabs underwear and picks up a pair of jeans and a T-shirt lying on the floor, pulling them on. She runs downstairs to the living room where Rob is pacing up and down.

'I don't know what to do. What should we do?' he says. 'I've been calling and calling but she's not answering her phone. I've got to go to work.' Usually so confident and buoyant, Rob seems lost and confused. His eyes are wild, and his hair is standing up on end. He looks like he's hardly slept at all. Abby has never seen him like this before. She realizes she's going to have to take charge of the situation.

'Call them and tell them you'll be late,' she says decisively. 'She probably stayed the night at Carla's. I'll phone the surgery. Maybe she's gone straight there.'

'But I don't understand. Why wouldn't she let us know where she was?'

Abby isn't worried. Not really. Not yet. She thinks she understands what has happened and feels a twinge of guilt but also of anger. Ellie is clearly still furious about what she said at the café, and she can see why she wouldn't tell her what she was doing, but it is weird that she hasn't let Rob know where she is either.

She boils the kettle and makes them both a cup of tea.

'It's okay,' she tells Rob. 'She'll be at work, you'll see.' But when she calls the surgery, no one answers. 'She's not there yet,' she says, disappointed.

'Have you got Carla's number?' asks Rob. He sips his tea, then stands up, raking agitated fingers through his hair. 'I can't remember it, but she must still be there, right?'

'Right. I haven't got her number, but I'll go around there after breakfast,' says Abby soothingly. 'You go to work. Don't worry, everything will be fine. She's probably just left her phone at work or something. You know what she's like.'

Rob nods and puts on his jacket. 'You'll call me as soon as you find out where she is?'

'Yes, don't worry. It'll be fine, you'll see.'

When Rob has gone she tries Ellie's number again. There's no answer. The phone just rings and rings. She pictures Ellie looking at her name flash up and ignoring it. *Damn you, Ellie,* she thinks. Then, after a few moments' thought she sends a text.

Ellie, I changed my mind. She's all yours. I'm not giving her up for adoption. Pls call me. Let's not fight.

A few minutes later she picks up her umbrella and heads out in the rain to Carla's house.

The lake in the park is overflowing and large sections are flooded right up to the bandstand. Carla's house is right next to the park. There are sodden toys scattered in the garden like the aftermath of a biblical disaster.

Carla opens the door, one baby in her arm and a toddler clinging to her leg. *Peppa Pig* is playing loudly from the living room. She looks harassed, her usually perfect make-up smudged and her hair slipping out of her ponytail.

'Abigail!' she exclaims, surprised. 'Come in. I'm sorry about the mess.'

'Actually, I just want to speak with Ellie. She's not answering her phone.'

Carla looks confused. 'Ellie? She's not here. Look, do you want to come in out of the rain?' She ushers Abby into a chaotic living room and clears a space on the sofa, throwing toys and baby clothes onto the floor.

Abby sits down. *Ellie must be on her way to work. They must have just missed each other*, she thinks. 'What time did she leave?'

Carla's eyes widen as she rocks the baby. 'What do you mean, what time did she leave? She hasn't been here.'

'She didn't come here after you went to dinner last night?'

'No. We didn't have dinner last night. Why?'

Abby's heart sinks. If Ellie didn't stay here last night, then where was she? A wave of sharp pain grips her belly and she clutches her stomach.

'Are you okay?'

'Yes, it's just Braxton Hicks, I think. I've been getting them for a week now.'

'Oh, you poor thing. They're horrible, aren't they? I had them for weeks with Oliver.' Carla puts the baby down in a car seat and it immediately starts bawling. She sits down and rocks the chair with her foot until he's quiet again.

Abby's pain subsides, and she thinks rapidly. She's trying to stay calm, trying not to panic. There must be some rational explanation for all this. 'Rob said Ellie was coming here for dinner last night.'

'Yes, well, that was the plan, but she rang me about lunch time and said she wasn't going to be able to make it.'

'Did she give any explanation? Did she say where she was going?'

Carla frowns. 'Not really. She just said something important had come up and that she needed to sort it out. I assumed it had something to do with work. She sounded a bit agitated, you know, like she didn't have much time to speak. Anyway, why are you asking? Has something happened?'

'She didn't come home last night,' Abby says. 'We don't know where she is . . .' She's trying hard not to cry, but her voice breaks a little. 'We had a fight the day before yesterday – a really serious fight.'

'Oh, sweetie.' Carla sits next to her and puts her arm round her. 'Don't worry. She's a grown woman. She can look after herself. And one thing I know about Ellie is that she loves you more than anything.'

This statement pushes Abby over the edge and she cries into Carla's shoulder, feeling bad for every unkind, ungenerous thought she's ever had about the woman.

'What you need is a cup of tea,' says Carla when Abby has calmed down a little. She heads to the kitchen.

Abby sips her tea distractedly while Carla makes a few phone calls to mutual friends. But no one seems to know where Ellie is. Abby's wasting her time here.

'Let me know if she contacts you,' Abby says, leaving her tea almost untouched and heading for the door.

'Of course – and can you tell me when you find her?' says Carla. 'Otherwise I'll worry.'

Where the hell are you, Ellie? How can you do this to us again? Abby thinks angrily as she walks back through the park. She feeds the anger. Anger is better than the alternative. Ellie has done this before. A few months after the baby died, during her worst period of depression, she took off without a word. Nobody knew where she was. Rob even reported her missing to the police and they were about to launch a search party when she reappeared as if nothing had happened. Abby and Rob never did find out where she'd been. It will be the same this time, Abby tells herself. Ellie will turn up when she's ready.

At home, she rings the surgery again and gets the receptionist, Nicky.

'Um, Ellie? I'm not sure. I haven't seen her. I'll check for you. Hold on a second.'

Abby waits, making a silent deal with a God she doesn't really believe in. But Nicky is back within a few seconds and the news isn't good.

'She's not in her office. She must be late. Do you want me to get her to call you when she gets in?'

'Yes, please.' Abby hangs up, her self-control melting. She's sobbing when Rob rings about five minutes later. She blows her nose and answers the phone with a flutter of hope. Maybe Rob has heard from her.

It's difficult to hear his voice over the shrieks of schoolkids in the background but it seems like Rob hasn't heard anything either. 'Have you found her yet? Was she at Carla's?' he asks.

'I'm afraid not. She wasn't there.' Abby sits on the stairs staring at a spider's web in the corner of the room.

'Oh, Jesus . . . Okay. I'm coming home. Stay there.'

Fifteen minutes later Rob is back. He flings his briefcase onto the sofa and sits down with his head in his hands. When he looks up, his eyes are red-rimmed and wild.

'What the hell are we going to do, Abigail? Should we go to the police? She promised she'd never, ever do this again. She's been so well recently. I never saw this coming.'

'I think there might be a reason.' Abby takes a deep breath. 'I think it might be my fault.'

Rob looks at her sharply. 'What makes you think that?'

Abby tells him about their argument, about the cruel and horrible things she said.

Rob shakes his head. 'She didn't seem that upset. I had the impression she was frustrated, more than anything. I also had the impression she was worried that she might have been unfair to you.' He stands up. 'There's no point in blaming yourself, Abby. We need to concentrate on finding her. Right, we need to think. Where else might she have gone?'

'I haven't tried Dad's yet. I didn't want to worry him unnecessarily, but I think I'm going to have to check.'

Rob nods enthusiastically. 'Yes, she might have gone there.' They both know they're clutching at straws. Ellie and Dad have never been that close, and with Sue round at Dad's all the time it seems like the last place Ellie would go.

Nevertheless, Abby picks up the phone and calls her dad.

He answers after a couple of rings, sounding a bit breathless. 'Oh . . . hello, Abigail. I'm just in the middle of something can I call you back?'

'No, Dad, it's important. It's about Ellie. We're trying to get hold of her.' Abby tries to make her voice calm. 'You know what she's like, she never answers her phone. We were just wondering if you've heard from her at all?'

Her dad sounds mildly alarmed. 'No. Why? Is everything okay?'

'Yes, yes, we're fine. It's just she's staying with a friend and we can't get hold of her.'

'Oh . . . well, no. I'll tell her to call you if I hear from her.'

Rob is hovering over her. 'No luck?' he says as she hangs up the phone.

Abby shakes her head. She's beginning to fear the worst.

Chapter Thirty-Five

'We'd like to report a missing person,' says Rob.

'Right.' The duty officer is not PC Whittaker this time, but a middle-aged woman with cropped brown hair and a brisk, efficient manner. She looks like the kind of tough no-nonsense person it's good to have on your side.

'How old is the missing person?' she asks. If she's shocked by their request she doesn't show it.

'She's thirty-three.'

'And what relation is she to you?'

'My wife.'

She looks enquiringly at Abby. Abby swallows. Reporting this to the police is bringing it home that something serious might have happened to Ellie and she's fighting back tears. 'She's my sister,' she manages.

The officer gives her a sympathetic smile.

'I'll have to fill in missing persons report,' she says more gently, opening the door and ushering them into the interview room. She gestures for Abby to sit down and pulls up a chair for Rob. 'Please sit down. I'm PC Mitchell, by the way,' she says, shaking their hands. 'Can I get you a coffee or a tea?'

'No, thanks,' Rob says, and Abby shakes her head. *Why is everything always so slow at this police station? Why is there never any sense of urgency? My sister is missing, maybe in danger, and all you can do is offer us tea,* she wants to shout. But she keeps her mouth shut. There's no point in antagonizing them.

'Right, okay then.' PC Mitchell takes out her phone and sits at the desk. She takes down a few basic details – Ellie's full name and address. Then she looks up at them both.

'And how long has she been missing?' she asks.

'About thirty-two hours,' says Rob. 'She didn't come home last night but we thought she might have stayed with a friend.'

'Oh?' PC Mitchell notes this down. 'And have you checked with the friend?'

Abby nods. 'Ellie was supposed to meet her for an evening meal, but she called her earlier in the day to say she couldn't make it.'

The officer chews her stylus thoughtfully. 'So, when was the last time you saw her?'

'Yesterday morning before work,' says Rob.

'And was her behaviour unusual in any way yesterday morning?'

'No . . .' He hesitates, looking at Abby. 'No.'

'And she turned up at work as usual?'

'Yes. She's a doctor. She works at the Church Road clinic.' Rob's eyelid is twitching, his face is pale. He looks, if it's possible, even worse than Abby feels. She takes his hand and squeezes it. His hand is cold and clammy, trembling slightly.

'So . . . what time did she leave work?'

'According to the receptionist, Ellie was still there when she left at seven o'clock,' Rob says.

PC Mitchell looks up, and tucks her hair behind her ear. 'Is that unusual?'

'No. She often stays late. She takes her job very seriously. She's a very responsible person generally. Something major would have had to have happened for her to miss work. That's why we're so worried about her.'

It's true, Abby thinks with a new lurch of fear. Ellie loves her work and is devoted to her patients. No matter how angry or upset she was, she would never let them down.

PC Mitchell nods. 'I see,' she says gravely. 'Well, we'll do all we can to help you find her. Can you tell me what she was wearing when she went missing?'

Rob frowns. 'I'm not sure. Her work clothes. She usually wears grey trousers and I think maybe a pink top. But I can't be sure.' He smacks himself in the head. 'God, I'm so useless!'

'Okay, don't worry, maybe someone will remember at her work. Does she have any medical conditions we should know about? Does she take any medication?'

'No . . .' Rob hesitates. 'She was on antidepressants for a while after we lost our baby a couple of years ago. But she's off them now.'

PC Mitchell puts her stylus down and folds her hands in front of her. She looks them both directly in the eyes. 'I'm sorry to have to ask this. But is there any reason to think she might be a danger to herself?'

'No,' says Rob uncertainly, then more emphatically, 'No, definitely not. I mean, she was upset that morning. But she was angry rather than anything else.'

'Angry?' PC Mitchell raises her eyebrows.

Abby feels sick with guilt. Is this all her fault? Did Ellie take off because of their argument?

'She was angry with me,' she says, and explains about the pregnancy and adoption, leaving out the part about the messages and her stalker. She doesn't want to complicate things. This isn't about her.

PC Mitchell listens without comment. When Abby's explanation is finished, she nods. 'Can you think of any places she might have gone? Places she likes to spend time?'

Rob and Abby exchange looks. Ellie doesn't really hang out anywhere. She's mostly at home or at work. 'She often goes walking in Ashridge Park,' says Abby eventually. 'But that's usually with the dog.'

PC Mitchell nods.

'Has she ever done anything like this before?'

Rob and Abby exchange a glance. They're both thinking the same thing: that if they tell the police officer about the last time, she will just assume that Ellie has run off again and give the case a lower priority. But then again, they are sure to have a record of the last time Rob reported her missing.

'Yes, but that was different,' says Rob. 'She'd just lost her baby, and even then, she turned up for work.'

'Where did she go on that occasion?'

Rob sighs. 'I don't know. She never told me.'

'Well.' PC Mitchell puts down her stylus and gives them a look that manages to convey empathy and resolve. 'So, overall, you think it's unlikely that she's gone missing voluntarily?'

'I don't know,' says Rob. Abby doesn't answer. Her mind is crowded with possibilities too terrible to contemplate. If Ellie hasn't taken off of her own accord, the alternative doesn't bear thinking about.

PC Mitchell sighs and sits back. 'Is there anything else you think we should know?'

Rob and Abby exchange glances. Abby thinks about her stalker – but there can't be a connection, can there? And she doesn't want to complicate the issue. She shakes her head. Rob runs a hand through his hair. 'Not that I can think of.'

'Well,' says PC Mitchell, and stands up. 'We'll do what we can here. We'll start off by ringing round the hospitals. In the meantime, there's quite a lot you can help us with. We need details of her bank account to see if she's spent any money. Also, you should go home and check what she's taken. Has she taken her credit card, for example? Clothes, toothbrush? Do you know where she keeps her passport?'

Rob nods.

'Good, check it's still there and check social media. Does she go on Facebook, Instagram, Twitter?'

'She's not into all that. She's a bit of a technophobe.'

'Look at her emails, then. Maybe they'll give you more of a clue as to what she's been thinking over the past few days.'

As they're leaving she says, 'Oh, and a recent photograph would be useful.'

It's raining again, a steady, dismal downpour, as they leave the police station.

'What now?' says Rob, standing outside in the porch, sheltering from the driving rain. He looks like a lost little boy.

'Do you think she could have gone walking in Ashridge Park and got lost?' Abby asks. She is gripped by a vision of Ellie lying in a ditch somewhere, injured.

'Maybe,' says Rob. 'It's worth a try. I'll take a look there once I've been to the bank. You go home and check what's missing. You might be better than me at noticing if any of her clothes are gone. See if you can find her passport too. It should be in the top drawer of the bedside table.'

She'll be back, Abby thinks as she trudges home through the rain. *She'll be back at home, sitting with her feet up in front of the telly as if nothing has happened. It'll be like last time.* She almost convinces herself this is true and hope blooms in her chest as she walks up the garden path.

But the emptiness of the silent house is palpable. Hector comes to greet her at the door, his tail wagging listlessly, and Abby pats him on the head. 'Where is she, eh, boy? Do you know?'

He pads back to his basket and slumps there with his head

on his paws, a reproachful look in his brown eyes, as if he knows that something is seriously wrong.

Evidence of Ellie is everywhere. Her cardigan draped over the back of a chair; her muddy trainers tossed by the door; the book she was reading, *Why Elephants Cry*, open face down on the coffee table. Abby picks it up and reads the page she was on, hoping for some kind of clue to her state of mind. But there's nothing useful in it.

'Oh, Ellie, where are you?' she says aloud. Now she's on her own, Abby is completely overwhelmed with fear. *What could have happened to her sister?* She sits down on the floor next to Hector and bursts into tears. Sobs rack her body and she clutches her belly, rocking backwards and forwards. After a few minutes she gives herself a shake and stands up. *This is no time to fall apart*, she thinks. *Ellie needs you.*

She rarely goes into Rob and Ellie's bedroom and it feels like an invasion of their privacy somehow, but she has to do this. Abby looks around the large messy room, wondering where to start. Hector's basket in the corner is covered in dog hairs. Ellie insisted on him sleeping in the room with them, but Rob put his foot down when she suggested he slept on their bed. Neither Ellie nor Rob are particularly tidy people. There are clothes on the floor and the bed is unmade. Ellie's dresser is a jumble of objects: her make-up case, her brush, her contact-lens case and glasses. Abby doesn't like that. If she'd intended to go away for a few days she would have taken at least her brush and contact lenses, wouldn't she? So, if she went away of her own accord, it must have been a spur-of-the-moment decision.

Next to the make-up case is a photo of Mum taken in a photographer's studio when she was in her early twenties. Abby picks it up. She looks so like Ellie in this photo, the same wavy blonde hair, the same determined chin. Abby feels self-control crumbling again, the pain of the loss of her mum mixing with and exacerbating her fears about Ellie.

'She's okay,' Abby says to her own reflection in the mirror. *She has to be.* Abby replaces the photograph and looks in Ellie's bedside drawer. There, as Rob had said she would, she finds Ellie's passport, along with an old diary from 2016. She flicks through it. There isn't much in there – a few birthdays, a vet's appointment. She flings it back in the drawer. How can an old diary help her? Next, she rifles through Ellie's wardrobe but it's impossible to tell if there's anything missing. In the en-suite, there are two toothbrushes still in the holder.

Perhaps her emails will reveal an appointment or a plan to visit a friend. Abby knows she's clutching at straws, but she's desperate.

She makes herself a cup of tea to try to steady her nerves as she waits for Rob and Ellie's computer to load. She connects to the internet and tries to log in to their emails. They have a shared account. A box flashes up asking for a password.

Shit. Of course. The email is password protected. She tries ringing Rob, but his phone rings upstairs. He's left it at home. What could the password be? It'll be something obvious, she's sure about that. She tries Rob and Ellie's date of birth, then 'Hector' and Ellie's date of birth in various combinations. Then she remembers the diary upstairs with all the notes and numbers in the back. *Of course*. Ellie has a terrible memory; she will have recorded her passwords.

Upstairs she looks in the diary and, sure enough, at the back Ellie has made a list of all her passwords. It's Ellie's date of birth, but combined with 'Ace', the name of the dog they had when they were kids. Abby runs downstairs, types it into the computer, and is rewarded by a revolving circle of white dots.

There are nine unread emails in the inbox. Abby starts with the most recent and works backwards. There are some general emails to Rob from school; and a couple of messages from Amazon suggesting items they might like to buy, and confirming the purchase of a baby carrier. There's a message from a friend called Heather asking if she wants to come to a school reunion at the end of October. Abby emails Heather explaining that Ellie has disappeared and asking her to contact them if she knows anything. Then she opens her own Facebook account and posts a message.

My beloved sister, Elizabeth Campbell, has been missing for two days now, and we are worried sick about her. If you know anything at all about where she might be, please let us know and please share this message.

She needs a photo of Ellie to attach to the message, so she goes back to the emails and clicks on the drive where Rob and Ellie keep most of their photos. She searches through the previous summer but there's nothing she can use. There are lots of photos of Hector, a few of Abby and Rob, but none of Ellie. Ellie is usually the one behind the camera. She tries another file, simply labelled *Photos*.

At first, she's confused, then embarrassed. It must be Rob's. But why would he keep his porn here, where Ellie can see it? Her first instinct is to close the file. It's not her business. But there's something odd about the pictures. She clicks on one, and it fills the screen. This is not your standard porn. Actually, it's quite artistic. It's a photo of a naked woman lying on a turquoise sheet. Her skin is pale and stark. She looks almost like a statue. There's something arresting about the light that makes Abby think it's a professionally taken shot. But there's also something disturbing. Maybe it's the way her face is hidden under a fan of brown hair, or the way the body seems so limp, as if she's asleep, or . . . dead. There's something about her. A horrible suspicion crawls in Abby's belly.

Heart hammering, she clicks on the next picture. This picture is undeniably pornographic. The woman's legs are splayed. But this time the face is clear. Her eyes are closed, her brown hair curling over her cheek, the large freckle on her right shoulder.

It's unmistakeable.

The picture is of Abby.

Chapter Thirty-Six

It must be a mistake.

The world tilts. Blackness curls at the edges of her mind and the room sways. She feels like she's about to faint. Hands shaking, she clicks through more photos. There are lots of them, all taken in different poses, arms and legs arranged like mannequins or like the victims of an ancient disaster – reminding her of pictures she's seen of the petrified bodies in Pompeii. In all of them her eyes are closed, or her head is turned away from the camera, her identity nullified. In one picture the photographer has left his finger over the lens. Abby stares at it for a long time. *Who owns that finger?* The answer seems inescapable. Only two people could have uploaded these photos. Ellie or Rob . . . and Abby is sure it wasn't Ellie.

But how is that even possible? Her mind recoils. The evidence in front of her eyes is too terrible to contemplate. Before she has time to gather her thoughts, she hears the squeak of the front gate. Someone crunches up the gravel pathway and there's the sound of the key scraping in the lock. He's back.

Shit. Heart thumping out of her chest, she closes the window with the photos and switches off the computer. The computer is turning itself off as Rob comes into the living room, kicks off his shoes and flings himself down on the sofa.

'She hasn't taken anything out of our joint account,' he says, his voice weary and flat.

Abby nods, not trusting herself to speak.

'Did you find anything?' he asks. 'What were you looking at just now?'

Abby shakes her head. *Stay calm. Stay calm.* 'Some emails,' she manages, her voice sounding surprisingly normal. 'There was nothing useful.'

'Jesus Christ.' Rob gives a heavy sigh. He puts his head in his hands. 'I can't believe this is happening.'

Abby feels cold and afraid. All she can see are the pictures – those disgusting pictures. She can't believe the man sitting in front of her took them. Rob, who she's always trusted, always thought of as a brother. The sense of betrayal is overwhelming. Inside her belly the baby kicks her hard and nausea grips her. She retches.

'Abby, are you okay?'

She dashes past him up the stairs to the bathroom and throws up repeatedly into the toilet. Then, with trembling hands, she locks the door and crouches with her back against the bath. For what feels like a long time she just sits there, rocking backwards and forwards, trying to control her breathing. What should she do? Then, just as she decides to move, she hears Rob's heavy footsteps on the stairs. She

311

freezes, panic gripping her. *There's nothing to be afraid of*, she tells herself. *It's only Rob.* But Rob is no longer the person she thought she knew. If he took those pictures, what else is he capable of?

Her heart is hammering through her chest as he knocks on the door.

'Abby, are you alright in there?'

She sits there, frozen.

'Come on, open the door. Talk to me. We've got to hold it together. Ellie's going to turn up. You'll see.'

He can't know anything's different. She mustn't let him suspect she knows. What would he do if he knew *she* knew? 'I'm just a bit queasy, that's all,' she says, trying to keep her voice from shaking. 'The baby's in an uncomfortable position.'

There's silence for a minute. Then, 'Oh, okay. Do you need anything?'

'No, thanks.'

He stands outside for a while, not moving. Abby waits, holding her breath. Then at last she hears him walk away downstairs, and then the sound of him clattering around in the kitchen. She scrabbles to her feet, unsure what to do. All she knows is she needs to get out of this house. Away from Rob.

Slowly, quietly, she opens the door and creeps across the landing and down the stairs.

He's in the kitchen on his laptop.

'You feeling better?' he asks, looking up and rubbing his

eyes. Abby forces herself to stop at the door, even though all her instincts are telling her to run. She must pretend everything is normal, or at least as normal as it can be with Ellie missing.

'I'm okay,' she says. 'It's just really hard being at home, with Ellie out there. I feel like I need to do something. I thought I'd go to the surgery. Maybe someone there will know something . . .' She heads for the door.

Rob stands up. 'Wait, I'll come with you.'

'No!' Abby says. Her voice comes out harsh and loud, and Rob blinks in surprise.

'I mean,' she says, trying to sound calm, 'someone should really wait here, in case she turns up or phones the landline.'

'You're right,' says Rob, sitting back down. 'Okay, I'll stay.'

Abby's breathing slows. 'I won't be long,' she says, slipping out of the door before he has the chance to change his mind.

Outside, the weather is still foul, and Abby welcomes the rain and wind battering her face. But no amount of rain can drive away the dirtiness and disgust she feels. She walks quickly, bending her head against the wind and rain. Every step taking her further away from the house – a place where she no longer feels safe.

'Wait!'

She's halfway down the road when she hears him shouting behind her. She pretends she hasn't heard and speeds up. But, too late, he comes running up and grabs her by the shoulder.

'Didn't you hear me?' he says.

'I . . .'

'Here, I just wanted to give you this.' She looks down and sees he's holding out an umbrella.

'You'll get soaked,' he says.

'Thank you,' she manages, and using all her self-control, she turns and walks away slowly down the road until she turns and sees he's back inside the house. Then, despite the fact she's eight months pregnant, she runs through the rain, not stopping to look back, all the way to Danny's house.

Twenty minutes later she's knocking on Danny's door.

'Abigail,' says Mark, standing awkwardly in the doorway, his arms hanging limply by his side. 'What are you doing here? Are you okay?'

Abby unfurls her umbrella, trying to catch her breath and clutching her belly. 'Is Danny around?' she gasps. 'I need to talk to him.'

'He's not here. He's been staying with Will.'

'Will?'

'Yes, Will, his new boyfriend.'

'Oh . . . yes.' Abby's been so wrapped up in her own concerns, she'd forgotten that Danny had a new man in his life.

'He should be back soon. He said he'd be back this evening. Do you want to come in and wait?' says Mark, standing back to let her in.

Abby takes off her cardigan, which is sopping wet, and follows him into the kitchen. 'I'll get you some dry clothes.

Hang on.' Mark disappears and then reappears with a T-shirt, a pair of shorts and a towel for her to dry her hair.

'You can change in my room.'

In Mark's room she pulls on the T-shirt and shorts which, with their elasticated waist, fit surprisingly well around her swollen belly. Then she rubs her hair dry. She catches a glance of herself in the mirror and gasps. She looks like a mad woman. Her hair is sticking out at strange angles and her mascara has run down her face. She wipes away the black smudges with a trembling hand and smooths down her hair.

It's okay, she says to herself, as if she were soothing a baby. *It's okay.*

But of course, she can't fool herself. Everything is far from okay.

Downstairs Mark is making a cup of tea. He slops a mug down on the table in front of her. Abby picks it up, but her hand is trembling so much she puts it down again without drinking it.

'Is everything alright, Abigail? You seem ... um ... a bit distracted.'

Where can she start? She's getting a headache. Pain gnawing at her temples.

'It's my sister, Ellie. She's gone missing.'

'Jesus.' He stares at her open mouthed. 'Since when?'

'Since the day before yesterday.'

Mark nods. He takes off his glasses and cleans them. Then he puts them back on and blinks at her.

'And you've got no idea where she is?'

'No, but I think it might be my fault.' She explains about the argument she had with Ellie over the baby. She doesn't mention the photos. She's not ready to talk about that yet, especially not with Mark. Even the thought of it makes her nauseous and dizzy.

Mark listens without comment. He doesn't say the usual things you might expect, like 'She'll turn up' or 'You can't blame yourself.' He just listens and sips his tea. 'You must be very worried,' he says at last, and he reaches out across the table and pats her hand awkwardly.

'Worried' isn't the word for what she's feeling right now. 'Broken', 'desperate' or 'overwhelmed' might be better words. And there's something about his clumsy sympathy that breaks her self-control. All the pent-up anxiety of the day – her fear for Ellie and the shock and horror of the photographs – bubbles to the surface and she bursts into tears.

Mark looks alarmed and fetches a box of tissues.

'Here,' he says, offering them to Abby.

Abby wipes her eyes and blows her nose. 'I should be out there right now looking for her, not sitting here being useless,' she says, trying to contain her tears. She stands up with a sudden determination, but as she does, a wave of pain washes over her and she clutches her belly.

'Are you okay? You're not going into labour, are you?' Mark hovers anxiously.

'No, it's just Braxton Hicks. They're like practice contractions,' she explains, because Mark looks confused. 'Do you have a raincoat I can borrow?' She heads towards the door.

'You're not well enough to go out!' Mark says firmly, taking her arm and steering her back to her seat. 'Why don't you have a rest for a bit? At least wait until your clothes are dry. You can use Danny's room.' Abby hesitates. She does feel unwell. Her head is pounding, and she feels sick – the stress of the past few hours catching up with her. She needs to calm down and clear her thoughts, before she'll be any use to anyone. 'Perhaps just for a few minutes.'

Mark shows her to Danny's room, and she crawls onto the bed and lies on top of the duvet.

'I'll be downstairs if you need anything,' he says.

Once he's gone, she lies on the bed, clutching her head, trying to empty her mind, but thoughts keep slithering in like snakes, and the photos she saw flash up in her mind like a horror movie. *When did Rob take them? He had plenty of opportunity*, she thinks. It would be easy enough for him to sneak into her bedroom at night, while she was asleep. That turquoise sheet she was lying on in the photo could easily be hers. She has a set exactly that shade. *But she would have woken up, surely – unless he'd drugged her.*

She sits up, her breath coming in short, shallow gasps, and she turns the idea over in her mind, looking for flaws. But, yes, it makes sense. It is possible and the idea that she was drugged has refused to go away. That evening when Andrew Wilson dropped her home from the party on New Year's Eve, Ellie was already in bed – but Rob was still up. He said himself he'd poured her a glass of water. How easy would it have been for him to slip something inside? There

317

are all sorts of drugs in Ellie's doctor's bag. Any after-effect she would put down to a hangover. Are the photos evidence of his rape – a sort of sick souvenir?

She clutches her head and groans in pain. The thought is abhorrent, disgusting, but it won't go away, and more thoughts follow. Maybe that wasn't the first time, either. Just before Christmas, Ellie was away at a conference. It was the day she'd had her biopsy. She'd sat up late in the evening with Rob drinking and woke up in the morning feeling like shit. At the time she'd put it down to the after-effects of mixing anaesthetic and alcohol, but what if it hadn't been that at all?

Anger and disgust curdle in her stomach. *How dare he?* she thinks. How could he do this to her? Sure, she's not always got on with him, but she would never have imagined he could do something like this. It leaves a sour taste in her mouth. And it's not just her that he's betrayed. He's betrayed Ellie, too. Because what would it do to Ellie if she knew? It would destroy her.

Then another thought comes, even more horrible. *What if Ellie does know? What if she found out somehow? Maybe she saw the photos. After all, they were on their shared account. It would explain why she'd run off and why she hadn't contacted Rob. Maybe she thinks that the photos were taken with Abby's consent. What if Ellie thinks that they were having an affair?* It doesn't bear thinking about.

Abby closes her eyes. *Where would Ellie go?* She pictures Ellie the day she told her about her pregnancy, standing in the dappled sunlight under a chestnut tree by the KEEP OUT sign. '*I used to come here a lot, after I lost the baby,*' she had said.

Of course! That's it. It must be.

Abby's just getting out of bed when she hears the front door open and the sound of Danny talking. She puts on her shoes and goes downstairs. Danny's in the kitchen talking to Mark. When Abby comes in, he turns, gives her a hug and kisses her on top of her head.

'Mark told me about Ellie,' he says. 'I'm so sorry, Abs. We'll find her, don't you worry.'

'Yes, thank you,' Abby says impatiently, picking up her umbrella. 'I think I know where she might have gone.'

'Oh?'

'There's a place in Ashridge Wood. I'm going to see if I can find her.'

'Wait, are you sure you're well enough?' Danny says, blocking her exit. 'At least let me come with you. I can drive you there.'

Abby nods. 'Fine, let's go.' She's anxious to get going. Every second could count if Ellie were injured or hurt.

The rain eases up and by the time they reach the park it's barely even spitting. Danny squeezes into a parking space and they get out of the car and head up the main ride in silence. Abby is so lost in her own thoughts she almost forgets Danny's there. How long has this whole thing with Rob been going on? She examines incidents in the past from this new perspective, turning them over in her mind. There was the time he accidentally walked in on

319

her in the shower, and there was the way he was so keen for her to move in with them, how he helped secure her job at Elmgrove Comprehensive. Was it all part of a plan? Had he meant to make her part of his sick fantasies right from the start?

'Which way?' says Danny as they reach the spot where the main path separates into two. One branches off through the woods, leading to the house and the lake, and the other leads to the top of the pathway and the polo fields beyond.

'This way,' says Abby, heading through the trees. She shakes off thoughts of Rob. She needs to focus on the here and now, on Ellie. What she's going to do about Rob can wait till later.

'Ellie!' she calls out every two minutes. Listening for an answering call. But there is no answer, just the coo of a wood pigeon, the steady drip of rainwater falling from the sodden trees.

'Here,' she says, as they reach the fields with the horses and the fenced-off part of the park.

Danny hangs back. 'But it says private property.'

'I know, but Ellie used to come here just after the baby died. She told me.'

There's a small gap in the fence and Abby squeezes through, holding up the barbed wire for Danny to follow. He hesitates, then ducks under. For a couple of minutes they walk through a wooded area, which opens into a small clearing with a view of the big house. There's a lake with a wooden jetty. Next to the lake, half hidden in the trees, there's an old ruined cottage. The door is hanging off its hinges and the windows are smashed.

'Ellie!' Abby calls out. She peers into the dark, dank interior. Nothing. Just a few crushed cans of Coke, cigarette butts and an empty crisp packet.

'She's not here,' she says. Disappointment weighs heavily on her. She was so sure. She sits on the wooden jetty and Danny sits next to her. It's getting dark. On the lake a heron dips its beak in the water, then spreads it wide wings and flaps away.

'You thought Ellie would be here?' Danny says. 'Why?'

'I thought maybe she'd come to be alone. I thought she'd found out . . .'

'Found out what?'

Then it all rushes out, bubbling to the surface like sewage from a blocked drain – finding the photographs, how she thinks Rob has raped her, may in fact be the father of the baby she's carrying.

Danny picks up a stone and throws it into the water. It lands, creating a spreading ripple of circles on the dark water. He looks shocked and confused.

'I sound insane, I know.'

'Not insane, no. So, it was Rob? I mean . . .' He tails off, shaking his head.

'It must have been. Who else could have uploaded them? The only other person with access is Ellie and that makes no sense.'

Danny nods slowly. 'What are you going to do?'

'I don't know yet. All I know is I can't go back there tonight. I can't face seeing him,' says Abby. 'Can I stay at your house?'

'Of course.'

When they get back to Danny's house he makes some beans on toast and tries to persuade her to eat. She's pushing the food around her plate when her phone rings. *Rob calling* flashes up on the screen.

'It's him.' She automatically hits END CALL and drops the phone as if a cockroach has flown into her hand.

'You should call him back,' says Danny. 'Or he'll wonder what's going on.'

She doesn't want to speak to Rob ever again. But Danny's right. If she doesn't, it will alert him to the fact that she knows what he's done.

'Would you rather I spoke to him?' asks Danny.

But she shakes her head. She can do this. She has to do this.

Rob answers the phone on the second ring.

'Abby, thank God. I've been trying to get hold of you for ages. Where the hell are you?'

The sound of his voice, so familiar and yet so unfamiliar, makes her feel sick. She struggles to sound normal.

'Um, I'm at a friend's house,' she says. 'I just needed to get away for a bit.'

'Oh . . . okay. Well, as long as you're alright.'

'I'm okay.'

322

'Well, I just wanted to tell you that the police are organizing a search party tomorrow morning in Ashridge Wood.'

'Ashridge Wood,' she repeats stupidly.

'Yes. Apparently, someone at her work said she mentioned going for a walk there. Anyway, I thought you'd want to know. Maybe you could put it up on Facebook? Get as many of your friends involved as possible. The more people the better.'

'Okay, I'll do that.' She puts down the phone trembling.

'I hate him,' she says to Danny. 'I hate him so much.'

Danny puts his arm around her. 'Rob, though? I just can't believe that Rob could ... Are you sure this isn't all some kind of misunderstanding?'

She shrugs him off impatiently. 'No, bring me your laptop. I want to show you what I found.'

She wishes she could erase the pictures from existence and it's humiliating for Danny to see them, but she knows that if Danny is to believe Rob could do this, she's going to have to show him.

She logs in to Ellie's email.

'There,' she says, opening the folder of photos.

Danny scrolls through, an increasingly grave expression on his face. 'You have no memory of these being taken?' he asks.

'No. He must have drugged me.' Abby moves away, so she can't see the pictures. She has no desire to see them again.

'Look at this,' says Danny suddenly. 'This isn't you, is it?'

Reluctantly, she moves behind him and looks over his

shoulder. The picture on the screen is posed in a similar way to the first picture of her. One leg bent, the other straight, her head turned away from the camera, hair fanning over her face. But it isn't Abby. It's a stranger: a blonde woman in her thirties, plump-thighed, heavy-breasted. Danny clicks through more photos of her, some of which show her face.

'Do you know who she is?' he asks.

Abby shakes her head. Danny carries on and they come to yet another woman, or girl. She looks heartbreakingly young, her caramel-coloured skin stark against the white sheet. In one photo her mouth is hanging open and there is the glint of braces on her teeth.

'Tanseela,' Abby breathes. *Her instincts were right all along*, she thinks. There *was* a connection. *But how could he? That sweet, young girl, so innocent, so trusting.* She turns away in disgust.

'We have to take these to the police,' Danny says grimly, switching off the laptop and snapping it shut.

'Yes, I know . . . but not yet.' Abby paces the room, torn between desire for justice and her fear for Ellie. But she must prioritize Ellie right now. 'I don't want to distract them from finding Ellie.'

'Are you sure?'

Abby nods. She feels suddenly overwhelmingly tired. 'I think I'm going to head to bed,' she says.

'Sure,' says Danny. 'You can sleep in my room.'

Abby lets him bundle her upstairs. She sits on the bed and he takes off her shoes and she collapses under the covers.

'See you in the morning,' he says, stroking her hair.

'Yes, thanks, Danny,' she murmurs, closing her eyes. The best thing she can do now is sleep so that her head is clear for the morning. Her last thought as she drifts off to sleep is that first thing tomorrow she'll go to Ellie's work and talk to Dr Rowe, Dr Samuel, the receptionist and the nurses for herself to check exactly what Ellie said about going to Ashridge Wood. Then, after that, she'll join the search party. The thought of seeing Rob again fills her with dread but she knows she has to face him for Ellie's sake.

In the middle of the night she wakes up gripped by terror, her heart pummelling against her chest. An idea has forced its way into her head, fully formed. It's an awful, terrifying idea but she can't shake it off as she lies there shivering in the dark.

What if Ellie had confronted Rob about the photos? Wouldn't that be a more likely thing for Ellie to do? Ellie's never been one to shy away from a confrontation. Maybe she threatened to go to the police and Rob couldn't let her.

What if Rob had killed Ellie?

Chapter Thirty-Seven

In the morning light the fears of last night seem absurd. Rob may be many things, but he would never hurt Ellie, she's sure of that. Abby gets out of bed feeling determined. Today is the day they will find Ellie. She needs to believe that. She gets out of bed, dresses and heads out of the house before Danny and Mark are awake.

There's a fragment of rainbow in the sky behind the surgery, vanishing in a large dark grey cloud. Maybe it's a good sign. Abby isn't one who generally believes in signs and omens, but just now she's clinging to whatever she can. She reaches the surgery door just as the receptionist, Nicky, pulls up and gets out of her car. 'Hello, Abigail. Any news of Ellie?' she asks, unlocking the front door.

'No. The search party is this morning.' Abby follows Nicky into reception. 'That's why I'm here, actually. You told the police she said she was going for a walk in Ashridge Park after work? Did she say where exactly?'

Nicky shakes her head. She hangs up her coat and turns on

her computer. 'No, it was Dr Rowe she spoke to. I left early on Tuesday. My son had a dentist's appointment.'

'Did you talk to her at all? Did she say or do anything out of the ordinary?'

The phone rings and Nicky answers it. '*Sorry,*' she mouths to Abby. 'The locum,' she says, hanging up. 'He got lost on his way here.' She twists the silver chain around her neck. 'No, I can't think of anything out of the ordinary. She seemed normal. A little bit stressed maybe. She got locked out of her computer and she was having problems accessing her patient files.'

Abby can all too easily imagine that.

'Do you want to wait and talk to Simon?' Nicky looks at her watch. 'He should be here any minute.'

Abby goes through to the waiting room. There is one other person in there, an elderly lady with wrinkled tights. Abby smiles at her vaguely and looks at her watch. She doesn't have much time before she needs to be in Ashridge Wood. But she doesn't have to wait long. About ten minutes later, Dr Rowe bustles in.

'Abigail. I'm so sorry. Is there any news about Ellie?' he asks, clasping her hands.

Abby shakes her head.

'Nicky said you wanted to talk to me?'

'Yes. You told the police you thought she'd gone to the park. What exactly did she say?'

'Let's go to my office where we can talk in private.' He steers her into his surgery. 'Take a seat.'

He turns on his computer. Then he sits opposite Abby, crossing his legs. Abby sits down, her eyes skimming over his desk and resting on the photograph of Dr Rowe with his family, smiling at the camera. She focuses on the daughter. There's something familiar about her – the fair hair, the slight stoop of the shoulders. She reminds her of Ellie, Abby realizes, and feels a pang of longing for her sister. She turns away, trying not to cry and looks into Dr Rowe's sympathetic blue eyes.

'Did Ellie say that she was definitely going to the park? Are you sure it was Ashridge?'

He frowns. 'I can't remember her exact words. But I had the impression that she was going there. To clear her head, I think she said.'

'Did she say which part? She didn't mention a lake?'

'I'm afraid not. Sorry.' His eyes skim down to her belly. 'You look ready to pop. How are you?'

Abby runs a hand over her belly. 'I'm not due for another two weeks.' She leans forward. 'What time did she leave?'

Dr Rowe frowns. 'Now, let me see, she was still here when I left. She's often the last to leave.' He looks at his watch. 'I'm sorry, Abigail, but I have a patient in a minute.'

'There's just one more thing I wanted to ask. Please.'

'Of course.'

'Was Ellie on any kind of medication? I know you're not meant to break doctor–patient confidentiality, but it could be important.'

He sighs. 'The police asked me about that too. The truth

is, she came to see me about feeling down a few months ago, around mid-May . . .' *About the time Abby first told her about her pregnancy.* Ellie had seemed to take it in her stride. *Had she been pretending all the time?* Abby shifts in her seat and there's a sharp pain, like an iron fist clenching. She clutches her stomach and groans.

'Are you okay?' Dr Rowe is watching her, his eyes full of concern.

Abby nods and grits her teeth. 'I think it's just Braxton Hicks,' she says. But this is more intense than any contractions she's experienced previously.

'What did you prescribe?' she asks, trying to focus on Ellie.

'I suggested a course of cognitive therapy and anti-depressants.'

'What kind?'

He scrawls down the name on a piece of paper for Abby.

'Who was the therapist?'

He clicks the computer. 'An excellent therapist. Michelle Harper.'

'Can you give me her number?'

'Sure.'

He scribbles a number beneath the name of the drug, and hands it to Abby. Abby folds it and puts it in her handbag. *It will probably amount to nothing but you never know what could be important.*

'Well, if that's all . . .'

But just then there is another contraction, even more

intense than the last. Abby's legs tremble and she doubles over in pain.

Dr Rowe looks at his watch, timing her. 'That's a minute since the last one,' he says. 'It looks like you're in labour. Let me have a look.'

'I can't be,' she says, but as she speaks an enormous tidal wave of pain washes over her and she blanks out for a minute.

When she comes round, Dr Rowe is smiling down at her.

'Well, thank you for your help,' she says staggering to her feet, trying to ignore the pain. 'I've got to go and join the search party.'

'Not now, you can't,' he says. 'We need to get you to a hospital.'

He makes a phone call. 'Hey, Nicky. Can you cancel my appointments? We've got an emergency here.'

'What about your patients?' Abby says weakly. 'You could just call an ambulance for me.'

'No, no, it's alright. They'll take forever. I can take you.'

It's odd, him insisting on taking her. But Abby is in too much pain to wonder why.

Chapter Thirty-Eight

Dr Rowe's black SUV is parked at the back of the surgery. He puts his bag in the boot and reluctantly Abby climbs up in the passenger seat.

'I feel better now,' she says. 'I think it was just Braxton Hicks. Maybe you could drop me at Ashridge Wood? The north gate?'

Dr Rowe chuckles gently. 'I'm afraid not, Abby. You're definitely in labour. Childbirth isn't something you can postpone.'

A brief flurry of rain splatters against the windscreen and Dr Rowe puts on the windscreen wipers as they drive through the town centre. The pain is bad, but Abby can manage it, she thinks. When she gets to hospital she'll ask for pain relief. *Why not? Why feel pain when you don't have to? There's enough pain and suffering in the world.* There's a thought at the back of her mind, niggling away, but the pain takes over and she doesn't have room for anything else.

'Do you want to call somebody? Your father? Your brother-in-law? I've got his number – I can call him?'

Abby shakes her head vehemently. The last person she wants at the birth is Rob. The only person she really wants is Ellie. Pain mingles with anger and grief, and she wipes away a tear. *Ellie will be so disappointed to miss this*, she thinks.

'Things aren't exactly good between me and Rob at the moment,' she says, making the understatement of the year. 'Did Ellie mention anything about photographs?'

'What?' says Dr Rowe sharply.

'The day before she went missing, she didn't mention some photos that Rob took, did she? Or being angry with me or Rob?'

'Oh, no.'

Of course Ellie wouldn't have shared something like that with Dr Rowe. If she'd have told anyone, it would have been Carla.

They drive past allotments and the golf club heading onto the old Cheltenham road. It's not the most direct route but Abby guesses that Dr Rowe is trying to avoid the traffic.

'I always wanted more children,' says Dr Rowe, 'but my wife didn't want any more after my daughter was born. She had two difficult pregnancies. Endometriosis. Have you thought of a name for her yet ... ?'

'Not yet,' says Abby. She'll leave that to Ellie. *Ellie can have whatever she wants, if only she'll come back.*

'*Her*,' she says slowly. 'How do you know it's a girl?'

'Oh?' Dr Rowe swerves to avoid a cyclist. 'It was in your medical files from the scan.'

Abby nods. 'I'll probably leave choosing the name to her adoptive parents.'

'I thought you had changed your mind about that? You were going to let Ellie adopt, no?'

There's a long silence. Abby is thinking hard. She stares straight ahead at the winding road as they drive through a tunnel of trees. Something is scuttling away at the back of her head. She tries to grasp it, but it slips away in another wave of pain. Then she has it.

Ellie is the only person she's told about her change of heart, and she only told her in a text, yesterday morning. Fourteen hours after Dr Rowe supposedly last saw her. The thought is slow to take root. Everything has to be looked at from a different angle. But then something else clicks into place inside her head: the photograph on Dr Rowe's desk of his daughter. She remembers now where she's seen her before. It was on the CCTV footage in the florist's. She was the girl buying the orchid.

Another memory comes hard on its heels, screaming for attention . . .

Just before her biopsy. Dr Rowe perched on the desk smiling down at her. Helen coming in clutching her head.

'I'm really not feeling well,' she said.

'It's okay, you go on home. I'll call the agency and get someone to cover you.' Dr Rowe smiled kindly. As Helen slipped out he picked up the phone. He stood with the phone to his ear, waiting silently. 'No answer I'm afraid,' he said after a while. 'But I should think that we'll manage without a nurse, so long as you're okay with that, Abigail?'

Abby nodded. She was too busy worrying about the knife she'd seen to think about the ethics or legality of him performing the surgery without a nurse present. Besides, she knew Dr Rowe. He was Ellie's colleague. She trusted him.

Dr Rowe looked at her expression and laughed.

'You don't have to look so afraid! I can sedate you if you like. Or put you under completely? You won't remember a thing.'

What if she's been looking at this whole thing from the wrong perspective all this time? What if this baby wasn't conceived on New Year's Eve? What if she conceived two weeks earlier when she had the biopsy? Hadn't the sonographer said the baby was unusually developed for its due date? And now here she was in labour exactly two weeks early.

Perhaps she's going insane. Suspicion is eating away at her like a worm. *First Rob, now Dr Rowe. It can't be true.* But there's no getting around the adoption thing. There's no way he can know about her decision unless he saw the phone message she sent to Ellie.

Abby is suddenly overwhelmed by a terrible, chilling certainty. *It's him: this is the man that raped her and now he's done something to Ellie, too.* Disgust and pain well up inside her and she vomits all over the dashboard.

'Oh dear,' says Dr Rowe. He swerves into a lay-by. He seems almost as agitated as Abby.

Abby acts instinctively, through fear. As soon as he stops, she opens the door and tries to get out. She needs to get out, away from this monster.

'Where do you think you're going?' he says, gripping her arm tightly, pulling her back into the car. He leans across her, slams the door shut and applies the centralized locking.

Keep calm, don't panic. Don't let him know you suspect anything.

'I just need to get out for a minute,' she says, trembling. 'I think I'm going to throw up again.'

But it's too late. *He knows.* Her face has given it away, or else he's realized his mistake about the adoption.

'You're shaking, Abigail. Don't worry, I'm not going to hurt you. You're the mother of my child. But you know that, don't you?' He opens the glove compartment, gets out a cloth and wipes the dashboard. Then tenderly, carefully, wipes her mouth.

You're the mother of my child. It's something else hearing it from his lips. No more pretending.

'It was you,' Abby blurts. 'You raped me, took photos of me while I was unconscious. And you've done it to other women too, haven't you?'

He doesn't answer immediately. He starts the engine again and drives on, his mouth set in a grim line. Abby looks out of the window at the gently rolling Cotswold hills. The sun has come out again; its rays dance and glitter on the river, mocking her.

Dr Rowe grips the wheel.

'There have been other women, Abigail, it's true, but you're special.' He's driving slowly, crawling along the road. A car behind hoots, swerves and overtakes on a blind corner. He doesn't seem to notice. 'Do you think things happen for a reason, Abigail?' he says dreamily. 'Because I do. When I found out you were pregnant, I knew it was all part of a plan. You were destined to be the mother of my child.'

'You sent me all those flowers and messages too. You made your daughter buy that orchid for me. Why?'

'I have to admit you were nothing to me at first. It was just sex. Like with all the others. But when you came to my surgery that day, I knew you were special then. This child is special. You must have felt it too. We are meant to be. I think you sense it too, deep inside, but you're afraid of it. That's why you decided to throw yourself away on that worthless young man.'

He's crazy, Abby realizes. *Completely deranged.*

They wind slowly through a small village past a country pub. There's a woman outside watering the window boxes. So near and yet so far. Could she bang on the window, attract her attention? No, that would only provoke him. She just needs to sit tight, go along with his lunacy until they reach the hospital. He's told her he won't hurt her. She holds on to that.

But just out of the village, he veers off the road onto a small lane into the woods, and Abby's heart plummets.

'Where are you going?' she asks, trying to stay calm.

He doesn't answer. Despite the sunshine the road goes through a dark tunnel of trees. The road gets narrower and there is no other traffic. They are driving further and further into the depths of the forest.

'This isn't the way to the hospital. I need to go to hospital,' she says.

'That's not possible I'm afraid.'

He turns again down a dirt track and the car bumps over

the muddy ground. And then another turning, down an even narrower road, almost a footpath. After what feels like forever, he pulls into a passing point and kills the engine. Abby looks around desperately. *Where the hell are they? It's the middle of the forest.* They are next to a small wooden gate, but no one has been through the gate for a long time. It's completely overgrown with weeds and stinging nettles.

'What are we doing here?' says Abby, and she hates herself for the way she sounds, her voice a small, scared whisper.

Dr Rowe drums his fingers on the wheel and turns to her sighing.

'I'd like to trust you, Abigail, but I don't think I can, can I? If I take you to hospital, you'll tell someone about us and they won't understand.'

'I won't tell anyone, I promise.' Abby has started crying, tears of terror and snot running down her nose. She wipes the snot away with her sleeve.

'Don't cry, Abigail. You'll spoil your beautiful face.'

She clambers out of the car. Her heart is firing off like a machine gun, her mind racing. She watches as he opens the boot, rummaging inside for something. This is her chance while he's distracted. She acts instinctively, running back along the path they've taken. But she gets no further than three metres before a wave of pain surges over her. She calls out in agony and frustration, and doubles over, clutching her belly. Her legs are shaking as if she's been electrocuted. She feels helpless, like livestock, as Dr Rowe strolls up behind her and calmly clamps his hand over her mouth.

'You silly girl,' he says. 'You're in labour. Where do you think you're going?' She doesn't struggle much after that, and she waits, docile, as he pushes the gate open and bundles her through. Then they are stumbling up an escarpment through dense trees. They don't go far, just until the path is out of sight. He stops and forces her roughly down to the ground against a tree trunk.

'You're too stubborn for your own good. Just like your sister,' he says.

At the mention of Ellie, Abby starts crying again.

'What have you done with Ellie?' she whimpers.

Dr Rowe sighs, and sits down next to her, placing his briefcase and his doctor's bag next to him on the ground. 'It's a shame. I didn't want to hurt her, you know that. I always liked Elizabeth. I thought she was a very fine doctor. But she had to go poking her nose into things that didn't concern her.'

'She found the photographs on your computer,' Abby says. She sees suddenly how it must have happened. When Ellie couldn't access her patient files on her own computer she must have tried Dr Rowe's. Instead of finding the files, she must have stumbled on the photos of Abby and the other women. Abby tries to imagine what she must have felt. *Shock? Horror? Had she tried to phone her then? Was that what the missed calls were? If only she had answered.* Whatever Ellie's feelings were, she'd had the presence of mind to save the pictures to her email. *Then what? Did she confront him?*

Oh, Ellie, she thinks. That's precisely what Ellie would have done – especially if she thought she was defending her little sister.

Dr Rowe puts his head in his hands. 'What a mess,' he says. After a while he lifts his head and rubs his eyes. 'She was going to tell the police. I couldn't let her. I would have lost everything. My job, my children. Our baby.'

'What did you do to her?' Abby stares at him in horror.

He stares straight ahead as if he's looking at something in the distance.

'The human skull is made up of twenty-two bones. It's surprisingly easy to break, considering it protects the brain. Bad design. The weakest point is where the four bones meet; the frontal, the parietal, the sphenoid and temporal bones.'

Abby bellows with rage. She tries to stand up. She would kill him now if she could. 'What the fuck did you do to her?' she screams.

'You need to shut the hell up,' he snaps, striding over and pushing her back down. He pulls a roll of tape from his bag, wrapping it around her mouth and wrists.

Abby's anger leaves her, replaced with a terrible hopelessness. She starts snivelling. Midges circle her head and small insects bite her thighs. She stares up at the sky, blue between a small gap in the trees.

Chapter Thirty-Nine

Pain. This pain is new, a monster obliterating everything else, even the horror of her situation, and she surrenders to it. This baby is coming regardless of what she does. Ellie is dead, and she needs to grieve, but right now there is no room for grief. The baby is ruthless in its blind struggle for life.

She's dimly aware of the passing of time, of the darkness encroaching, of Dr Rowe pacing up and down. The trees look sinister in the dusk, with their twisted black branches. The only light comes from his phone and when he switches it off it's almost completely dark. For a while he drops off to sleep and she considers an escape attempt, but it's impossible to move. She's paralysed by the pain. Instead she looks up at the sky. Just a small patch of black sky studded with stars. Most of the time, though, she's absorbed by pain and the pain is absorbed by her. It seems to become part of her, like it's always been there.

When the baby starts crowning at daybreak, she's so exhausted and worn down, she's almost grateful to Dr Rowe.

As he delivers the baby he barks instructions to her – when to push and when to breathe – and she is powerless to do anything but what he says.

The baby finally comes as the first glint of sunlight appears through the trees and it's like a cork popping. Suddenly, there is no pain anymore and a huge feeling of relief. But the relief doesn't last long. She's quickly on her guard again as, with the pain gone, comes the realization of the danger she's in. And it's not just her. It's this tiny, helpless creature too. She watches warily as Dr Rowe cuts the umbilical cord with surgical scissors.

'I've only done this once before at medical school,' he says conversationally as he ties the cord, and then he lays the baby gently on the ground, on the damp leaves. The baby makes a mewling noise. Abby stares at it. It's a small, red wriggling thing, covered in mucus and blood. Abby feels a strong urge to protect it at all costs. She is rigid with fear as Dr Rowe picks the baby up and rocks her gently in his arms.

'A fine, healthy baby girl,' he pronounces. 'How about we call her Sophie? I've always liked that name. I wanted to call my daughter Sophie, but my wife didn't like it.'

He carries on talking as if they're a normal couple with their first child, and more than ever Abby realizes how completely detached from reality he is.

'I'm so proud of you,' he says. Then, to her horror, he rips the tape off her mouth and pecks her on the lips. Abby tries not to gag. She even kisses him back. Maybe she can convince him that she really is in love with him too.

'We should take her to the hospital,' she says, 'to check that everything's okay.'

'She's fine. Ten fingers, ten toes. Perfect in every way.'

'Can I hold her?' She struggles to her feet.

'Lie down. You haven't passed the afterbirth yet.' He pushes her back down and something slithers out between her legs. He holds the most disgusting thing she's ever seen. He waves it in her face, a translucent, slimy sack of veins and globules of what looks like clotted blood, and he laughs as she recoils.

'Some people like to eat it. It's meant to be very good for you.'

Abby tries standing again. 'Please . . .' she says.

'Lie down. You're losing a lot of blood.'

She looks down, and sure enough, there is a puddle of blood soaking into the mulch on the forest floor. Abby ignores it. She feels fine. She feels strong and determined. 'Please let me hold her,' she says, taking a step towards him. 'If you untied my hands I would be able to hold her.' Her eyes flicker down to the surgical scissors lying on the ground where he has left them. If she can persuade him to untie her hands maybe she can pick them up and take him by surprise.

But he sees where she's looking, and the smile vanishes from his face, and morphs into rage. Abby has never seen anyone's mood change so swiftly and dramatically.

'You think I was born yesterday?' he says, picking up the scissors. He runs his hand over the blade. 'You stupid bitch. Do you? *Do you?!*'

'No . . . I just want to hold the baby . . . *our* baby.' Abigail forces herself to smile at him desperately. 'We could take her home, together. Nobody ever need know about this . . . Like you said, we love each other . . .'

For a second, she thinks he's buying it. He listens with his head on one side; his expression softens. But then he shakes his head violently and his face twists in anger. 'You never loved me, did you? It was always him. That loser.' He lunges towards her with the scissors and Abby dodges him.

'Help!' she screams, staggering towards the gate. 'Help! Somebody help!'

'Shut the fuck up,' he hisses, dragging her back to the tree. He shoves her down and presses surgical tape over her mouth again.

'What am I going to do with you, Abigail?' He sighs. And Abby freezes with fear as he picks up the surgical scissors from where he's dropped them, and crouches down beside her, holding the scissors to her throat.

'I don't want to hurt you, but it would be so easy,' he says softly. 'There's the jugular vein here and the carotid artery here.' He presses her neck with his thumb. 'If I slice through those, you'll be dead in minutes.'

Abby shakes her head. Tears of terror are running down her cheeks.

'I don't want to do it. I love you, Abigail, but I don't know what else to do. I can't trust you. Oh God . . .' He sits back on his haunches and rocks backwards and forwards, dropping the scissors. He's crying, Abigail realizes, feeling a flicker of hope. Maybe he's having a change of heart. But then he makes a sudden snorting noise, stands up and strides over.

'You leave me with no choice,' he says. He puts his hands around her throat and she feels him begin to squeeze.

No, no, no. Not like this. Please God, not like this. She's choking. She can't breathe. The pain is intense. She thrashes wildly like a trapped animal, kicking and struggling desperately to free her arms. His eyes are far away. Unreachable. Somewhere in the background she's aware of the baby screaming.

No, no, no. She's losing consciousness. There's a loud ringing in her ears and everything blurs. She looks up at the trees, the green leaves. Stars seem to be bursting in the sky. Then, like a mirage of normality in this night-mare, a grey, shaggy dog comes bounding over the bank. She blinks. *Is it a hallucination? A product of her brain shutting down? A lack of oxygen?* The dog stops short, whimpers, then starts barking. Dr Rowe's grip loosens and Abby gasps for breath.

'Toby, where the hell are you?' a woman's voice, plummy, exasperated, clearly calls out. 'Toby, come here, you bloody dog!'

The sound is so mundane, and Abby has never been so glad to hear anything in her life. Dr Rowe lets go and stands up on alert. Abby coughs and splutters, gulping the air. Then she struggles to her feet and tries to call out. But it comes out as a grunt through the surgical tape.

'Shut up, you bitch,' hisses Dr Rowe, crouching low. He tries to scare the dog away, waving his arms threateningly but it's already too late. A few seconds later an elderly lady in green wellingtons and a green anorak comes scrambling up the slope.

Time stands still. Abby later remembers every tiny detail of this woman, from the stray grey hair on her coat to the way her mouth hangs open, looking from Abby to Dr Rowe to the baby, eyes wide with shock.

'What on earth . . .' she starts. Then she reaches in her pocket and pulls out a phone, fumbling with the buttons. At the same time, in one swift movement, Dr Rowe lunges at her, knocking her phone out of her hand.

Abby watches in horror as he wrestles her to the ground, his hands at her throat. The woman screams, kicks and scratches and the dog barks and bites at his leg. But Dr Rowe is too strong.

Abby keeps struggling to free her hands. *She has to help her. She can't let him kill her.* Then out of nowhere she remembers . . . *Danny. Danny in the staff room talking to her replacement* – the two of them talking about the way to escape if someone has tied your hands. She has no idea if it really works, but she has to try. She raises her hands high above her head and brings her elbows down rapidly. The tape is supposed to tear, but it doesn't work. She tries again, bringing her arms down as hard as she can. The tape stretches a bit. Again, and there is finally enough room for her to wriggle her hands free. She has no time to think. She snatches the scissors from where they're lying on the ground and lunges at Dr Rowe. She acts instinctively, raising the blades and plunging them into his neck, right into the artery. Then she staggers back, horrified, as blood fountains out, spurting all over her.

'What the . . . ?' Dr Rowe says. He reels backwards, staring at her and clutching his neck, trying to stem the blood. Blood gushes out of his neck and trails down his chest.

Abby stands transfixed, appalled. He takes a step towards her, then he keels over and lies on the ground, still holding his neck and making a gurgling noise. The dog is barking wildly now. The woman is gasping for breath. She struggles to her feet and grabs Abby's hand.

'We need to get out of here,' she says.

'Yes.' Abby stands for a minute, stunned, paralysed with shock. Then the baby's crying brings her to her senses.

'The baby,' she says, and she scoops her up in her arms. Together they head for the road. They don't look back. Every second is time for Dr Rowe to recover and follow them, and with every breath she expects to hear him behind them. But they reach the road without incident and almost immediately manage to flag down a car.

The driver screeches to a halt in the lay-by and winds down the window.

'You okay, love?' he asks.

Abby is unable to answer. She feels faint and scared. The driver's face is blurring, and his voice seems to be coming from a long way off. She feels herself swaying, clutching the baby close to her, afraid to drop her.

Luckily, the old woman takes charge of the situation. 'This

young lady has just given birth. We need to get to the hospital as quickly as possible,' she says.

'Hop in, then,' he says.

Abby sits slumped in the back of the car, hardly able to believe that she is safe. The baby wriggles against her chest and she closes her eyes. The last thing she hears is the old lady on the phone to the police before she passes out.

Chapter Forty

Abby wakes with a jolt, opening her eyes to see an unfamiliar white ceiling. *Where the hell is she?* There's pain in her head and a strange tightness in her chest. She sits up and looks around, blinking at the light from the window in confusion. There's another empty bed next to hers, a blue plastic curtain partially drawn. It's a hospital curtain.

She's in hospital.

Everything comes crashing back – the nightmare of the past twenty-four hours, Dr Rowe, and the terror of her ordeal. And she throws up all over the sheets.

'No worries, these things happen.' A nurse with an Australian accent appears by her bedside and serene, blue eyes smile down at her. 'I'll get you a pan.'

Abby sits up. She clambers out of bed. Terror seizes her, adrenaline coursing through her body.

'Where is he . . . ?'

'It's okay. Get back into bed. He's gone. You're safe here.'

'I'm safe? You're sure?'

'Yes.'

'But . . .' Abby looks around, panic choking her. 'He killed Ellie. He tried to kill me . . .'

The nurse hesitates and looks around over her shoulder. She lowers her voice. 'I probably shouldn't be telling you this, but by the time the paramedics got there he was already dead. You don't need to worry about him anymore. He can't hurt you again.'

I killed him, Abby thinks in horror, but there is no room for pity in her heart for the man who murdered her sister.

'And the baby. Where's my baby?' she asks, as the nurse whips the top sheet off the bed, changing it swiftly and expertly.

'She's fine. She's right here. Look.'

The nurse wheels over a transparent cot. The baby is asleep inside, a tiny, red, raw thing wrapped in a blanket, with tiny white mittens on her hands. Abby gazes at her transfixed, and the baby opens her filmy blue eyes, and makes a tiny mewling noise.

'Would you like to hold her?' The nurse picks up the baby and holds her out to Abby, smiling.

Abby is too dazed to refuse. She takes the baby in her arms and sits down on the bed, gazing at its tiny face. The baby moves its head and nuzzles her chest.

The nurse laughs gently. 'She wants to feed. Would you like to try?'

'No.' Abby shakes her head violently because she's remembered Ellie. Her beloved sister is dead. This creature's father killed her. She starts to cry, great heaving sobs that shake her whole body.

'That's it, let it all out,' says the nurse, taking the baby from her. 'You've been through a terrible ordeal.'

'My sister,' she says between sobs. The pain of her loss feels too big to contain in one small body. 'He killed her.'

The nurse sits next to her on the bed and puts her arm around her, saying nothing. It seems impossible that Ellie no longer exists, her beautiful, vibrant presence lost forever. Abby rests her face on the nurse's shoulder and cries for a long time.

It's only later she remembers the woman who saved her.

'There was someone else with me . . . she helped me . . .'

'You mean Pamela? Yes, she's fine. She had a few cuts, some bruising around her neck, and obviously she was shaken up, but otherwise unhurt. She's a remarkable woman.'

Abby can't help but agree.

Abby stays in hospital for the next couple of days. The doctors and nurses insist that she needs time to rest and heal, and she's too exhausted and broken to argue. She's also too exhausted to argue when they gently but persistently push the baby on her. And the first time she feeds her, Abby knows she will have to keep her.

As the baby clamps her tiny mouth around Abby's nipple it's surprisingly sharp, like the edge of a shellfish. But it doesn't hurt. Not really. And it feels right, as if a part of her that had always been missing has been returned to her. They need each other now – her and the baby. She feels sorry for Joel and Maria, who she knows will be heartbroken, but it's too late now.

The next few days in hospital are a blur. Dad comes to visit with a book of crosswords. Grief is etched on his face. He's aged about ten years since she last saw him. He sits and holds her hand, something he hasn't done since she was about eight years old, tears rolling down his cheeks.

'She was so like her mother,' he says. 'Always wanting to help, always standing up for what she believed in.' He squeezes her hand. 'At least I didn't lose you too.' It's the closest he's ever come to telling her he loves her.

Rob comes too, bearing a large box of chocolates. 'I didn't think you'd appreciate flowers,' he says, smiling weakly, even now trying to make a joke. Rob too looks older. His curly hair is threaded with grey and his face is drawn. At the sight of him, Abby feels a deep well of affection she hadn't even known existed. She can't believe she ever suspected him or doubted his love for Ellie. He stays with her for the whole visiting hour and they hardly talk. Rob, never usually lost for words, is unable to speak.

Chapter Forty-One

The crematorium is packed. Hundreds of people are crammed into the small room, spilling out into the hallway. Ellie's friends, colleagues and patients all have turned up to pay their respects, and everyone seems to have some poignant memory to share. Ellie has touched so many people in her short life.

Abby can't take it all in. She feels numb, drained of emotion. It's impossible to believe that Ellie has really gone. Impossible to conceive of a world without her big sister. She sits in the front row clutching Danny's hand as Ellie's coffin vanishes behind a velvet curtain. It seems like a conjuring trick – as if Ellie will suddenly appear, laughing and bowing. 'Fooled you,' she'll say, laughing that deep belly laugh of hers. And she will be the irrepressible Ellie from before – before she lost her baby and some of her sparkle along with it.

But Ellie won't appear ever again. Abby knows that. She just can't *feel* it yet.

One of Ellie's college friends relates an anecdote. It's a story about when they were training together, how Ellie stood up for her to a bullying senior surgeon. 'And that just sums Ellie up,' concludes the friend, biting back tears. 'She was truthful, brave, fair . . . and one of the kindest people I ever met.'

Abby's vision blurs. She's dimly aware that Rob, sitting next to her, is sobbing, his head in his hands, and that Dad, sitting across the aisle, looks completely bewildered, his eyes darting from place to place, as though if he looks hard enough he'll find Ellie in the crowd. Abby is dry-eyed. She doesn't cry. She knows that if she cries now she'll never stop.

After the funeral they head back home with close friends and family. Sue greets them at the door, Abby's baby screaming in her arms. She's been so helpful the last few days, preparing a huge spread for all the guests and looking after the baby while Abby was preparing for the funeral. Abby's beginning to think she might have misjudged her.

'She was asleep most of the time, the little angel,' Sue says to Abby, stroking the baby's cheek and cooing. 'You know I think she looks a little like your sister.' She wipes away a tear. 'I wish I could have known her better . . .'

Sue is only trying to be kind, but Abby can't face her, or the mountain of food that she's prepared. As soon as she can, she slips outside into the garden, into the fresh air and the misty rain.

She sits on the old, wooden bench and stares at a damp hole in the earth under the apple tree. Hector has been digging again and has dug up all the lavender Ellie planted in the spring. *Ellie's going to be furious*, Abby thinks vaguely. Then,

But Ellie's not here. She's not coming back. The thought hits her like a tsunami.

She's crying so hard she doesn't hear Rob approach until he's right up to her.

'I thought I'd find you here,' he says, sitting next to her on the bench. Then he stays with her for a while in silence until she stops crying.

'The police said that she wouldn't have suffered much,' he says. 'A blow to the head like that. It would have been over very quickly.'

Abby hopes this is true. She can't bear to think of Ellie afraid and hurt. She thinks of the man that did this. She thinks of him clutching his neck and the blood spurting through his fingers.

'I killed him,' she whispers. Still the horror of it is difficult to process.

'I'm glad you did,' says Rob grimly. There's a new steel in his voice she's never heard before. 'If you hadn't killed him I would have had to.'

Abby nods. There's something in his tone that makes her believe him.

'They searched his house,' Rob continues. 'They found her body covered in leaves in the woods near where he took you. They think he meant to go back later and bury her.' He stops for a minute, unable to carry on. Abby puts her hand over his and he takes a deep, shuddering breath. 'They also found more pictures of patients on his hard drive. Pictures like the ones Ellie found of you . . . dating back years.'

Abby shivers. 'How did he get away with it for so long? That's what I don't understand.'

'He was very good at pulling the wool over people's eyes. He exploited people's weaknesses too. Helen knew something. Or if she didn't know, then she at least suspected, but turned a blind eye. He used what he knew about her drug habit to keep her quiet.'

They sit side by side, oblivious to the rain that is pattering down, getting heavier now, dripping off the leaves of the apple tree.

'What are your plans?' Rob asks eventually.

'I don't know.'

'You know you're welcome to stay with me and Hector as long as you want.'

It's a tempting offer in many ways but Abby knows she can't stay here, with all that has happened. She knows it will break her.

'Thank you, I appreciate that, but I think it's time I found my own place and started taking responsibility for my own life. Will you be okay by yourself though?'

'What, without your wonderful culinary skills?' Rob gives her a lopsided smile.

And Abby gives a short hiccuping laugh and then starts crying again. Rob bursts into tears too and wraps her in his arms.

They've been sitting like that for a while, just crying and holding on to each other as if they can stop one another from drowning, when Sue comes bustling down the path.

From the open kitchen door there's the sound of the baby bawling.

'I think the wee one needs feeding,' Sue says breathlessly to Abby. 'She won't stop crying.'

Abby stands up and rubs her eyes. In a way it's a blessing, this responsibility. She can't just give up. She has to keep going for the baby.

'Okay I'm coming,' she says.

Three Years Later

Though it's October already, the sun is still strong in Cyprus, and it glares out of a clear blue sky, glittering on the sea and burning Abby's cheek as she drives along the highway towards the airport.

'Where are we going, Mummy?'

Abby glances over her shoulder at Beth who is sitting in her car seat, head turned away from the sun, chubby little legs flexing.

'To pick up your Uncle Danny and Uncle Will from the airport.'

'Why?' Beth demands.

'Because they're coming to stay for a while.'

'Why?'

Abby sighs. Beth has recently learned the power of the word 'Why?' and she uses it all the time. 'Why do I have to go to bed?' 'Why do you have boobies, Mummy?' 'Why did you turn off the sun?' But, thank God, she still hasn't asked the question Abby is dreading. 'Why haven't I got a daddy like all my friends?'

Danny and Will are already through baggage claim and sitting on their suitcases outside the airport when Abby pulls up in the car park.

'How's my little cherub?' Danny says, crouching down by Beth's pushchair and tickling her neck.

'I'm not a cherub,' Beth giggles, squirming in the chair. 'I'm Beth.'

'Are you sure you're not a cherub?' Danny teases her. 'You look like a cherub to me.'

'I think someone's getting broody,' Will comments drily, kissing Abby on the cheek.

Abby smiles. She likes Will. He's quite a bit older than Danny, calm and quiet. He seems to be good for him. She doesn't think she's ever known Danny as happy as he's been these past few years with Will.

'Everyone at school sends their love,' says Danny once they've squashed their suitcases into Abby's tiny boot and are driving back along the highway to her house.

'And Rob?' Abby asks anxiously. She knows the past three years have been tough for Rob and they haven't been in touch as much as she would like.

'He's doing okay,' says Danny, staring out of the window at the dry, chalky hills and the sad-looking goats crammed into their pens.

'You wouldn't recognize him,' adds Will. 'He's shaved his beard and he's lost so much weight. He's been training for this marathon. He's collected quite a bit of money so far.'

Abby nods. Rob has been doing fun runs and marathons

for the past couple of years like he's on some kind of mission, furiously raising money for charities he knows Ellie would approve of.

'Is he seeing anyone?' Abby asks. As far as she knows, Rob hasn't been involved with another woman since Ellie died and she knows Ellie wouldn't have wanted him to be on his own.

Danny grins. 'Well . . . you'll never guess . . .'

'Oh my God! What?' Abby glances over at him in the passenger seat.

'He probably wouldn't want me to tell you this, but he's been having this on-off thing with Gina.'

'Gina!' Abby exclaims, astonished.

'I know. They're the last two people you'd put together, aren't they? Thea thinks he's after a promotion.'

Abby snorts with laughter. She can't imagine Rob with Gina, but whatever makes him happy is a good thing in her view.

Later, when Danny and Will have unpacked, Abby takes them down to the seafront and they sit in Fini's beach bar watching the huge, orange sun sink below the horizon.

Beth is asleep in her pushchair, breathing softly. She looks so pure and innocent when she's asleep. Looking down at her, Abby feels a pang. She can't bear the thought of anything ever hurting her, but she knows it will be impossible to protect her forever.

'She's adorable,' says Danny. 'You know, she reminds me a lot of Ellie.'

'Yes.' Abby nods. There *is* a lot of Ellie in Beth – in her stubbornness, her quick laughter and her fearless blue eyes.

'How are *you*, anyway?' Danny sits back and gives her a searching look.

Abby shrugs. 'Me? Oh, I'm okay.'

It's true, she thinks. *She's okay. It's been a struggle but she's okay.* She has a job she enjoys, teaching the children of army personnel at the British army base, and she's even started dating again – a Cypriot dentist called Andreas. It's early days, of course, but he seems to get on well with Beth, so that's a good sign.

Every day is a choice. A choice to get up. A choice to see the good in life. A choice to love. And mostly she makes the right choice, but it would be a lie to say she doesn't have the occasional dark moment. Moments when she wakes up from nightmares, sweating with terror, and moments when she looks at Beth and wonders about things like nature versus nurture.

In her darkest moments she thinks she catches a glimpse of *him* in Beth – in her flashes of anger or in a charming dimple. But then again, she sees a lot of different people in Beth – Ellie's eyes and smile, her own nose, Dad's chin.

And mostly, when she looks at her daughter all she sees is Beth – that unique little girl, who brings so much joy to her life.

ACKNOWLEDGEMENTS

Firstly, I would like to thank the amazing team at Quercus, Emily Yau, Nick de Somogyi and, in particular, the brilliant and tactful Rachel Neely whose feedback has been invaluable.

I'm grateful also to Catherine Johnson and the lovely, talented fellow members of my Curtis Brown course for helping me to develop as a writer, especially Jenny Ireland. Thomas Abraham, Pauline Dawes and Robert Easton, who took the time to read and comment on the first three chapters of *Deliver Me*.

Next, I'd like to thank the friendly and helpful Sergeant Garrett Gloyn, who made me realize that the police are far more efficient than I would have liked!

My thanks too, to Toby Lodge and Caitlin John, my first and most encouraging readers, and Max Lodge for inspirational conversation and for making me laugh.

Finally, my love and gratitude go to the best man I know, Jim Lodge, for his insightful comments, patience and endless cups of tea!